AUTUMN

A NOVEL

Marc MacDonald

FriesenPress

One Printers Way
Altona, MB R0G 0B0
Canada

www.friesenpress.com

First Edition — 2024

ISBN
978-1-03-831189-4 (Hardcover)
978-1-03-831188-7 (Paperback)
978-1-03-831190-0 (eBook)

1. FICTION, LITERARY

Distributed to the trade by The Ingram Book Company

AUTUMN

A NOVEL

For Tricia, who always saw the writer in me, even when I lost sight of it.

And for my boys, may your boundless imaginations and curiosities ignite stories that will captivate and inspire the world.

CHAPTER 1

The question was a perfectly valid one. Yes, a perfectly valid question indeed. Yet despite its rationality, I was still unable to summon the courage to respond with even a crumb of truth. Hell, I was barely ready to lie about it. But, as I said, the question itself—it really was perfectly valid.

Unrelated, but no less a factor for consideration, was Phil, the asker of said perfectly valid question, who happened to be a total stranger. As a personal rule—and one I feel more people should adopt—I never share too much with strangers. I mean, let's face it, that's just sound practice. And today, especially, wasn't the time to deviate from my longstanding philosophy.

I pictured Phil sporting a mustache and a furrowed brow. Of course, I had no idea the extent of furrow on Phil's brow or if he even had the faintest hint of whiskers staking claim across his upper lip. These were just features I took upon myself to impose on him based on the rattling sound of loose gravel in his voice. I don't consciously attach these types of assumptions to someone's appearance, it's just something I've done since I was a kid. It's a habit born from long family road trips; a creative way to pass the time with my younger sister. We would play a modified game of Guess Who, attributing hair and eye colour, shape of jaw and nose, and even how much excess weight might be dangling from under their chin to every voice on the radio—disc jockeys, as my Dad was wont to call them, as if compelled to verbalize the meaning of DJ.

After all, this was a time when the car radio was one of the few means to break up the monotony of the front-seat discussions of adults: taxes, mortgage rates, conservative politics. A toothless DJ with green hair and no fewer than seventeen moles on their face was preferred fodder to amortizations and debates on whether gay marriage should be permitted. It should, and it has.

As we traversed the open roads—we would have never predicted the volume of congestion the highways would amass today—my sister, who retained the creative genes in the family, could always be counted on to ascribe some of the oddest attributes to the voices we heard. Having some life experience behind me now, I've taken to the belief that these weren't weird descriptions—it was just that at the time, I'd never seen anyone with a nose, eyebrow, or lip ring, for example. As an adult, these piercings and others are commonplace, nothing more than an expression of one's self. And brave expressions at that because, let's be honest, the world remains too judgmental for its own good. The best part of this game was when we finally had a chance to see what these people looked like; they never—not even once, not even closely—looked like they sounded coming through the speakers of Mom and Dad's Lincoln. To the youth of today, this fun little game is probably unthinkable, not so much because they lack imagination, though having their faces connected to a screen since birth certainly suggests their creativity has been stunted in comparison, but because they can't envision a world before music or videos being instantly available at their fingertips. And even if they remember CD players, this was before those too, at least in cars. If you were lucky, you had a tape deck, but even then, you needed cassettes to play in it. The idea of skipping to a specific song probably wasn't even a dream at this point.

And so, on long road trips, when families still piled into the family car and drove day and night, we would listen to these strange, captivating voices crackling through the speakers. As I applied this old habit to Phil, I was reminded of just how easily we paint a picture of someone's appearance based on little more information than how smooth or aged their voice is. As stated in Phil's case, his voice sounded like loose change whirring in a blender. Vin Scully, he was not. I was further reminded just how unfair this is to the other person. In the grand scheme of things, who cares what they look or sound like?

Coarse voice aside, Phil's valid question hung in the air, and I would have to address it. But just what the hell *was* I doing here?

In my defence, I thought I knew, or at the very least, I had a pretty good inclination, but as is the case with much of my life, I had no concrete idea what I was doing or if I'd even know when I realized I was doing it.

It was a late September afternoon, and the rain, which had followed me like a faithful four-legged stray during my drive to Silver Springs, transformed its mist into an assault of steady, thick drops pounding the roof of my car like the fists of a drunk Irishman on a pub table when trying to prove a point. These weighty, unremitting thumps became the soundtrack to one of the biggest decisions I'd made in recent memory, perhaps my life. It was more Randy Newman than Alexandre Desplat, which could account for my frayed decision-making abilities.

The bulbs encased within the exterior plastic of the sign for Silver Springs Health and Rehabilitation Centre hadn't yet burst to life and remained a measure behind the rapid darkness descending upon its aged façade and the surrounding area. Nestled in the trees and flanked by sloping hills and serpentine rivers, Silver Springs was home to, among its physical bodies, a picturesque landscape and climate that could produce, at the drop of a dime, weather that prevented the most enthusiastic windshield wiper blades from keeping up with cascading streams and tiny exploding grenades of water.

The building itself was once an architectural marvel, and scores of photos and corresponding accolades splayed across the pages of old magazines and newspapers existed as proof—it just took some searching, which I had diligently done. The timeworn then-hotel was purchased sometime in the 1970s by a man named Billy Springs, who hailed from old oil money—didn't they all?—and painstakingly developed it into one of the country's most sought-after physical rehabilitation centres. That was when unfettered money flowed into the place, of course. I discovered through my research, while edging closer to the brink of making my life-altering decision, that Springs's two adult children, who now wielded joint control over the budget, keep the place running, albeit at the bare minimum and only because a clause in their inheritance documents dictate they do so. Saying they perform the bare minimum might even be a generous stretch, given the condition of the pothole-filled parking lot my car had ambled over and now floated in.

Balconies ran along the top floor, which, unlike most traditional hotels, was only eight storeys high, and the rooms up there were the only ones boasting this feature. Again, they were a hot ticket back in the day, so said my research. The triangle peaks of the twin corner towers were adorned with green flags that flapped furiously in the prevailing storm's wind. Everything appeared symmetrical, even if it wasn't precisely so. The driveway that once ran to the front door valet had been repurposed into an interlocking brick walking path that kept all vehicular traffic a healthy distance away from the building.

Despite nature's decades-long toll, what had been said about the building's architecture and design remained true. It was still a marvel to take in, further amplified by the expanse of the natural world acting as its backdrop. The trees stood tall, protecting the castle from outsiders like a moat in reverse. The hills rolled like waves. The streams cut a path as Mother Earth, not man, dictated. Everything was lush and green for now. This would be my new home.

After stalling for as long as uncomfortably possible, I finally summoned a reasonable, even if vague, response to Phil, informing him that I was here as a volunteer. This was true, of course, but the answer's validity barely scratched the surface of my current reasoning for sitting in a well-driven Chevy Malibu, in the midst of a late summer thunderstorm, in a near-empty parking lot, in a place most people had long forgotten about.

"Bullshit," said Phil, reflecting what I perceived to be genuine disdain for what he sensed to be a ruse.

"Bull or otherwise, my good man, there's no shit, I'm here to volunteer." *My good man? Who was I, George Banks?* My nerves were cloaking themselves in poor repartee.

"Okay, if you're legit, bring your court papers in, and we'll get you signed off and on file," huffed Phil.

"Court papers?"

"Oh Jesus. Listen, kid, I don't have time for this. No one has willingly volunteered here in like twenty years unless court-ordered because of some dumbass white-collar crime that isn't worth anyone's time to actually prosecute. And even then, that ain't exactly volunteering, is it? It's being volun-told. You been volun-told, kid?"

Kid? Who did he think I was, Kevin McCallister? Though that would be a compliment—that kid was a ruthless genius, if not a bit whiny. Whether my mouth spoke the words or they stayed in my mind, I knew I should just relax and move forward or risk developing a case of cinematic schizophrenia.

"Well, Phil, my good man"—shit, there it was again—"you know what they say, there's a first time for everything." Now I was being smug. I knew I was being smug. I thought it would work. I don't know why I thought this. It cost me.

Click.

"Phil? Phil? Hello?" Son of a bitch hung up on me.

I peered out the windshield, doing that thing where you crane your neck to get a view of the sky from the driver's seat. It was a kind of duck-and-twist manoeuvre. It was an incredibly awkward movement and certainly not natural. The dark, heavy clouds offered no indication the rain would let up before I exited the dry comfort of my vehicle. I wallowed in my instant weather analysis. To add insult to my thus-far less-than-stellar arrival, I had no umbrella, no jacket readily available. The digital clock on the dashboard ticked—or did it flip? What does a digital clock do? It was undoubtedly reminding me that time was not on my side and that the next click I heard wouldn't be Phil's repeated hang-up but the sound of the doors locking for the day; no one in, no one out, unless accompanied by law enforcement or medical care professionals.

It was time.

Building up the courage, as if I was about to dip paper-cut hands into a jar of vinegar to fish out a key, I took a few deep breaths and convinced myself one last time that this was what I needed to do, where I needed to be. I opened the door and made a break for it.

Puddles exploded beneath my feet as I sprinted the hundred metres from the closest parking space in the lot to the front entrance. A covered entryway greeted me upon arrival, providing shelter from the rain. The front doors were heavy, clad with tall, thick brass handles that had long since lost their sheen, and stood as the last obstacle between me and my new friend Phil. Gathering myself under the burgundy overhang, short of breath and nearly soaked completely through, two things happened: the rain stopped, as if Mother Nature had grown bored with playing her watery joke, and I experienced a brief panic attack, the latter of which requiring me to take a seat on an iron-slatted bench and practise the breathing exercises my therapist suggested I employ when faced with the sudden shortness of breath.

It had been a while since my last attack, but they usually struck me under similar circumstances: embarking on a new situation that could significantly impact my life—or, as my therapist enjoyed pointing out, *perceived* consequences. Perceived because I couldn't possibly know what an outcome would be before I had experienced it. Sometimes I hated that guy.

As the clouds dispersed and the sun broke through, a warm breeze rolled in on the absence of precipitation. It wasn't nearly strong enough to dry my clothes, but it offered a persistent enough gust to at least assist in calming my nerves.

Vigorously shaking my head, much like a dog does tip to tail after a bath, I tried to create the impression of someone who was more or less put together. My hair had grown slightly shaggy and, having been doused with rain, was now plastered to my skull in a most unflattering manner. I didn't need a mirror to confirm this as I ran my fingers through soaking clumps of hair, pulling them away from my scalp. I was quickly gaining an appreciation for why women loathe the wind and rain, at least as it related to their locks.

I opened the front doors and made my approach, Phil's furrowing brow—I knew it—telling me this improvised grooming endeavour had failed, at least by his standards. Let's be honest, it failed the standards of anyone with eyesight. I knew I looked like shit. He wore no mustache but did possess a stiff upper lip that furnished his resting face with a dutiful pissed-off look.

"Why are you so wet?" asked Phil, deadpan and somewhat disgusted.

"What? Seriously?" I glanced behind me at the trail of water I had trudged in. "It has been pouring, and I do mean *pouring*, for the past half hour, and I had to run the length of a football field just to get to the door. What gives on the distance from the parking lot?"

Phil leaned to his right, peering around my soaked frame, and saw only sunshine.

"Looks pretty *noice* to me," he said, a hint of a smile curling the corners of his mouth in a sociopathic I-am-going-to-kill-you-later type of look. I was hoping he'd kill his pronunciation of the word *nice*. I could come to terms with my life's demise if I could be assured of that.

"Yeah, well, it was raining when I—never mind, it doesn't matter. I'm here for the volunteer position on the third floor. Alex Chambers."

Phil studied me. I mean, he really studied me. I felt my soul shudder as his dark, beady eyes bored into me. I felt an urge to hold my arms across the front of my body, as if I was standing there naked and trying to avoid further shame, but I summoned the inner strength to appear resilient.

"Sorry, Chief, that spot's taken. Besides, you said you ain't got any papers. You don't really want to be here. In fact, I suggest you get going before someone finds out you're here of your own free will; they might try to have you committed. We got a whole floor for that kind of thing."

Phil chuckled to himself and patted the robust cushion of a belly that overflowed the waist of his pants, daring the buttons on his shirt to pop off like Tony Montana at the end of *Scarface*.

"No, no. When I talked to, uh, Susanne, I think it was, she said she was holding the position for me. I'll have you know, she was quite taken that I was making the call of my own volition."

Before I could finish the sentence, Phil had picked up the phone, stopped listening to me, and presumably contacted Susanne. Looking to get past this situation as quickly as he could, Phil paid me no mind. As soon as he heard Susanne's name, he dialed. His actions betrayed his thoughts; if someone else could deal with me, let them.

"Yeah, Suz—sorry, Susanne. Got some kid here says he wants to volunteer on the third floor. Yep. Okay. Right. Thanks."

Phil returned the receiver to its cradle, leaned back in his chair, testing the structural integrity of the seat, and released a heavy, satisfactory sigh.

"Susanne is coming, but she ain't going to tell you anything more than I already told you. But you seem to think you know more about what's available here than me. Not the case, buddy boy. I've been here fourteen years. Count 'em, fourteen." He held up his fingers, all ten of them, but did so as if there were fourteen. "I know this place in and out: the people, the hallways, the positions—available or *filled*. But hey, maybe you can't take instruction from a man, some type of reverse sexism or something, I don't know what you millennials believe in these days. I can't keep up."

"Phil, you're an interesting guy, you know that?" I said.

"Yeah, I am. I'm *choice*." He pronounced choice like he did nice, drawing out the 'oice,' and it made me want to slap him. I mean really slap him—a nice, swift, open-handed, five-fingered handshake with his face. A grown man should not be using the dialect of a teenage douchebag.

Thankfully, Susanne was coming to square away the misunderstanding, but I was still trying to process what Phil had just told me. I thought back to Phil's original question and realized that it held more merit than I had known ten minutes ago.

What the hell *was* I doing here?

CHAPTER 2

Susanne Rogers exited a pair of doors fit for an emergency room, one opening in and one opening out, which, given the nature of the clientele here, weren't entirely out of place. Her hair, had it not been tied back and knotted in one of those buns you can wedge a pencil in—I only note this because there was, in fact, a pencil crammed in her hair—would have bounced with her steps; it looked to be of considerable length with a natural wave, even tied up.

She wore navy-blue heels, which, even at their modest height, offered an unnatural obstacle to her natural stride. The rest of her attire matched what you would expect of the prototypical director of community services and resident care: navy-blue pencil skirt with matching blazer, white blouse buttoned nearly to the top, shiny but noticeably inexpensive costume jewellery around the neck and wrist and adorning both ears, lanyard with credentials and swipe access, and, of course, a clipboard. The clipboard also had a pencil, only this one was tied with a string and fastened with masking tape. Susanne was a grown-up camp counsellor, and she was about to prove it.

On the phone, she had seemed genuinely supportive of my willingness to volunteer, appreciative even, thus making me think Phil's misguided assurances of his being in the know were just a speed bump or an arrogant charade—a stunt to pull on the new guy.

"Mr. Chambers, I am Ms. Rogers, we spoke on the phone a few days ago." She extended her hand as she drew close enough to offer it. "Thank you for coming."

"Alex," I said, feeling too young and even further unaccomplished to be labelled as a Mr. "And yes, we did speak on the phone. I'm glad you remember. I'm hoping you also remember the arrangement we came to at that time. My friend Bill here seems to think it's non-existent."

"My name's Phil," he objected, gruffer than I had anticipated.

Susanne looked at me. Silence. Her facial expression whispered bad news was on its way. Her eyes screamed it.

"No, no, no, no," I repeated as if I were a child's toy, my pull string stuck. "We had an agreement. I've come all this way."

"I am sorry, Mr. Chambers—"

"Alex," I interrupted, feeling increasingly uncomfortable by what was playing out before me. If I was about to have my legs taken out from under me, I might as well nip the unnecessary formalities in the bud.

"I am very sorry, Mr. Chambers, but that volunteer position has indeed been filled and is no longer available."

I could see Phil in my peripheral view, forming a shit-eating grin. If I felt inclined to slap him before, I was absolutely certain that I wanted to slap him now; maybe even a double delivery of five across the cheeks. He had this look on his face, the kind that suggested he was rehearsing a story to tell his buddies over flat beer at the bar about how he had schooled some young city boy in the ways of Silver Springs's ethos—a not-in-my-house tale. Chest puffed out. Heels dug in. Always the alpha male.

In short order, he was dead to me now. Bye, Phil.

"Listen, Mr. Chambers," Susanne said as she gently collected my forearm and guided me out of Phil's earshot. "We here at Silver

Springs are not immune to the nepotism that larger corporations face. Yes, we have a touch more latitude with those we bring on, but there is simply nothing I can do for you regarding the volunteer position we previously spoke of. We appreciate all persons who wish to volunteer with our wonderful residents, but sometimes we cannot take everyone."

Her spiel felt rehearsed and uninspired, and had my eyes not been fixed on hers, burning a hole through them, I would have bet good money she was reading a script. Any originality for smoothing the situation over was non-existent, which only led to further frustration and my growing condemnation of Phil. He, of course, had nothing to do with this part of the conversation, but he was at fault somehow. He became my sworn enemy, my rival, my nemesis; he'd been resurrected solely to serve this fatalistic purpose.

Fuck you, Phil!

This screamed expletive exploded in my mind as I glanced over Susanne's shoulder at the frumpy doorman casting his faux tough-guy glare my way.

"I am very sorry, truly, I am," she continued. "And I am sorry you came all this way for a position that is no longer available." Susanne was steadier now, just slightly, and only if you closely observed her body language would you have noticed her stiffening, cautiously anticipating what her corporate manual advised would be a round or two of mounting tension and escalating insults.

"I don't understand, I just don't," I managed in response, pinching the bridge of my nose as if this would somehow further convey my incomprehension of the situation. "Two days ago, the position was there. I completed your background check, you accepted me, you told me when to arrive, which, by the way, is now. I'm here as we agreed and you're telling me nothing we discussed is available. Moreover, if you filled that spot after we spoke, why didn't you call me? Why let me drive all the way here, endure a brief monsoon just to get in the damn doors, and then promptly tell me to hit the road?"

"That is a fair criticism, Mr. Chambers. And you are right, I should have called to let you know that the position you applied for had been filled. For that, I sincerely apologize."

Damn straight. I'm gaining the edge, I thought. *Take that, Phil.*

We stood in silence for a few seconds, me savouring the glory of my infinitesimal victory and Susanne contemplating her next move. The chess game was on, and having convinced myself I was on my way to checkmate, I wasn't prepared for her next move: queen to e4 (or some such chess move that makes an opponent's jaw drop in awe and bewilderment).

"Well now, let us just hold on a second," suggested Susanne, looking as though she were in the midst of an epiphany. "There is another position available, and if we are being truthful, I was hoping that by offering it in this fashion, you would be more likely to accept it. I am sorry for the cloak-and-dagger approach. If you are so inclined, we have something for you on the fourth floor."

Susanne's clutch on her clipboard loosened, the white draining from her knuckles signalling a feeling that she was on her way to deescalating the situation.

"The fourth floor?" This wasn't ideal, but it was something—a foot in the door. I knew enough about Silver Springs to know the residents were grouped by floor, with requirements specifically tended to by the appropriate staff and appointed service providers. And given the clientele, a merry-go-round of employee and volunteer faces was the last thing patients at Silver Springs needed. It wasn't my first choice—I didn't even have a second choice—but I wasn't in much of a position to negotiate. Anything less than being here would pose an impediment to my overall plan. Therefore, I was taking it no matter what. I could recalibrate later.

Hear that, Phil? Fourth floor, big guy.

"As I am sure you are aware, and in the event you are not, I will enlighten you now. We generally keep our staff and volunteers on the same floor so as to guard against our patients experiencing added levels of stress by a rotation of new faces and personalities caring for them. I am sure you understand."

Everything out of Susanne's mouth, at least in person, was automated, straight out of the care-provider textbook that I was certain was her bedtime reading material. She was prepared for every conversation, loaded with pre-recorded scripts for every likely scenario. Stick to the script, make the sale.

"Yeah, sure, makes sense, I guess." I was quickly losing interest in continuing this stale conversation. It was time to move on, to get things underway.

"The fourth floor is where you will find our older guests here at Silver Springs," she said. "This group, particularly, requires consistency and familiarity as many have begun experiencing the progression of dementia and other forms of memory loss, though certainly not all of them. So, if you are in fact interested, I would like you to take a moment to think about this before you commit to anything. I cannot stress enough that if you choose to accept this position, I fully expect that you will be with us for some time. These folks need stability and not a tourist who will look around and walk away. Do you understand?"

Well, that answers my question about who inhabits the fourth floor. Up to this point, I had only bothered to learn who resided on the third floor. But the older guests it would be. Bring it on.

Forgetting for a moment that I was completely soaked through, I pretended to contemplate this offer as if I were somehow in the driver's seat with options, which, of course, couldn't have been further from reality.

"Okay," I said. "I'm in. Fourth floor it is. Where do I sign?"

"Excellent! We are thrilled to have you, Mr. Chambers. We hope you will enjoy your time with us."

Who was this woman, this non-violent T-800 machine? Had the entirety of the last few minutes been nothing more than a series of ones and zeroes for her to compute before generating a corporately trite response?

For the sake of the residents, I certainly hoped the foot soldiers on staff were more in tune with that little emotion most of us know as empathy. "Mr. Abner here will get you started on the paperwork, and once again, Mr. Chambers, we are so happy to have you."

Autobot.

Phil, whose last name I just learned was Abner, held an expression that was likely his default: grumpy. Not just grumpy, but sour, like having a lemon soaking your taste buds around the clock. I'm only moderately ashamed to say I took some pleasure in this.

"Well then, Doubleday, let's get that paperwork started for my *choice* volunteer position, shall we?"

"Doubleday?" he snarked.

"Obviously, you're not a baseball fan." He didn't need to give me another reason not to like him, but he did, which made designating him my nemesis all the more real.

A bonus, if you wanted to look at it that way, was that staff and volunteers were provided complimentary residence, complete with meal service and in-house laundry. Given the facility's proximity to anything other than trees, rivers, rocks, and hills for a few hours in all directions, there really was no other option, unless your business model included the expectation that people be eager and willing to commute each day from the closest hint of civilization in order to join the employee ranks at Silver Springs. And we're not talking a major city centre either. We're talking the basics: church, school, bar, general store.

Instead of escorting me to my room as Susanne had instructed with her parting words, Phil gave me brief and vague directions, which turned out to be wrong, of course.

I chalked this up to Phil being a poor loser but an avid gamesman. We were in the trenches now, and my respect for his commitment to the game deepened. Walking the halls, I could hear the slosh of my footsteps, each compression of my foot on the sole of my shoe spewing murky liquid like water cresting the bow of a boat on the high seas. The sound was unsettling but was nothing compared to the feeling. It was like stepping on a sheet of wet cat fur and wiggling your toes until the fur wrapped around each one.

I found room 409 at the end of the hallway, near a stairwell but as far from the elevator as you could get.

I inserted my key, a literal key, not a magnetic key card like most modern lodging establishments, and turned it. And by turned it, I mean I tried to turn it. It didn't move more than a hair.

Phil. Fucking Phil.

Back in the lobby, my adversary launched into hysterics as he watched my zigzagging journey and unsuccessful attempts to enter my room, courtesy of the cameras above beaming their digital feed directly to the monitors on his desk.

"Looks like your key doesn't work," came Phil's voice from a ceiling speaker.

I looked at the camera and replied. "Yes, it would appear that way, wouldn't it?"

"If you come back to the front desk, we can reissue the key for room 408."

"I'm in room 409, Phil."

"Oh yeah, well how 'bout that. I guess that's the problem now, innit? I gave you the key for 408. I'm not usually one to mess up a little detail like that. Guess you got me on an off day."

After making my way back to the main floor, retrieving the correct key from a still-splitting-a-gut Phil, and retracing my steps, I returned to what would be my new room, the door permitting my entry with the familiar click of the lock's pins releasing.

I pushed the door forward and entered what could have been any room at any Howard Johnson in any city in the world. It was a standard template. It was just fine.

Walking in, I was greeted by an open closet to my left, home to four hangers dangling from their holsters, securely fastened to the stainless-steel bar, guaranteed to never be stolen from their mounts. The bathroom door was ajar, providing a view of the wall-mounted hair dryer and a supply of basic toiletries and soaps arranged on the counter. It smelled like week-old pine trees, which could have been residual cleaning solution or simply a default musky, aged fragrance, but the tile floor was void of cracks and permanent stains, and the faucet and toilet appeared to be relatively new. A few metres ahead sat a queen-size bed bookended by small wooden tables. One housed a lamp, the other a phone, coiled cord and all. The walls were a colour I could best describe as dried mustard. There was a framed photo on each wall, all animal-themed and equally disquieting, even for an avowed animal lover.

The television mounted on the wall was a most surprising sight. It was a flat-screen that had to be at least sixty inches. Under normal circumstances, such as any living room I've ever been in, this would have been a detail not worth mentioning. Here, however, it was the pièce de résistance. Below it, a credenza with a built-in minifridge I was surprised to see was already well stocked. I unzipped my duffle bag to add a few things of my own. Heavy, dusty curtains were pulled back to reveal the room's most redeeming quality outside the consumer electronics: a remarkable view of rolling hills and tall trees that seemed to go on forever and, given Silver Springs's location essentially in the middle of nowhere, probably did. I tested the window and it opened, thank God. I pulled the heavy pane of glass upwards, hoping to cleanse the room of its dank aroma. The multipurpose unit providing both air conditioning and heat gave a low grumble, even though, upon inspection, the power switch was visibly turned to the off position.

All in all, the room was rather likeable—much nicer than what I would have expected given the antiquated theme and accoutrements throughout the rest of the place. It made me think that anything new, for whatever reason, ended up in room 409, but the renovation was piecemeal instead of complete. I wasn't about to complain.

I tossed my belongings on the bed with a soft thud and followed suit with the weight of my clothed, rain-soaked body. Both luggage and body gathered in the now-noticeable dip in the middle of the mattress.

Sitting up, I opened the bedside table drawer and, sure enough, found a Holy Bible. Maybe I *was* in a Howard Johnson and this whole thing was being played out in some alternate timeline. Maybe Phil was a concierge at the hotel, and my being here was just a weekend getaway reservation that I never made.

Maybe Phil was right. Maybe I ended up here without realizing how it happened because, as he said, nobody comes here on their own.

The shrill ring of the phone snapped me back to the present moment.

"Hello?"

"Yeah, new guy, dinner's in half an hour."

"Thanks, Doubleday. Where's the cafeteria?"

"Follow your nose; it'll take you there," he said, laughing that same hyena-like laugh he did with his key-switcheroo joke. "And don't call me Doubleday. I don't get it." And then he hung up.

I followed suit, hopeful the shower had enough hot water for a cleansing rinse before dinner.

CHAPTER 3

The cafeteria reminded me—as did the entire building, at least in its current state—of a college dormitory. Taking stock of the furniture, décor, and layout, it was a fair comparison, and given that it once hosted hundreds of bodies at any given time in its prime, I could not be convicted of a prejudicial assessment. To those who once revered this place during its golden days, seeing the building in its present-day condition would undoubtedly be slightly disconcerting, especially the room that had been converted into the fourth-floor cafeteria. The eatery, as it existed, should have been circular, curved in the corners and wallpapered with the memories of the once-upon-a-time hot spot for late-night soirées and high rollers; this was no exaggeration as I had seen the pictures. Instead, it was squared off, made to look like any other room, perhaps to persuade the current clientele to spend more time resting their hips than gyrating them.

Staff in need of nourishment were corralled in lines designed to keep people advancing forward, leaving little time for sifting through the pre-made food options. You got in, grabbed something, and moved along. Red plastic cups that reminded me of Pizza Hut back in the '90s were available in stacks by the fountain machine, begging to be filled with Coke or Fresca or iced tea. Plain, dull-looking metal cutlery wrapped in napkins sat in a duller plastic bin at the end of the line.

The tables, give or take ten in total and spaced out considerably further than necessary, were round and seated maybe six people at most, four comfortably. The chairs, tucked neatly under the lip of the table, were the same hard, blue, plastic seats I remember awaiting me in my college seminars. They were designed to bear people for a time and dismiss them as soon as their primary objective was complete. Whether in a cramped seminar room or the cafeteria at Silver Springs, loitering, it seemed, was most definitely discouraged.

Dinner was served in shifts, and at 6:30 p.m. it was our turn, the fourth-floor staff and volunteers. The residents also ate at this time but did so in the opposite tower's cafeteria, which I presumed was also squared off and made to look like any other room. I'd find out later this separation was more about giving staff and volunteers a break than curtailing any lingering tensions that may arise throughout the day.

We had an hour to eat. Surveying the evening's spread, I opted for what looked to be a hot roast-beef sandwich—a decision I would regret later that night; you will thank me for sparing you the gastric details—with a side salad and some seasonal vegetables. I grabbed my red cup and filled it with Coke. After the fizz dissipated, I was left with about half a glass. I didn't bother trying to get it full.

I exited the food line like a camper in the mess hall, tray in hand and desperately seeking a friend or two to sit with. I, however, scanned the room for the opposite: an empty table. I didn't have any friends here and wasn't intent on making any. I wanted to eat and get back to my room. A budding headache and body ache were on the precipice of significantly derailing my first hours at Silver Springs. And these were crucial hours. I was banking on a good night's rest to alleviate these symptoms but feared the anxious excitement of finally arriving here would preclude any such endeavour.

"Hey, new guy, over here," came a voice and welcoming wave from the person sitting at a table to my left.

Shit. There goes anonymity.

I had a split decision to make: be polite and kindly dismiss the invitation or accept and possibly be pulled into the labyrinth of Silver Springs politicking. My therapist would not be pleased with this thought. I was creating an outcome, a negative outcome, to a situation I had not yet experienced. But still, I mean, how was this place unlike high school? I'd already relived several moments from my burgeoning youth, and I'd only been on the premises a very short time.

Despite my initial design to refrain from engraining myself here and settling into any type of friendly routine with the staff, I chose the latter, giving Dr. Chartner a small victory. If nothing else, maybe I could get a leg up on Phil, some useful ammunition I could put in my back pocket. This, too, would not please the good doctor. This would be exhibiting vindictive behaviour, he would say.

"Hey, I'm Alex," I said to the lone patron at the table, extending my hand and brushing therapy under the rug.

"Hey, Alex, nice to meet you. You can call me Fred."

I looked at him, slightly confused. Figuring my social status would never reach the level of warranting much concern about my place in the Silver Springs milieu, I chose to dig into this curious statement.

"Alright, Fred it is," I said. "But if you don't mind me asking, what do other people call you?"

"What do you mean?" replied the young man who wanted to be called Fred.

"Well, usually when people say call me, in this case, Fred, it's because they have a name that's difficult to pronounce or they fear having a name that would be associated with a certain profession, like Destiny—and you don't strike me as a Destiny, but no judgments if that's your moniker."

Fred laughed. At least my first impression on him had been positive. My two other attempts at a good first impression had not gone particularly well downstairs.

"Well, in case you didn't notice, I'm half Asian," he said. "And if you're thinking that my name is actually Xuong Ng and I've chosen to adopt the North American name of Fred, you'd be wrong. Unfortunately, my full name is Freddy Jim Kruger due to my father's heritage and my mother's love for Queen's music."

"You're fucking with me," I said cautiously, not wanting to have the wool pulled over me on day one. "I mean, your name's not really Freddy Krueger, is it?"

"It is," he said, calm and measured as if he'd told this story a thousand times, and with a name like Freddy Krueger, a thousand might be an underestimate. "My dad is of German descent, hence Kruger. Except it's spelled K-R-U-G-E-R. But never mind that it's spelled different, that argument is just a waste of breath. When they were choosing my name, my parents had never heard of *A Nightmare on Elm Street*, so a horrifically disfigured, metal-clawed murderer who terrorizes dreams was not in their realm of thought when signing my birth certificate. I like my name, believe it or not, despite the years of ridicule and cheap jokes, so I go by Fred. It's still me, and it makes me feel a little more unique and a lot less murdery."

"Wow, okay then, Fred it is. But wouldn't it be easier to just introduce yourself as Fred and leave the follow-up questions behind?"

"I've tried that, but eventually, and especially in the places I spend a lot of time, it comes out, as things so often do, and I found it was easier to head it off at the pass. Approaching it the way I did with you gets it all out of the way pretty much in exactly this fashion. It's a tried-and-true method."

Fred had to be no more than twenty-two or twenty-three years old. He looked like a kid, and his features only served to accentuate his youth: smooth skin, bright eyes, and the genuine energy and friendliness of someone who had not been exposed to the harsher elements of the social circles most people run in during their early twenties.

I began to cut at my sandwich, a feeble attempt given my blunted cutlery, but I persevered. Pangs of hunger inspired my resilience and interrupted my thought patterns, causing me to push down harder on my knife, scratching the plate and causing both Fred and me to wince from the acoustic pain akin to nails on a chalkboard.

It was nice of Fred to invite me to sit with him. It reminded me of when I was the new kid in tenth grade. I hadn't known anybody, and nobody had known me. I'd been the foreigner in a foreign cafeteria among people who had grown up together. No one had been looking to expand their circle of friends to include the new guy. High school kids can be mean, but more than that, they can be ignorant. It's not their fault, exactly. They're preoccupied with who hooked up with who at which party and how they are going to sneak out of the house the next time a good time presents itself. Making a new kid feel comfortable doesn't rank high on the priority list.

But some people, every now and then, just get it. Maybe it's innate, or maybe their parents did one hell of a job in raising fine, accepting, welcoming young humans. One of these people was a kid named Reeves. It was my third day in a new town and attending a new high school, and Reeves happened to notice my solitary lunchtime routine of reading a book, or at least pretending to, and invited me to the cool-kids table. I sat there the rest of my high school days, quickly and forever cementing myself in the upper echelon of cliques at Riverview High School. Looking back, I can't help but think what a ridiculous concept a cool-kids anything was, but in high school, it was everything, and I was fortunate to land there.

"So what brings you here under the employment of the all-wonderful Silver Springs?" Fred asked me.

"I'm just volunteering," I said. "I was supposed to be on the third floor, but there was a mix-up, and I'm pretty set on being here, so a quick change of plans and fourth floor it is."

"Oh," he said, a little surprised. "I figured, you know, with the scrubs and lanyard, you were a new full-timer."

After my warm, not-so-hot shower, I came to find most of the contents of my luggage soaked through. How this had happened in such a short sprint from the parking lot to the front doors was beyond me, but I had three options at that point: go hungry the rest of the night, attend dinner in a towel, or don the scrubs that were folded in the drawer and make my way to where I was at this very moment.

"Short story but not worth telling," I said, hand-ironing out a crease on my pants that refused to diminish. "This is all I had available to me in the room, so here I am. How's it look?"

"It was in the room. You're volunteering, fourth floor." He said this more like a statement than a question. "They don't have you in 409 by chance, do they?"

I stopped mid-gnaw of my dry roast beef. How did he know I was in room 409?

"Yes. Yes. And yes." I looked at him intently, waiting for his expression to give something away. Things were starting to feel suspect. He remained expressionless, and my anxiety kicked in, knocking the gate open to the negative thought patterns clambering to rush in.

"That's good, man. Welcome. I hear it's the nicest room on the floor, flat-screen and all."

He lowered his gaze as he took a bite of his macaroni and cheese, and as he did, I noticed a slight curl at the side of his mouth. The son of a bitch was on the inside of a joke I would soon be the butt of. I could feel it. My negative thought patterns were right.

Take that, Dr. Chartner. Maybe you aren't as smart as you think.

"You know Phil, from downstairs?" I asked, certain they were in cahoots.

"Yeah, I know Phil. Everyone knows Phil. He's kind of an asshole, but he means well, for the most part anyway. Why?"

"Just wondering what was up with that guy, but like you said, kind of an asshole."

So help me, Fred, if you and Phil are in on whatever is happening right now.

Fred and I finished our meals, exchanging a few topical details about our lives. Before coming here, I'd been a teacher at a small college for a few years, and he'd taken this job after dropping out of high school. School wasn't for him, he said, and his decision to drop out was heartbreaking to his mother. He made some reference to an aged stereotype, but I quickly dismissed it as there was no point in perpetuating it further.

We cleaned off our plates, loaded them on the conveyor belt carrying discarded trays with the remnants of a variety of meals to a room behind the wall, ready to be washed and stacked for tomorrow's breakfast, and made our way out of the cafeteria with about ten minutes to spare.

"Not much going on tonight, being Tuesday, but later in the week, usually more often than not, we get together outside as a staff for some fun. You know, bonfires, drinks, cards, that sort of thing. Tell you what, get yourself settled and meet me for breakfast tomorrow. I can try to show you the ropes a little."

"Appreciate it, Fred, thanks." Fred was at least a decade my junior, yet I had somehow landed under *his* wing. Thankfully, pride was never a sin I battled. I was happy to have a contact and someone I could lean on to help fulfill my goals while I was here.

I went back to my room and opened the window as wide as possible before flopping on the bed. The sun was still up but not nearly as high in the late-summer sky as it had been at this same hour just a few short weeks ago. The treetops swayed to the soft tune of the breeze, and the soothing sounds of early evening began to fill the room.

From a horizontal position, I looked around my quarters. Room 409.

What's so special about you?

The answer to this question was simple: Mae Seasons. And I was a few hours away from meeting the most exquisitely unique, infuriating, charming, and heartbreaking woman of my life.

CHAPTER 4

I woke early the next morning, craning my neck towards the window, witnessing the sun slowly making its ascent above the treeline. The light was still working to penetrate the dense forest wall surrounding Silver Springs. Despite the hour, and the body-consuming divot in the mattress, I felt rested for the first time in a long time. I stretched long and wide—arms and legs, fingers and toes splayed out and wiggling awake. While doing this, I yawned and blinked hard, willing the moisture in my eyes to remove the scratchiness that had taken root, a direct result of whatever dander or allergenic toxin had wafted through the open window as I slept. The fresh air circulating through the room all night was both poison and antidote this time of year.

Today is the day.

I swung my legs over the side of the bed and let my feet experience the worn, coarse carpet. It beat concrete, but not by much. I supposed new carpet, let alone underpadding, wasn't at the top of the list of the room's upgrades. My body rebelled against my waking movements, joints audibly cracking and popping as I stood up and shuffled to the bathroom. With darkness still consuming much of the room, I let my feet tell me when I'd arrived, the abrasive flooring giving way to a chilled tile. The instant temperature change on my feet shot up my body. If I wasn't fully awake before, I was now.

I turned the knob in the shower and let the hot water run, waiting to enter until steam overflowed from atop the robin's-egg-blue shower curtain and condensed on the smudged mirror I was intensely staring into.

Today is the day.

The hot water was intense but brief, and I ended up rinsing shampoo out of my hair in lukewarm water. Once clean, I dried off with a towel that was too small to effectively wrap around my waste as I shaved. Trying to keep the towel on—though for what reason, I'm not sure, as I possessed all the privacy required to perform the task in any state of dress—I ended up nicking myself a few times. Like an amateur shaver, I patched up my wounds with tiny squares of toilet paper that quickly absorbed the blood and turned from white to bright red. I brushed my teeth and was thankful to find the cool overnight breeze had dried the clothes I'd laid out by the open window.

Despite getting an early start to my morning and feeling good, it suddenly dawned on me that I had nowhere to go, nothing to do. It wasn't so much that I was a prisoner, it was that I couldn't go anywhere without someone first unlocking some doors for me and laying down a few guidelines and expectations. Okay, so I was kind of like a prisoner. But in a good way.

I grabbed my phone—which hadn't kept a charge overnight and was only at forty-three percent—off the table and scrolled through the dearth of good news the world was pumping out. It was a quick scroll. Every headline chosen for me was a murder, a political leader dividing their citizens, or some white-collar prick being accused of some type of misconduct—racial, sexual, or otherwise. Was this really my algorithm?

Depressed by the current trends of modern-day life, I tossed my phone back on the table and kept a watchful eye on the red digital numbers of the alarm clock instead. They seemed to change slowly, but change they did. Eventually, they flickered from 6:59 to 7:00. It was time.

I was certain I heard a click, as if the lockdown was over and gen pop could resume daytime activity, but it was probably in my head. Steadying myself as I stood, ready to seize the day, my positive self-talk was interrupted by the shrill sound of the standard-issue rotary phone at the far side of the room.

"Rise and shine, pretty boy." It was Phil. Of course it was Phil.

"Does your shift not end?" I inquired.

"Sometimes I like to pull a double, just because I can," he replied. Was he bragging? He made it sound like this was some great feat, but in actuality, it seemed a little sad to me, if not exhausting.

"Well, it's a real pleasure to start my day talking to you, Phil. What do you have in store for me today?"

Silence. Five seconds of it.

"Your breakfast slot is at seven ten. Goodbye."

I hung up and thought about just how strange people can be, Phil in particular, but I wasn't about to let him interfere with the day I had long awaited.

As peculiar as Phil seemed, he wasn't totally out of place here, as there was a general incongruity about the entire establishment. I had felt it the moment my sprint brought me through the front doors. There aren't many places I know of that are basically a catch-all for mild to moderate cases of mental, physical, and basic health needs.

It was a place for the forgotten, or so I dubbed it after hours of research; a place to go when other institutes determined that a patient was no longer a viable candidate to continue their stay at a hospital, care centre, or any other facility that requires payment.

When I researched Silver Springs—and I kid you not when I tell you I did this at the local library like I was in *The Pelican Brief*, microfiche and all—I learned that Billy Springs, who did a fascinating job of hiding his wealth from friends, created Silver

Springs because his best friend, Jameson Tilbert, was in a horrific car crash. In fact, the entire Tilbert family was in the vehicle when it happened.

The internet, despite being a quagmire of some of the most depressing and conspiratorial garbage known to man, was still a handy tool when it came to research. It got me started anyway, but it really just led me to the microfiche. The archives of old newspaper clippings not yet digitized were the symptom of meager funding and resources, not the unavailability of library technology. I had read through what seemed like hundreds of articles about Billy Springs and his purchase of what was then known as Silvertip Manor.

SPRINGS BUYS OLD HOTEL FOR FRIEND

Though they all survived, the Tilbert children were sent to one hospital, the adults to another. Surgeries of varying significance and invasiveness were performed, and each member of the family had unique requirements of physical and mental therapy to complete before any sense of normalcy could return. Given that Springs never flaunted his vast wealth—in fact, he never had a desire to let anyone know he had money—he chose to run in the circles of those who had nothing, came from nothing. The Tilberts fit this mold, and Billy was immediately captivated by their carefree existence, their enjoyment of life for what it was, not what it could be if only they had more.

HOPE SPRINGS ETERNAL FOR PATIENTS WHO HAVE NOTHING

As recoveries were made, the Tilberts found themselves being forced to separate as a family. Each individual had different needs for rehabilitation and there was no single institution that offered such an expansive range of multi-therapy expertise. The family would have to make a decision: heal separately or suffer together. This, of course, was entirely unacceptable to close family friend and multi-millionaire Billy Springs. He would not let his friend lose his family or continue to suffer.

PHILANTRHOPRIC SAVIOUR BILLY SPRINGS SAVES LIVES AND A HOTEL

Springs had been quietly paying the medical bills for the Tilberts and was happy to do so. In conversations with hospital staff as he wrote cheques and covered expenses, he was informed that the Tilbert's situation was not terribly uncommon; families unable to pay for clinical care were moved out for those who could, inducing a long and circular line of pain and suffering amongst the less financially sound. In fact, families that endured the same accident, whether a house fire or car crash, often ended up requiring different treatments not offered at the same place.

As I read on, it was clear, by every standard, that the healthcare system as it existed at the time was simply not acceptable to Springs. He began researching, much like I had, but with different mechanisms given the era. Facilities that could house patients of all kinds who couldn't afford their bills or costly treatments were a necessity, but practically impossible to find. There would need to be a large building with plenty of rooms, ample outdoor space for physical activity and recuperation, and scenic views for those who may only have their eyesight left. Needless to say, this narrowed Springs's options.

> *SPRINGS BUYS SILVERTIP MANOR*
>
> *When Springs stumbled upon the old Silvertip Manor, which had been the most exquisite and exclusive hotel in the country in the early 1950s, he immediately knew his search was over. What was once an operation requiring a minimum six-month wait for a reservation was, at the time of Springs's purchase, a dilapidated memory of its former glory.*

According to Springs, the physical state of the hotel was nothing more than a hiccup in his ultimate goal of buying the building. The place was perfect, or so he proclaimed in several interviews at the time of the acquisition. He had enough money to run the place in perpetuity, he said, even long after he was gone. And this was true—though upon his passing, his children, who had received the facility as part of their inheritance, failed to display the same charitable, let alone noble, vision as their father. With strict guidelines as to what should be done with Silver Springs, the children, now in charge of the budget's final sign-off each year, made sure to approve just slightly more than the minimum amount it would take to keep the facility operational. This frugalness, to express it politely, explained the building's slow-healing bruises.

But all the depressing shit aside, there was a bounce in my step. None of the Billy Springs story mattered much to me in this particular moment, though it would later on. I could feel a wave of energy pulse through my limbs as if I were a boxer entering the ring to a chorus of cheers. I felt good. I felt alive.

Today was the day.

I saw Fred already seated at the same table as the night before. He glanced in my direction and gave me a friendly, inviting wave to join him. I nodded, indicating my acceptance, and made my way to the spread of bacon, eggs, pancakes, cereals, muffins, and the remaining medley of the usual morning food options. Breakfast was much more appealing than dinner.

My appetite was barely registering, but I knew I should eat something. I grabbed a carrot muffin, a glass of orange juice, and a cup of coffee. I steadied my fare on my tray and made my way to Fred.

"How'd you sleep?" he asked in a way that sent a ping of concern through my body.

"You know what, all things considered, I slept not too bad. The bed leaves a little something to be desired, but the fresh air up here is therapeutic, even if it triggered my allergies."

Fred looked at me, studying my face for the tiniest giveaway that I was full of shit, which I very well could have been.

"So let me ask you," I said, settling into my seat and looking for answers. "What exactly is the day-to-day process here? No one really told me much on the phone, and after I got here yesterday, well, there wasn't a whole lot of direction."

Fred again studied me, certain I could not be who I said I was, that I must have been sent here to play some twisted joke on him. Neither was true, at least not to my knowledge.

"Well, breakfast ends about seven forty. The residents are in their own dining hall around six thirty or seven, those who are awake anyway. Some don't make it out until lunch. Basically, we wrap up here, head down the hall to the rec room and get started on the day. The staff who are with residents at breakfast are finishing the night shift, and they're more or less just there to keep an eye at a distance. They've got it pretty easy, despite the up-all-night thing, but by morning they're pretty tired. Once we arrive, we work with whoever needs a hand or needs to talk;

we're always on the move. Volunteers, like you, on the other hand, usually get paired up with someone for the day, week, or however long you're here."

That didn't sound too bad, I thought. Spend the day with an elderly patient who was afflicted with anything from Alzheimer's to severe depression or someone who just needed help walking from point A to point B or working on a jigsaw puzzle. Again, there was no real prescription to fit in here; from the second floor to the eighth, each level was its own island of misfit toys.

"Anyone you recommend staying away from?" I asked, looking for a little first day assist.

"You won't get a choice today, my friend," said Fred. "You're the new guy; you don't get to pick. You get whoever is left. You get Mae."

"Who's Mae?" I said.

"Mae. Mae Seasons. You're staying in the room volunteers working with Mae get. We call it the Seasons room."

"Do many guests have rooms named after them?" I asked, confident I knew the answer.

"Oh no, the Seasons room is special. And so is Mae. You'll see for yourself soon enough."

Fred lowered his gaze to his food as he took a bite of his yellowish scrambled eggs, and as he did, I was certain I saw him smile, just like last night. He knew something. I knew he knew something. Phil knew something. Everyone was in on it.

And soon, I would be too.

After disposing of our breakfast remnants, we made our way down the long hallway adorned with a leaf-patterned carpet. The walls appeared stained from the bygone days of permissible smoking, which very well could have been the case given the place's glory days were during the height of carefree and rampant social smoking. The overhead fluorescent lights were out of place, clashing with the antique-style sconces that lined the walls.

Much like my room, everything seemed to be in slow transition from dated to mildly modern, like a young married couple who furnished the majority of their first home with assorted hand-me-downs but also bought a few new things from HomeSense to make it look more modern than it really was.

A group of about fifteen of us marched towards the common room where I was about to meet Mae Seasons for the first time. We fell into walking in lockstep without even noticing, or at least I didn't. The only thing missing from a massive misunderstanding was the goose step.

Fred was ahead of me by four or five other staff members, so I couldn't see the smirk that was undoubtedly smeared across his face. His coy performance at breakfast had me on guard, but really, how bad could it be up here? This was the fourth floor, the older guests. How bad could Mae really be? I mean, this was the *fourth floor*. The *older* guests. It bears repeating.

Whoever was in the lead opened the doors when we arrived at the common room. They opened with a click, and everyone seemed to straighten up ever so slightly. It was an odd sight, but deferring to the fact that this group of staff was in possession of the one thing I was not—knowledge of what was behind these doors—I followed suit. It was at this point that I felt the hairs on the back of my neck stand up. I'd never really understood the saying before, not realizing that it was, in fact, more than just words, that it was the actual feeling of the cosmos shifting at the top of your spine. It was equally exhilarating and terrifying.

The group moved in with swift assurance, like a SWAT team entering a hostile building, minus the battering ram, flashbangs, and orders for those occupying the inside to get down on the floor. Upon my entry, I realized that everything leading up to this moment was not cause for concern.

A fairly sizeable group of elderly residents moved about the common room, offering low murmurs of competing conversations and escalated decibels of voices yelling at conversation partners an arm's length away. There were plaid armchairs, abandoned walkers and canes, and at least, by my count, a dozen cribbage boards on various tables throughout the room. It was a commercial for senior living if there ever was one.

Staff members dispersed, my safety-in-numbers strategy dissipating as quickly as my confidence in my ability to actually see this through. Before I had time to catch Fred and ask him any last questions, I found myself standing in the doorway alone, taking in the scene before me and inhaling what I was hoping was fugitive hard-boiled eggs from breakfast.

My face contorted and my eyes burned. I held my breath to avoid breathing in more of the putrid stench and looked for a safe haven in the room. As I was about to take my first step towards decontaminated air, a weathered voice broke the silence and my concentration.

"Yep. That was me."

Mae Seasons then let out a hearty laugh and instructed me to follow her.

CHAPTER 5

"So you're the new guy they told me was coming—word travels fast," said Mae, eyeing me from head to toe as we reached a bookshelf filled with a litany of old paperbacks, everything from Danielle Steel to Mark Twain. Most of the books bore tattered spines, a crime, I thought, but one that gave credence to my belief they were like old teddy bears: even when their softness was long lost, they remained a loved and treasured item rarely put down for long.

Mae had the look of someone who, in another lifetime, turned heads. Her hair, now painted by the silver brushstrokes that come with age and experience, was sleek and thick, and her features were soft, with a network of time-earned creases around her mouth and eyes. She was tall, even for ninety-one years of age. I may have been flattered to have gotten the old up-and-down by a twenty-something Mae Seasons, but now, at her age, it felt slightly uncomfortable. I took solace in the fact there would be zero physical or sexual undertones to her gaze.

"I've seen worse," she said. "Play your cards right and who knows." This was followed by a wink, a jerk of the head indicating to once again follow her, and what I would later learn was her trademark laugh: a light but jovial chortle that was nothing if not distinct. Her rapid and self-assured movements left no room for a proper introduction. So, once again, I did as I was told and followed Mae to the far end of the room where a drip coffee maker sat on a small table, percolating the "bitter swill that will be the death of us all," at least according to Mae. Tiny plastic cups of cream and milk formed a fortress around the sugar cubes, neatly displayed in a dish sitting on a doily.

Despite her dire warning, she pulled the carafe mid-brew and poured a cup, not realizing, or simply not caring, that the machine, fittingly old, did not have an automatic stop. Coffee dripped and sizzled on the boilerplate, ignored completely by its current operator.

"Here, drink this," she said, offering me a mug. "Get a cup down now and another in a few minutes. It'll become easier—if you stick around for more than a day, that is."

I tried to study her face, but she was appraising the room, not looking at me.

"I plan on being here for a while. My name is Alex. Alex Chambers. It's nice to meet you. You must be Mae Seasons?" I asked this as if I didn't already know. It was hard not to know.

"Well, aren't you a quick study," she responded, oozing sarcasm. "I'm sorry. Listen. I'm sure you mean well, but no one usually sticks around that long. The staff, sure. They're paid to be here. Paid a pittance, mind you, but paid nonetheless. The volunteers, my volunteers, they maybe last a week, and honestly, you look like you won't make it to the end of the day. No offense. Well, some maybe. I don't really care if you're offended. You reek of indignation, by the way."

Trying to process this first interaction, I wasn't sure of a response. I was on the verge of one when my eyes started to burn again. Without shame, Mae smiled, pleased with herself.

Someone named Walter walked by and grimaced at the foul odour, raising his hand, not to cover his nose, but to give Mae a high-five. Mae obliged, and I was certain I saw her slip something into his hand as the high-five morphed into a grasp. She did this with the elegance and subtly of someone who'd been greasing palms at this very hotel in the '70s. Apparently, she was the Ellis Boyd Redding of Silver Springs, but meaner and without the smooth tone of Morgan Freeman.

"Jesus, Mae," said Walter. "You've still got it."

The rancid wave began to drift through the room, leaving most in stitches, shouting praise and encouragement at their geriatric hero. Seemingly, this was her thing, what she was known for. And most surprisingly, no one seemed to mind.

Great. My volunteer assignment took unapologetic pleasure in stinkingly perfuming a room, I thought.

Evidently, Mae was known for something else in these hallowed hallways and rooms, something my new friend Fred could have informed me about but chose not to. As Mae caught me analyzing her exchange with Walter, she neared close enough to quietly indicate that I had seen nothing.

She then kicked me in the shin. Hard.

"Hey, how's it going?" It was Fred, grinning, but with a dollop of compassion.

"Yeah. I—I—I'm just getting to know Mae," I said, wincing in pain, trying not to scream in agony and wrath at my abuser.

"Mae, it's so nice to see you up and about this morning," said Fred. "Have you told Alex you've been here going on fourteen years now? I must say, each year, you get a little more animated, but we wouldn't have it any other way."

I glanced at Fred and then the clock. It was just past eight in the morning, and despite my previous pledge to Mae Seasons that I would be here a while, it seemed like she had a better read on the situation. I wasn't sure if I would make it the rest of the day. My head was spinning and lower leg throbbing.

Mae wandered off shortly thereafter, telling me this time *not* to follow. Once more, I did as I was told. This reprieve offered time to observe the rest of the room, the ebb and flow of a typical day on the fourth floor at Silver Springs; it allowed me to get an aerial view of what exactly I was getting into and, more importantly, who I was getting into it with. I observed Mae interact with others on the floor, and she was proving to be something of an enigma. One minute she was helping someone who appeared to be a friend pick things up off the floor, and the next, she was talking trash as she skunked her opponent in a game of cribbage.

As the morning progressed and my dossier on Mae began to fill, a simple chess game provided the ultimate surveillance. Mae was sitting across from a woman named Francine, give or take Mae's age, and the game seemed to be moving along at a fairly reasonable pace. It seemed friendly too. There was no clock, and I'm not sure all the pieces were even on the board, but the two of them swapped pawns, knights, and whatever the other pieces are with fluidity. My knowledge of chess begins and ends with the phrase 'checkmate.'

As I watched the two engage in their back and forth, Mae grew increasingly agitated. It could be that she was losing. It could be constipation. With Mae, you just never knew.

"For crying out loud, Francine," cried Mae. "You can't move your rook there." I trusted Mae knew what she was talking about and listened to the exchange with the little information I took to be accurate.

"Oh dear, Mae, you're right. My mistake," said Francine.

I took and released a deep breath; the fire was snuffed before it ignited. Or so I thought.

"You cheating son of a bitch!" Mae declared, escalating the situation.

Francine tried to explain what was a simple, innocent mistake, but Mae wasn't having any of it. I mean none of it. I couldn't imagine a friendly game of chess getting to this point, especially at their age, but here we were, at the threshold of senior-citizen fisticuffs.

A few of the staff came over to check in on the commotion, eventually drawing Mae aside to speak with her privately, trying to prevent a further scene.

I took this opportunity to introduce myself to Francine, hoping, if nothing else, I could get a sense of what had just occurred and better understand what made the woman I was now tasked with babysitting tick.

"Hello, Francine, is it?" I asked in as non-threatening a manner as I could.

Francine looked up at me with a bit of a blank stare. Her large, circular glasses magnified her hazel eyes so they looked as if they were bulging. Her hair was short and curly and snow white. Her movements were cautious and unsteady. As she placed the game pieces back to their appropriate spots on the board for the next match, she told me that what just happened was nothing more than Mae being Mae.

Having asked what exactly that meant, Francine gave me little in the way of illumination.

"Oh, poor Mae just has a short fuse," said Francine. "She always has, ever since she arrived here all that time ago. I came here a year before her, and things were relatively calm. Needless to say, things haven't been the same since Mae arrived. She's lovely, but she can also be a bitch. She's like a sister to me."

Hearing someone a decade away from one hundred years old call one of their own a bitch was a little like hearing a nun narrate a sex tape: it just shouldn't happen, and if and when it did, it was unsettling.

I thanked Francine for what little insight she'd given me and went about observing everything else I could for the rest of the morning.

During this time, Mae was ushered in and out of the common room, removed each time for some type of verbal assault or lewd behaviour. Thankfully, no more of it was directed my way. Others seemed to be on the same page as Francine, as the name-calling, both under the breath and not, was astonishing coming from the crowd populating the room. It seemed like Mae had more enemies than friends. It also seemed that everyone loved her and loathed her in equal measure.

A headache was forming.

CHAPTER 6

Later that day, Fred filled me in on exactly how, and more importantly why, the new guy ends up with Mae. To his credit, he admitted that staff were the ones who arranged for new volunteers to be paired with the eccentric resident. They did this for two reasons, he said. The first was because it gave them all a good laugh, knowing that most people wouldn't expect Mae to be, well, Mae. The second reason was for the staff's own sanity. They had all tried giving their time and attention to Mae in a fashion that would coax her into an easy rhythm. It seemed that management at Silver Springs hoped that one day someone would come in and things would just click for her, that she'd ease off the pedal that propelled her hardened exterior and difficult-to-manage personality. They'd seen it before with other residents, Fred explained. It was an earnest hope, a wish that had yet to come true. I was the shiny new penny tossed in the wishing well.

The longest anyone had stayed volunteering with Mae was three weeks, and by the end of those twenty-one days, the volunteer had left with diminished self-esteem and significant questions about the decency of humanity, not to mention a few scrapes and bruises, physical and emotional. While I could appreciate the candor of these statements, I did wonder if the people who had been paired with her before just weren't quite thick-skinned enough. I mean, sure, Mae was a little abrupt when she was worked up, maybe even a little mean, but overall, she didn't seem *that* bad. Then again, it was only day one, and I was now over-the-top self-conscious about my perceived indignation.

As the day revealed itself, I noticed a pattern to hurricane Mae; once she made landfall, it took about ten minutes for her to dissipate, returning to a state of nonchalant normalcy, which for her was reminiscent of someone who was experiencing Mondays on a loop.

I was reading quietly in the common room, making myself available should any resident need my assistance, when Fred came with the message that Mae wanted to see me in her room.

Giving room 4H—residents' rooms had numbers and letters; staff's and volunteer's rooms had numbers only—the familiar rhythmic knock we all seem to use, I waited on entirely the wrong kind of bated breath outside the door. Instead of the door handle turning to greet my arrival, I was welcomed with a muffled "Come in," emitted from the other side.

Upon entering Mae's room, I was instantly transported back to every room in every home my grandmother had ever lived. The wallpaper was a textured, abstract floral pattern, the carpet a soft pink, and the lamps, furniture, and decorations hearkened back to generations gone by. There was a small RCA radio on the ledge near the window, once white but now stained yellow through years of being touched with greasy fingertips and faded from the kiss of the sun. Coming through its speakers was classic country music, with its distinguishable twang and full-throated, southern-accented voices. There was a pleasing smell in her room that was familiar and made me think of my grandmother. The scent was a mixture of vanilla and peppermint, and in a way, it was comforting, momentarily disarming my trepidation of being alone with Mae.

I took small steps as I moved closer, my gait unintentionally turning minimalist. Mae was sitting in an old armchair complete with green velvet arm covers and a worn Afghan blanket draped over the back. She had a cup of tea on the table beside her, the bag's tag clinging to the outside of the white ceramic mug. She didn't offer me any. She didn't offer much in the way of a greeting either.

"What are you doing here?" she asked, picking up her cup and stirring a spoon in an almost hypnotic fashion.

"I was told you wanted to see me, I—"

"Not *here*. At Silver Springs. Why are you here? Why did you come?"

For the second time in as many days, I was confronted with telling my truth to a complete stranger. And for the second time in two days, I lied through my teeth.

"I wanted to give back, spend some time with people who may need someone to spend their time with," I said, proud of my delivery, staunch in my belief that it was convincing.

"You're full of shit. Let's get that right," she said, sounding like Gordon Ramsay and taking a sip of her tea before putting it back on the saucer. "If you're going to be here, if I'm going to be stuck with you, you will cut the shit. Do you understand? Nod if you understand."

I nodded, more out of fear than agreement. The way she said "nod, if you understand" made me feel like I was an expat in an interrogation scene with a terrorist.

"Good. Let's try this again, shall we? *Why* are you here?"

Prior to arriving, I had rehearsed my lines so many times it would have been easy to offer any of my go-to monologues in this moment, but it was obvious Mae saw through me. I don't know how, exactly, but sure as the sun had come up that morning, she knew I was full of shit. My motives, however, were mine and mine alone, and Mae, despite inducing my current state of fear, was not going to pry the full story out of me.

I unconsciously blurted out the first thing that was moderately true. "I was supposed to be on the third floor, but there was a mix-up and—"

Cut off again. "The mutes? You were supposed to be on the third floor with all the zombies? What the hell do you want to be down there for?"

"I thought it would be a good place to collect my thoughts, work out the details of my YA fantasy novel without much interruption or questions," I quipped. My modest chuckle was met with a cold stare. "Look, I wanted to be on the third floor because I thought it would be a good way to help out and reflect on my own life, alright. I'm going through what you might call a crisis of faith—"

Cut off. Again. "Oh, for fuck's sake, Adam, it—"

"Alex," I corrected her, cutting her off this time, which she quickly dismissed.

"It won't much matter what your name is if you don't cut the shit like I literally just told you to. You're not having a crisis of faith; you're too young and likely too stupid to even know what that means. You don't have the miles on you to have a crisis of anything."

Her blunt response startled me. I was saved from floundering for a reply by a knock at the door and an incoming staff member named James. He was tall and lean and would qualify as handsome to anyone with a set of eyes, including, and perhaps especially, Mae, whose sour expression turned sweet at his arrival. She gave me an unsettling wink. James was there to take Mae to her in-house doctor's appointment.

"We're not done here," she said to me, getting up to go with James. As he moved ahead of her, she followed. Looking back at me, Mae put both her hands to the sides of her pelvis, gesturing what could only be discerned as a sexual thrust.

No, I thought, *we most certainly aren't done here.*

Despite her aggression, intolerance for my shit, and suggestively lecherous nature, I felt, for the first time in close to twenty years, that someone might actually be able to understand me, even if

I had only been scolded, berated, and physically harmed up to that point.

As Mae left the room, I took one more inhalation of what was surrounding me, both in nostalgic fragrance and physical structure. Despite hurricane Mae's destructive path, she somehow offered a measure of calm. Don't ask me to explain it because I can't. It was ineffable. Ineffable but eerily reassuring.

What was I doing here? The question was a perfectly valid one. Yes, a perfectly valid question indeed.

But I too had a question: what was Mae doing here? Neither of us *belonged* at Silver Springs, but it was exactly where we needed to be.

CHAPTER 7

Walking back to my room after Mae had been escorted to her doctor's appointment, Susanne lobbied my attention from near the elevator, requesting a word that, although promised, I knew wouldn't be quick.

Great, I thought. *What fresh hell does she have in store for me now?* Was she coming, with her corporate language, to add salt to my very fresh shin wound?

Susanne was dressed in her self-styled uniform. Nearly everything was exactly the same as the day before, but instead of a navy-blue ensemble, it was charcoal grey. Even her hair looked the exact same. If her tone indicated she was operated by levers, her attire confirmed it.

"Mr. Chambers, how are you this fine afternoon?" she asked cheerily. Fake, but cheerily.

"I'm good, Susanne." Thanks for asking. I guess.

"I heard you had a little mishap with Ms. Seasons this morning. I do hope you will try not to rile her up like that in the future."

Stunned at where she could have possibly received such misguided information as to the morning's events, my mouth opened to respond, but no words formed.

"Very well then. I just wanted to check in on you and remind you that our older guests here at Silver Spring can be very sensitive. Many of them have lived a life you and I could never dream of enduring. We need to be mindful of that at all times. I do hope you will remember and conduct yourself accordingly."

I felt my jaw inching closer to the floor.

"Yes, very good. If you need anything, please let Mr. Abner at the front know. He can assist you with whatever you require. Though, in the future, do try to be a little kinder to him as well. We want to make sure we treat everyone here at Silver Springs, whether staff or resident, with the utmost respect, care, and love."

Jaw met floor.

Upon repositioning it back to its original location, my lips finally started moving. "There is one thing, Susanne. A spot on the third floor."

"Sorry, Mr. Chambers, still nothing available."

Susanne strode back to the elevator, no doubt on her way to harangue another staff member or hapless volunteer.

I spent the better part of the afternoon walking the building, familiarizing myself with the compound's layout, at least in places I was granted access. Sorting this out was a game of trial and error, with some keypads turning green at my ID card's tap and others flashing a shall-not-pass red.

When I finally retired back to my room, I noticed the door was slightly ajar, a sliver of light casting a faint glow into the hallway. My instincts told me that my door hadn't closed tightly when I last left, that these aging doors were likely to swell and retract with the changing of the seasons, keeping them slightly off-kilter and not always level. When I heard a noise coming from the other side of the old door, I realized my instincts, which have always left something to be desired, were incorrect. Maybe someone was in the midst of pranking or plundering the room of the new guy. Or maybe it was some curious woodland creature that had infiltrated my chamber through the open window.

Thankfully, my belongings were few and invaluable. My iPhone was in my front pocket, my wallet in the back. What was left in my room included some clothes, a couple of books, and a six-pack of beer I thought might come in handy to take an edge off.

Pushing the door open confirmed I was partially right: someone was ransacking the room, though not a cute woodland creature. It was Mae, her cold, thin fingers wrapped around a colder beer. She was laughing. Of course she was laughing. She was, as I was growing to suspect, certifiable.

"You spineless little shite," she greeted me. "You let Robot Rogers tell you all the things you did wrong, when in fact, you didn't do a single one of them."

Her eyes shifted from mine down to my crotch. She pointed her free hand in the same direction and twirled it in a circular motion like she was casting a spell.

"I'm not sure there's anything there between those skinny legs of yours, Sonny."

"Mae, you're supposed to be—I don't know where, but I'm sure it's not here. What are you doing here? And how did you get into my room? And why are you drinking?" I had more questions, but I left it at those three for the time being.

"That miserable twat of a doctor isn't worth my time. I told him what he needed to hear in order to prescribe me some of these little friends and I was on my way." She held up an easy-to-open prescription bottle and gave it a rhythmic shake. I couldn't tell what was on the label, but Mae seemed quite pleased with her pharmaceutical score. "So, I decided to come and pay you a little visit. It took you long enough to get back. As for how I got in, well, I told those boys in white that I wanted to see the room named after me. Who are they to say no to a little old lady? They're young, and some of them pretty, but there's a reason they're working here—they're not too bright, you know? And finally, as for the drinking, well, I don't owe you an explanation, but here's one anyway, since we both know you'll be a persistent nag: I do what I want when I want. And I wanted a beer. It's a good thing you had some in the fridge. The way I see it, you have two choices. You can march your ass right through that door there and carry on with your day, or you can sit down next to me, have a drink, and get on with cutting through the bullshit you tried to pull earlier."

Who *was* this woman?

In a matter of a few short hours, she'd managed to assault me, break into my room, and take the first sips towards tying one on, all the while insulting my manhood and rationale for being here. Damn if that wasn't kind of impressive. Sadistic perhaps, but impressive nonetheless.

"Okay, Mae," I said, sizing up the ninety-one-year-old force of nature. "But this isn't a one-way conversation. You've got to give me something too—like an apology for this nice little bruise you gave me this morning, for starters." I lifted my pant leg, showing off my first Seasons battle scar. This would be the last time I took my eyes off Mae when talking to her.

"Sure thing, Sonny." She tossed me a beer, smiling.

As I cracked the tab, the usual soft click signalling the first breath of the brew within was replaced with a rush of frothy pressure exploding in my face, on my clothes, and all over the carpet.

Mae howled. And I don't mean she just laughed with great force; she released a knee-slapping, gut-busting howl. Wiping the dripping beer from my face, I saw Mae keeled over with laughter.

"You dummy," she managed through the tears now streaming down her cheeks. "I can't believe you fell for that."

"Why wouldn't I fall for that?" I exclaimed. "Why, of all the possible outcomes, would that have been one that would have, or even should have, entered my mind?"

For the second time in the last ten minutes, I was stunned, barely able to comprehend what was happening. I kept thinking back to the recurring question of what the hell I was doing here.

Deep down, I knew the answer, but on the surface, I was preparing to run. Fast.

"Oh, don't take it so personally, you Nancy," chided Mae. "It's all in good fun. Or are you not the type who is capable of having any fun? You do look a bit rigid, you know, like you've got a nice, stiff, straight pole wedged right up that arse of yours."

Mae's candid, and vivid, language flustered me. If she was trying to coax information out of me, she was taking the path less travelled. I told Mae I needed to change and mustered as much politeness as possible to ask if she would give me a minute to do so. I grabbed a new set of clothes from the drawer and shuffled to the bathroom.

Looking into the smudged mirror, I noticed the residue of Coors Light lining my face. I took a stiff, scratchy washcloth from the rack on the wall and turned the tap on to soak it. The warm water took its time but eventually arrived. Wiping my face and neck, I peeled off my shirt and tossed it on the crumpled towel that lay on the floor. I had no idea what the laundry schedule was here, but figured it was something that could be handled later. For now, I wanted to rid myself of the scent of beer seeping into my pores and cottons.

I opted to fully change even though my pants were spared any liquid shrapnel from the exploding can. As I slid them down past my knees, I heard the door creak.

"Jesus Christ, Mae, shut the door!" I screamed, hurriedly pulling my pants back up.

Once more, Mae snickered. "Oh, lighten up. You should be thankful a woman wants to see you in your skivvies. There's going to come a day when that young body of yours will be shrivelled up and not worth the eyes of anyone but your proctologist."

"Well, I guess you'd know from experience." *Ha, take that. There's something between these legs after all, you old shrew.*

"Oh no, Sonny, this train still has plenty of steam in the engine."

I gagged and nearly threw up. I tasted the sour bile swimming in my throat. My manhood may be intact, barely, but trading barbs with Mae Seasons was never going to be a game in which I could compete.

I pushed the door tightly into its frame and turned the lock from vertical to horizontal, securing my privacy. As I did this, I quickly realized that my guard would have to be up at all times with Mae. Emerging from the bathroom, I now sported a pair of khaki shorts and a T-shirt with the word 'EXPLORE' written upside down and ending with a backwards E. I'm sure there was some type of irony or metaphor woven in it, but I've never found it. I just liked the colour and feel: a soft blue with softer threads.

I stood about two metres away from Mae, now sitting in the armchair near the open window, her hair moving in the slight breeze. It was cooler than yesterday, which made for a comfortable temperature in the room, despite the red-hot cells elevating my blood pressure higher and higher.

Mae's hands were now folded in her lap, her feet flat on the floor, a position that was non-threatening. She looked as if she were at an interview, waiting to be called in and grilled about her experience, competencies, and ethics. In this moment, I thought of an old joke that seemed to fit Mae perfectly in such a scenario.

A man walks into a job interview with all the skills and experience required for the position. The interview goes well, and upon its conclusion, the interviewer asks one final question: what would you say is your weakness? The man thinks and replies earnestly—his weakness is that he's honest. The interviewer says that's hardly something that should be considered a weakness but rather a great strength. The man replies, "I don't give a shit what you think."

To me, this was Mae. She didn't give a shit about me or anyone else at Silver Springs. She was here for herself, for whatever reason, and she was looking out for number one. I can't say I fully blame that mindset, given the environment, but surely her desire to have some comfort in friendship had to exist.

I sat opposite her and studied her face, hoping to learn something, anything, that would give me the upper hand in our future exchanges. I knew I would be pummelled into submission if not prepared, so anything that would help me stay above water was welcome.

And then I saw it, high up on her wrist. The playing field was shifting back to even.

CHAPTER 8

"Okay, Mae," I said. "What exactly would you like to know about me?"

"Oh, Jesus H. Christ Almighty, how many times must I repeat myself? I want to know *why you're here*. I don't care why you're here with me; they pair me up with people like you all the time. They come; they go. It's a revolving door. I don't know why they think I need a babysitter, but here you are, same as all the rest. And so I ask you again: Why. Are. You. Here?"

There was something about Mae's voice as she made her request that suggested there was more to *her* story. It seemed odd to have endured so many unsuccessful pairings. Perhaps it wasn't my place to know, but I let the thought linger. If I was supposed to know, maybe I would in due time. I was, after all, sticking around. I was determined.

"Well, Mae, like I said, I'm here to volunteer. That's the God's honest truth."

Her eyes flashed with an insolent disappointment. Before she could take a verbal swipe, I continued. "But does it really matter? I'm here. That's it. I'm here. Why do you need a reason? What does it matter why I'm here? In the two-plus hours I've known you, I can't think of a single moment that would indicate you'd actually care why I'm here. Why are *you* here? Why is anyone here? Their reasons are their own, or everyone's, it doesn't matter. Susanne and company managed to screw things up and put me on this floor with you instead of the third floor, and I'm going to make the most of it. So, what do you say *you* cut the shit and we make this pairing as enjoyable as we can for the time it lasts?"

Mae sat quietly, either impressed or totally impervious. I was certain I would have been interrupted, scolded, or possibly kicked again, but none of those things happened. Instead, Mae just sat there. I have to be honest, given her age, I would have genuinely wondered if she had peacefully died in the very chair before me if not for her blinking.

"Let's go then, to the third floor," she said.

"What?"

"Did I stutter? To the third floor, dummy. Let's go."

Mae rose to her feet steadily and smoothly. Her age was an insignificant factor in anything about her.

"Mae, I have a question for you," I said, not yet standing up or believing that we were actually making our way to the third floor. "What's your connection with the armed forces?"

If Mae's eyes had flashed disappointment earlier, they were now a roiling storm of contempt. She adjusted her sweater, pulling her sleeves down to her wrists.

"If you're coming, let's go. I'm not waiting for you." And with that, Mae walked towards the door, not looking back.

"Now listen, we're not supposed to be down here; we're supposed to stick to our own floors," said Mae, speaking to me in a tone that suggested we were some type of dynamic duo pulling hijinks on the school principal.

We were in a stairwell that needed no description and barely offered enough features to provide one. The floors were separated by thick concrete and the needs of the patients inhabiting them.

Apparently, in the interest of efficiency and focused assistance, there was little to no habitual mixing of residents, unless you were related. I supposed this made sense given the varying ailments and degrees of specialized care that sent people to Silver Springs. On some level, though, it was sadly segregating, but then again, aren't most places like this a little bit sad?

"Mae, listen, I'm sorry if I—"

"Shut up and pay attention," said Mae, barking orders like a drill sergeant. "We're down here because you have some paltry need to be on this floor. You won't tell me what it is, but I'll figure it out. Yes, I will. If we get busted, I'll scream obscenities at you, kick you in the shin, and claim you kidnapped me and brought me here. You can say you followed me as I went AWOL. They will believe you over me, so don't worry, you're not in any real danger of picking up an abduction charge."

"Well, that shouldn't be too hard to believe seeing as you did exactly that this morning." I winced, still feeling lingering pain in my shin. "Wait, this morning, was that a—"

"Let's go, now or never, Sonny."

Mae leaned into the silver, horizontal push bar on the door in front of us, her efforts granting entry to the floor I was hoping to eventually become a permanent fixture on. Mae moved quickly, surprisingly quickly, which was not great for my cover, as I had to spend more time watching her than getting my bearings and finding the blind spots to keep our mission as stealthy as possible. I was able to discern, however, that the hallway was a replica of the floor directly above it—and likely the one below as well. Presumably, all floors were identical in décor and layout, the only real difference being the inhabitants.

We had entered at the far end of the hall, which meant we needed to make it the length of the building to get to the third-floor common room. Upon Mae's suggestion, this would be the consummate location to survey the populace. To do this, we'd have to pass Phil's eye-in-the-sky as we manoeuvred down the hallway, which we did like a couple of idiots, ducking into doorframes and crouching behind planters. This was a fairly stark corridor, but we treated it like an invasion of the Eagle's Nest. Mae informed me that the third floor had a veranda off the common room, offering pristine views of the countryside, an immense clearing of lush green hills to drink in before the forest swallowed the grassland. Why she volunteered this information at the moment she did was beyond me, and to be honest, I couldn't have cared less, prompting my one-word reply.

"Okay."

Halfway down the hall, I felt a rush of adrenaline. Or maybe it was antsy nausea disguised as adrenaline. The confusing euphoria was caused by sneaking around on the floor and anticipating what was potentially waiting behind the double doors directly ahead.

With each passing step, I expected to hear the forbidding voice of God, a.k.a. Phil, come booming through the speakers, alerting the authorities to the pair of escapees on the third floor. The voice never came. Part of me wished it had.

We made it the length of the hallway undetected. My breathing was noticeably heavier as we reached our destination—and not because of the energy expended to make it there. Sure, I was a little gassed from the expedited pace to get from point A to point B, but my heart raced faster as we stood facing the common-room doors. I'd never had a heart attack but figured this is what it must feel like to be on the brink of one.

Mae hadn't said a single word to me as we made our way down the hall. She hadn't said a single word to me as we reached the common-room doors. And she didn't say a single word to me as she collapsed to the floor just as we were about to enter the third-floor common room.

CHAPTER 9

Staff members rushed to the doorway as Phil's voice resonated from the overhead speakers. Code yellow, red alert, blue lobster. I don't know what words were actually being used or what any of it meant, but there was a memorable colour-coded system, that much I was sure of. My concern was solely for the lifeless body slumped at my feet.

I was forced out of the way as at least six people in Silver Springs-issued scrubs knelt beside Mae, checking her vitals.

Their words were indistinct and muffled, not because they weren't speaking clearly, but because everything in that moment sounded as if it were being said on a scratched-up cassette tape.

Before I was able to truly get a sense of what was happening, Susanne appeared.

Fuck.

"Mr. Chambers!" she called out with more than a spoonful of admonishment. "I thought we spoke about this. What on earth are you doing on the third floor with Ms. Seasons? You, both of you, are required to stay on the fourth floor, no exceptions."

"Susanne, listen, I—"

"Ms. Rogers," she snapped back, with an emphasis on *mizz.*

"Ms. Rogers. Mae and I were taking a walk on the fourth floor, where you so rightly point out we are supposed to remain; however, she began down the stairwell and I followed her. I feared she was going AWOL." I had no idea if our story would stick, but it was literally the only thing I had, and I was not terribly quick on my feet.

As Susanne recited from the manual—what to do when a volunteer goes rogue—staff members continued to work on Mae. They announced she was still breathing, which was a relief. They then wrapped that Velcro blood pressure contraption around her upper arm and began pumping the little rubber squeeze ball. Another staff member had a stethoscope placed on her heart or lungs or whatever they checked in that general chest area.

I wasn't fully listening to Susanne, though I was looking directly at her. My ears betrayed me, unable to focus on any single voice. I glanced down at Mae to check how she was doing, and I could've sworn she was grinning. I looked back at Susanne and then back at Mae. She was definitely grinning. I would have been convinced she'd died happy, sporting a grin like she knew a secret she was in sole possession of, or it could be another move in the irrational game we were playing. Accompanying the knowing facial expression was Mae's trademark hard-boiled egg smell. Both things could have signalled the same in death as they did in her life.

Her eyes now open, she gave me a subtle wink as staff members helped her to her feet and into a wheelchair.

"Head to my office please, Mr. Chambers," said Susanne, my hearing picking back up where it had left off during her spiel on safety. "We will have to discuss this incident, write up a report, and determine just what exactly we are going to do with whatever time you have left here."

Having not been here long, but long enough to know that countering with anything other than a silent nod of agreement would have been poor judgment, I began the lonely walk down the corridor, the bustle of excitement growing behind me as people from the third floor came out of the common room to inspect what was happening. I turned back to look at the faces in the crowd, but they were indistinguishable this far away.

"Time is wasting, Mr. Chambers," came the echo from down the hall. "I do not like to be kept waiting."

No, *Mizz* Rogers, I'm sure you do not.

"Nice going, new guy."

It was the voice of God.

"Shut up, Phil. Just shut up," I muttered. I was in absolutely no mood for his or anyone else's bullshit.

"Oh, well aren't you the sensitive one? What, new guy can't take a little ribbing? If you're going to make it here at the ol' SS, you'll have to grow some skin as thick as Kim K's behind." The sound of Phil enjoying his own joke filled the air.

Isolating individual speakers within the system, Phil's voice literally followed me as I walked towards Susanne's office. I felt like I was going to the principal's office for something I didn't do. Granted, I was partially liable for what had happened, but it wasn't my idea, and there was nothing I noticed that could have caused Mae's sudden collapse.

I knocked on the door that had Susanne's name and title prominently stencilled on the frosted glass. Once. Twice. Three times. There was no answer from within, so I took the initiative to enter. For reasons unknown, I sat down immediately, as if this would somehow relieve me of feeling like I was breaking and entering. A sitting man is not a threatening man. I rested in the incredibly uncomfortable chair across from Susanne's desk. My guess was that this was some type of power play she used to keep her guests on edge. Try as I might, I could not get comfortable.

Looking around the room, I noticed not one, not two, but three degrees from various universities, several certificates of competency, and what looked like a homemade employee-of-the-year plaque. A tall, worn wooden bookshelf held court in the corner, filled with—and I couldn't actually believe it—a full set of Silver Springs binders, each labelled and organized alphabetically.

There were no personal photos on her desk, walls, anywhere. Not a son or daughter or partner—not even a cat. Without question, Susanne was a cat person. It's not a judgment, it's just a painfully obvious characteristic for some.

There was a clock on the wall that obnoxiously ticked away each passing second. Had Susanne not arrived when she did, she would have had to use her wristwatch to tell time from then on.

"Mr. Chambers, the good news is that Ms. Seasons is going to be just fine. She simply experienced a minor dizzy spell," she said, making her way from my rear side to settle into her plush office chair. "However, we do not know what caused it, and given the delicate age of Ms. Seasons, even a small episode like what just happened could be very bad. We cannot be too careful. I am sure you understand."

"Yes, of course. But, Susanne—Ms. Rogers, I have no idea what happened. I didn't do anything to cause whatever happened to Mae. Ask Phil; I'm sure he was watching. Go check the tapes. I followed her down to the third floor, and at the common-room doors, she just went down."

My suggestion of watching the tapes would effectively out our intentions on floor number three. We did, after all, attempt our infiltration like a couple of rookie FBI agents clearing a room; peaking around corners, using hand signals to communicate forward motion, and so on. But still, the tapes would resolve any question as to my direct involvement in the incident. Taking the lesser charge would be a victory.

"We most certainly will review the tapes, Mr. Chambers. It is protocol. And I will, at your suggestion, speak with Mr. Abner to inquire about whether he witnessed anything of consequence. For now, however, we need to determine what we are going to do with you. You have had quite the first day."

Susanne spoke with a tepid desire to help me, but there was no way she was going to discover any substantiation that my time with Mae was a direct correlation with what happened, and I think she knew that. I hoped she knew that.

She picked up a pen from a blue, tin writing-utensil holder and began to twirl it between her thumb and forefinger, spinning the instrument like the rotors on a helicopter. She did this for a few seconds before asking me the same question I was now getting quite tired of being asked.

"Why do you want to be here, Mr. Chambers? I recall on the phone it was something about wanting to volunteer your time, to spend it with those who do not have anyone else to spend theirs with. Is that still the case?" Her keen eyes appraised my every movement.

"It is," I said with as much conviction as I could muster. "That's why I'm here. That's why I'd like to stay here."

After a few beats, Susanne let out a heavy sigh, the kind that usually signals bad news after thoughtful consideration.

"Maybe Silver Springs is not the best fit for you." She paused before moving on, letting the full weight of the idea land. "I must say, I have never seen a first day like this. Yes, Ms. Seasons can be, at times, a bit of a handful, but you have really put unnecessary strain on her today. And please be mindful that we have permitted you to be here solely to spend time with Ms. Seasons. For your information, not many people do."

Gee, I couldn't imagine why.

"Susanne—Ms. Rogers, I would very much like to stay here. I was supposed to be on the third floor. Maybe that's all this is; I'm in the right place but on the wrong floor. Maybe there's a way to switch me to the—"

"No, no. The third floor is full. We have discussed this already, Mr. Chambers, you surely recall. I am not in the habit of bending rules for anyone, especially troublemakers, which I am hoping you are not, though you are proving you may just be."

I was losing count, in such a short period, of how many times I had contemplated what I was doing here and if it was truly worth it. Was it worth the time, the effort, and, most of all, the frustration of putting up with Phil, Susanne, and Mae Seasons?

The answer, which I was thankful I kept returning to, was a resounding yes, though damn if it didn't put on a very good disguise in moments like this.

"Mr. Chambers, do you know how long I have been doing this?" She didn't give me a chance to hazard a guess before continuing. "I was born to do this job. It was made for me. I have completed the training, graduated top of my class. Simply put, I am the Tiger Woods of the rehabilitation game. Silver Springs may not be what it once was, but I will be darned if I do not show up every day to make this place as safe and homelike as possible for the lost souls who inhabit these floors."

I wasn't completely sure what Susanne's sermon was getting at, but interrupting was not in my best interest.

"I have given my life to this job. It may come as a surprise to you, but the people here are my family. Like many, we are all each other have. It can be a lonely place, and part of my job is to make it feel less lonely for as much time as I can. I cannot, will not, run this place like a fraternity or a sorority, bending rules, turning a blind eye, or being party to shenanigans that jeopardize the well-being of those who call this place home."

I don't know if Susanne meant to get the engine revving to travel this far down the track, but hitting the brakes now was out of the question. In for a penny and all that. What was becoming clear, however, was that Susanne, the rule-abiding director that she was, was less this way because of her wiring or genetic makeup and more because of her steadfast commitment to the people who took up residence at Silver Springs. She fell among those who provided a service greater than any desk jockey pushing paper at a nine-to-five. Respect, Susanne. Respect.

Susanne's cell phone rang—a Taylor Swift ringtone that was set far too loud for public settings. Glancing at the caller ID and picking it up on the precise conclusion of the third ring, she answered.

"Yes. I see. Okay. Very good. That is excellent news indeed. I will send him up. Thank you."

As Susanne hung up the phone, I stared at her. I don't just mean I looked at her intently, I mean I stared at her as if I were trying to perform some Jedi mind trick to make her spontaneously combust. I don't think that's what Jedi do exactly, but I appeared to be summoning some type of otherworldly force.

Speak, woman. Speak!

And then she did.

CHAPTER 10

I could feel Phil's eyes peering through the cameras, watching my every step as I made my way to Mae's room. What he was watching for, I didn't know, and quite frankly, at this point, I didn't much care. But I could feel them, and it was unpleasant.

Thankfully, the residents' rooms were not rigged with hidden cameras, though would it be entirely surprising if they were? I preferred not to spend too much time on this voyeuristic, particularly unsettling thought.

Mae's door was open, and a staff member named Dwayne waited outside.

"You Alex?" he asked as I approached.

"That'd be me."

"Go on in. Mae is waiting for you. She's lying down in the bedroom. I'm out of here, so you're on your own."

The words echoed behind Dwayne, who was in stride down the hall before he finished them: you're on your own.

Thanks, Dwayne, but this was not something that required any reminding.

I called Mae's name in a tone that was soft and warm but loud enough to be heard. It was the type of call-out your mom gave you when waking you up for school as a child, gentle enough to avoid startling you but with enough energy to make sure you heard.

Mae responded and welcomed me in, her face breaking into a wide, full smile.

"So, Alex, are you ready to cut the shit now?" At this point, Mae was upright in her bed. By all accounts, she was fine. Absolutely, unequivocally fine.

"Mae, what the actual fuck?" I quickly begged her pardon for the language.

"No, no, this is good. Let it out, my boy. Right now, every curse word you know. Go."

In what was becoming second nature, I searched Mae's face for a sign of—I don't even know. At this point, it was like grasping at straws in the wind. Fuck it. Here we go.

As I rattled off all the curse words I could think of, Mae exhibited an almost giddy temperament. With each word a little more offensive than the last, her excitement surged. As I was nearing the end of my list of vulgar vocabulary, Mae got out of bed, inching closer with the sharing of each unseemly syllable.

I recited words and off-colour combinations so quickly that I was breathless by the time I stopped.

"There. Satisfied?" I asked, sucking in oxygen.

Despite my question being directed at the slight lady in front of me, I was prepared to answer it for myself: yes, in some ways, I felt lighter, happy even, just letting all formality and pretense go. I don't know why, as I had no pent-up rage, no lingering, built-up frustration that required such a release of these linguistic taboos. Surely, Mae hadn't even heard of half the words I had just said.

"Now, there's one more, Sonny. Say it."

Mae's stare was intent and piercing, a look that creased the lines around her mouth and eyes, raising the corners of her mouth like the Grinch.

"Mae, that's all of them. That's all I'm going to say."

"No, it's not. Say the last one. It's cathartic, and you know it. We're cutting through all your shit right now. Say the word."

"Mae, I can't say *that* word in front of you. A lot of what I just said was bad enough. I cannot—I will not say it."

"That's too bad. I guess our friend Ms. Rogers will have to hear about how you spewed so much foul language you made an old lady pass out—again." Her eyes flickered with mischief. Mae was nuts. Calculated and nuts.

I contemplated letting Mae play her game, going back to my room, packing my bag, and leaving Silver Springs forever. Susanne had given me another chance, but another episode in such short order would all but drive the final nail deep into my volunteering coffin. And Mae knew. She knew as well as I did, I couldn't leave. Not yet.

"Okay, Mae, I'll say it. But I'd like to go on record as saying that while the last list of words came out with relative ease, this is not a word that I use. Ever. I'm not a prude, but I think we both know it's one of the worst words that can be spoken."

"Oh, don't be such a wanker. The Brits use it all the time. Everyone is so politically correct these days, it makes me sick. Say the damn word and we'll be on our way."

I stood motionless, willing my mouth to form the word, pleading with my vocal cords to make it audible enough to mollify Satan, who was before me in the guise of a ninety-one-year-old woman.

"C—u—n—"

Before I could sound the last letter, a wrinkled, aged palm delivered white-hot pain across my cheek.

"Don't you *ever* say that word in front of a lady, do you hear me? Disgusting. Did you grow up in a barn? Sweet Jesus, Alex, what's wrong with you?"

My face, equally red with embarrassment and the sting of the first slap I'd received in my entire life, couldn't contort in an appropriate way to convey the simple state of shock I was in.

Mae moved past me, shook her hand out, and told me it was dinnertime. Her laughter lingered in the room as I remained, unable to move.

Dinner, like all meals, had staff and volunteers separated from the residents. There were a few staff on hand who only worked the resident cafeteria meal shift, helping those with whatever dietary or feeding requirements they had. To be honest, this separation was a welcome break, and I was only on day one.

Fred was nowhere to be found. In fact, the cafeteria was emptier than it had been at breakfast and lunch. Maybe the day's menu was a deterrent—it featured meatloaf, but that was a generous description of the grey meat block hardening under the heat lamp. I grabbed a tray, filled it up with anything that looked edible, and took a seat at a table near the back of the room, close to the windows lining the far wall and overlooking the courtyard.

The view was majestic. It seemed that regardless of the window you looked out, the view was the same. Different, but the same. Hilltops appeared to rise into the sky, and the branches of the trees were hinting at their yearly transition from lush greens to vibrant yellows and reds and oranges. More than nature, it was the view directly below that really caught my eye.

The grounds of the courtyard were neatly trimmed, designed with an engineer's mind and manicured with an artist's touch. The lawn was thick and green and would have made my father jealous. There was not an errant dandelion or patch of crabgrass anywhere. There were no dead patches, and every blade looked uniform in length, as if trimmed with a pair of scissors. I gazed down upon the familiar configuration of bodies I recalled coming out of the third-floor common room when Mae decided to perform her morning improv. As far as I could tell, this was some type of recreation time, or more accurately, simply some outdoors time. The group just kind of sauntered about slowly or didn't move at all. I hated to admit it, but I could appreciate why Mae referred to them as zombies. The third-floor patients seemed content to let the refreshing air wash over them in the same fashion as the angel statues scattered throughout the grounds.

Time was passing without my knowing. My food remained on the tray, untouched. Just as Mae's wallop had caused jolts of shock and pain in the not-so-distant past, so too did a figure that stood out as I observed the walking dead.

It wasn't as if this was a total surprise; I knew she was here. It's why I was here.

But to see her, to really see her with my own eyes again, caused a paralysis that could only be broken by—Mae?

"Mae, what are you doing in here? I thought this room was only for staff and volunteers."

"Yeah, well, if you haven't caught on by now, I do what I want and go where I please. What are you looking at down there?"

"Nothing. Just kind of taking in the view. I guess it distracted me. I mean, it's pretty breathtaking up here. The hills, the trees, it's absolutely beautiful. Everywhere you look, it's like a Bob Ross painting."

Mae laboured through a deep, dramatic sigh. "Must we do this again?" It was said almost as a plea as opposed to a demand.

"Okay, okay. I know someone down there, alright?"

Mae smiled. "Now we're getting somewhere. Now we're cutting through the shit."

She didn't press the issue or quiz me about who it was. She was satisfied with my kernel of truth, my peace offering, and her backing off was an olive branch, or so I took it to be one.

I sensed an odd familiarity about Mae. Sure, some of it could be chalked up to her being an old woman my grandmother's age; therefore, Mae was basically the same as her. But it was more complex than that. There seemed to be something broken in Mae in the same way there was something broken in me. I had caught a glimpse of the break when I saw her tattoo and asked about it, but there would be time later to figure that puzzle out. And just as I had given her some space, she was now reciprocating.

"Well, good news for you, Alex: you've got the rest of the night off. My performance this afternoon has me booked with the white coats this evening. Full physical for me. But hey, it's not all bad. Have you seen the young Dr. Green? Maybe I'll ask *him* to turn his head and cough when he's done with me."

Gross, Mae. Just gross, I thought. But dammit if she wasn't one of a kind and just the slightest bit charming.

Mae put her hand on my shoulder, laughed, and trundled off. Once more, her laugh lingered while I remained unable to move. This was becoming a disturbing pattern.

CHAPTER 11

I spent the rest of the night in my room. I zoned out. I read a book—well, part of one anyway. I watched TV—if you classify mindlessly channel surfing as watching. Mostly, I stared out the window, gazing upon the trees and seeing an ominous curtain before me. My emotions were tempestuous and indistinguishable. I was looking forward to having the night to process whatever this cornucopia of anxiety, unease, guilt, and excitement was all about.

It had been sixteen years. *Sixteen years.*

I know life is as full of regrets as it is anything else, and sometimes the regrets stand a little taller, push back a little stronger, and thrust their way into memories, overtaking what once was good and turning it into a heaping pile of shame.

Just as my dinnertime zone out had been interrupted, so too was my Zen moment of deeply inhaling the fresh forest air and summoning the memories of someone I used to love. Still loved. Will forever love.

The phone on the night table pierced through the silence. It was either Phil or Susanne, neither of whom I was particularly interested in speaking to. I let it go to voicemail. But instead of a blinking red light offering notice of an awaiting message, the phone rang again. And again.

"Hello?!" I barked after deciding to pick up the phone in lieu of tossing it across the room in a childish tantrum.

"Mr. Chambers? Ms. Rogers. How are you?"

Susanne, not Phil. A small victory is still a victory, though this was won by the slimmest of margins.

"I'm fine. It's been quite the day." Fewer statements were truer.

"Yes, indeed it has. I am sorry to bother you during your own private time and at this hour. I do hope I am not interrupting, but the reason for my call this evening is to inform you that I owe you an apology." Susanne barely took a breath as she spoke. "I now realize, after reviewing the tapes and speaking with the doctors and Ms. Seasons herself, that you, in fact, had nothing to do with her collapsing earlier this morning, but please understand that I was coming from a place of great concern, of responsibility. I have to take care of my staff and my patients."

Small victory growing loftier by the word.

"You must understand, our residents are of the utmost importance to us. Attentiveness to their health and well-being are what we are known for, what we pride ourselves on, and, well, when someone new comes in and has near-catastrophic interactions with one of our own, one must wonder."

I would hardly categorize the morning's events as near catastrophic, but best to let sleeping dogs lie.

"But, nonetheless, things are now squared away, and Ms. Seasons was singing your praises. She even suggested I give you financial compensation for your time here. I hope you are not responsible for this idea of hers, as you surely know this is not possible and your being here is strictly on a volunteer basis."

I waited a few seconds just to make sure she was indeed finished speaking. "Yes, I'm aware," I said. "I have no expectation of payment. I'm sure Mae was just saying some nice things and pushing them as far as she could. She seems to have a penchant for such a thing."

"Well, in any matter, thank you for your time. Enjoy your evening. Goodbye."

It seemed that every conversation I had was odd, if not downright puzzling, save for those with Fred, and even they had a hint of peculiar.

I placed the phone back on the cradle and allowed myself a triumphant smile. The day had started out as a certified mess but was turning around, giving credence to my belief that I was doing the right thing in the right place, even if I hadn't fully convinced myself of it yet.

I flopped on the bed, closed my eyes, and slept until morning. It was the first night I had slept uninterrupted by nightmares in sixteen years.

Fred put down a stack of twenties and slid them in my direction.

"This is yours," he said, a tone of defeat carried in his voice. "We all lost the pool."

"The pool? What are you talking about?" I asked through bites of Honey Nut Cheerios.

"You made it three weeks, congratulations." He stuck out his hand and shook mine with the firmness of an enemy conquered and ready to meet their honourable fate while still respecting the warrior in their victory. "No one had you lasting more than five days. When we heard you were here, and knowing we'd pair you up with Mae, we all figured one of us would bank an easy payday. But you did it somehow. Are you here against your will? You can tell me. Blink twice if you are," he said with a grin.

"Five days, huh?" I replied, feeling underestimated and ever so slighted. "That's not a ton of respect for the new guy. Why so low? I mean, Mae hasn't been *that* bad."

"Listen, man, when I first got here, Mae was my first assignment, and I was a *paid* employee," said Fred. "I lasted two and a half days before I threatened to quit. They were short-staffed at the time, and I was the first new hire in over four months, and not due to a lack of openings. Needless to say, Susanne did everything in her power to keep me here. It's a tough spot to fill, you know, even with a paycheque."

Fred offered me a brief peek behind the curtain as he recounted his first days at Silver Springs. He had just left home—or rather, been forced out—after calling it quits in his junior year of high school. He had felt the steady pressure of academic success his whole life, and it had been breaking him, causing him a mental distress he simply could not bear any longer. He lost all interest in studying and academics in general. He packed up his Honda Civic—a sixteenth birthday present his parents threatened to take away if he dropped out—and took the first job he could find, even if it was in the middle of nowhere. Seems he made his escape before his parents could make good on their threat.

It didn't hurt, of course, that the employment he settled on included food, lodging, and laundry. It was like a full ride at the university he never attended. In fact, he said it was the sole reason he submitted his application. He had no discernable skills as a caregiver, but an able body was a body, and Susanne and company were desperate. The Springs children were getting greedier, cutting the budget at every turn. Good help left; subpar help slowly rolled in to fill their shoes. But Fred worked hard and helped turn the culture around.

He was young, yes, but he was committed to carving his own path, parents be damned. He enjoyed what he did and often enjoyed working with the likes of Mae, even if she, too, had introduced herself to Fred with a swift kick or two in the shins. Fred admitted that Mae wasn't as bad as some of the others made her out to be, that there was something buried within her that was pure, a core of love and affection. Granted, it would have to be chiselled out like a fossil buried in the depths of the earth, but it was there, somewhere.

"I've gotten to know the stories of a few people here," I said, "and I understand why they're at Silver Springs, but why is Mae here?"

"That, my friend, is a question I cannot answer," said Fred, taking a sip of his coffee, which was more milk and sugar than ground bean.

"First of all, how can you drink that? And second, what do you mean you can't answer that question?"

"What, this?" Fred lifted his mug. "I've never been able to really get on the coffee train; it's too bitter for me. But the caffeine is helpful, and it feels too weird having a Coke or Red Bull this early in the morning. And I can't tell you why Mae is here because I have no earthly idea. I'm not sure anyone does, other than maybe Susanne, but her lips are sealed tighter than a nun's—well, you get the picture."

"Gotcha, say no more. Seriously, please, say no more."

Fred was a good guy, and we seemed to have established a good repartee. I hadn't anticipated making a friend while I was here, but it was nice to have a friendship organically materialize.

It had been three weeks since I'd arrived at Silver Springs, and thankfully, no other day had even come close to the maelstrom that was day one. I had settled into an agreeable groove and was starting to understand what made Mae tick, even if I didn't know why she was here. I think she was feeling the same about me, but it was hard to tell. Either way, we were getting along. There was still a lingering uncertainty as to how long it would last, but I was going to ride it out.

I had been kicked in the shins a few times now, the bruises never quite fully healing before the tender and bright shades of yellow, blue, and purple sprouted back up in vibrancy. I was occasionally yelled at, and in one instance, I was scratched on the forearm to the point of bleeding. Each physical altercation required Mae to be carted off to see the doctors, though not Dr. Green who, I had heard after their appointment on day one, requested to never treat Mae again. I can only imagine why.

I hadn't made it back to the third floor and was relegated to viewing those residents from the fourth-floor cafeteria. It wasn't much, but it was something. Hell, it was everything.

As breakfast wore on and I watched Fred inject two more servings of sugar into a serving of coffee, I felt better and better about what was happening.

"Sorry to disappoint, but I'm here for the long haul," I said, collecting my stack and counting my winnings. I folded the bills and put them in my pocket. The extra cash was nice, though I had no dire need for it. Money wasn't an issue; it's why I was able to volunteer.

Fred, or anyone else for that matter, didn't need to know that I had inherited enough money from my grandparents to last several lifetimes. Maybe I'd give my newfound winnings to Mae, but what could she possibly need a hundred and forty bucks for? I'm sure she'd find a way to double or triple it, running some slick gambling scheme on her unsuspecting *friends*. I decided that aiding and abetting this type of behaviour would only land me back in the principal's office.

"Well, at any rate, it'll come in handy for your upcoming weekend off," said Fred.

"Weekend off? I didn't think volunteers got weekends off. I thought this was a seven-days-a-week thing. I mean, we're not expected to put in eight hours every day, but I don't think I've seen anyone leave."

"Last weekend of September, residents with passes get to head out. Granted, not many here have anyone to visit, let alone come pick them up and take them out for a weekend, but Mae, she's out of here every year. You can set your watch to it."

This was the first I had heard anything about this, but then again, I'd only been here a few weeks and there was still plenty I wasn't aware of. The thought of a weekend off held less appeal to me, here by my own volition, than those paid to be here. Fred had a look of envy when he told me, and I felt for him.

"I had no idea," I said. "I guess I'll have to figure out what to do with a few unexpected days off." The truth was, I didn't want to go anywhere. I wanted to perch in a cafeteria chair on the fourth floor and peer down below.

"Well, either way, lucky you," said Fred. "With the remaining group we have, Mae is the only one scheduled to go anywhere, which means nothing changes for us. But hey, that's life, right?"

We ate the rest of our breakfast in silence. Fred now looked like he held some animosity towards me for having a few days off. Considering what Mae puts me through, her handler, of all people, ought to have the right to a few days of rest, relaxation, and physical and mental recovery. Maybe I was reading too much into it. Perhaps it was just an exhausted employee who was in desperate need of a break that wasn't coming any time soon. Either way, what to do with a few days off?

That night I got a glimpse into the underbelly of staff life at Silver Springs. It was Friday, and I had been convinced by Fred that it was time to join in. I connected with a group of about twenty staff members in one of the outdoor gardens that couldn't be seen from the cafeteria windows—or from any of the overlooking windows.

It was a capacious area decked out with card tables, lawn chairs, and tiki torches to light the way. It was a BYOB type of thing, and thankfully, Fred hooked me up from his personal stash. I felt like a teenager again, sneaking booze from my parents' liquor cabinet, and Fred made it feel that way too as we sneaked into the garden where we now stood.

"We're all adults. We're not on the clock, but for some reason we all feel like Susanne is watching, so we have to be sneaky," Fred said, surveying the crowd before us.

We were close to being the last arrivals for the night's carefree, made-it-through-another-week festivities. Other staff members were caught up in various conversations, many imitating the crazy shit they'd dealt with during the past five days. There was lots of laughter and an overall cheerful vibe. It was a nice reprieve from the grind of the week.

"So, I hear you're heading off with Mae for the weekend," said Dwayne, sidling up to Fred and me.

"What are you talking about?" I asked him. "Apparently Mae is off somewhere, but as for me, I'm just here for the weekend. Maybe I'll sign up for the tour." I took a draw from my mickey of Canadian Club whisky.

"Guess my informant got some bad intel." Dwayne laughed and pointed in the direction of none other than Phil.

What the hell was *he* doing here? *Narc!* I wanted to yell out. I refrained.

"What's he doing here? I thought this was staff only," I asked Fred. "He's probably recording us as evidence."

"Phil is a bit of a savant with the technology," said Fred, failing to assuage my panic. "Although truth be told, given how he acts, he's really just more of a smart idiot."

It made sense, hearing it from Fred, given how Phil had followed me in isolated audio along the hallways, whispering over the speakers as he switched from one to another with ease, no one else seemingly able to hear him. A smart idiot indeed.

"He means well, he really does," Fred continued. "But he takes his job very seriously, and his social skills are inadequate at best. Though his tech skills have saved us from many a colossal problem."

I was curious about my nemesis and any information I could obtain that would help me prevail over him; I was playing the long game. "If you don't mind me asking, what kind of scrapes did he get you out of?" I pried.

"Too many to count," said Fred. "But Susanne basically owes him her career, which is why she looks out for him and builds him up and asks everyone to give him a chance, you know?"

Fred seemed at ease in this space, drink in hand, amongst friends and colleagues, and without the worry of Mae's or anyone else's shenanigans. He always seemed pretty at ease, but there was a discernable difference in the laid-back way he carried himself in this particular setting.

The wind sighed through the trees as the moon offered luminous support to the tiki torches. The air was crisp and chilled. The swigs of alcohol helped to keep the belly warm. The nights had seemingly dropped in temperature quicker than the day's warmth would have suggested was possible. These pendulum-like swings of the mercury were very much a northern phenomenon.

"So when you say Susanne *owes* Phil her career, what exactly do you mean?"

"Well, it was about three years ago now, or thereabouts. Susanne wasn't the director yet, but she was on track, and she wanted it bad. Oh boy, did she want it bad. She had never met the Springs kids—we don't mention their names, by the way. They're like Voldemort in tandem, but worse. Anyway, the little devils were coming for a site visit. No one knew why, but everyone was on high alert. With Tweedle Dee and Tweedle Dum holding our purse strings, we all wanted to make sure our presentation of Silver Springs was memorable. We figured if we could wow them, we might scrape a few more pennies out of the budget that year for some much-needed operating costs. They're pretty good with capital expenditures, but a penny more for operating is like trying to squeeze blood from a stone."

Fred recounted the day the Springs kids came. Their names are Davis and Danielle. I wasn't afraid to say them, but I had read enough about these two to understand why the permanent staff would take offense. The story, however, was mundane, and I was beginning to wonder what the big deal was, especially with Susanne.

"So, as the day was wrapping up, the Springs duo decided to do a random locker check, so to speak. The oldest asked Susanne, who had accompanied them throughout the day, to go to her office for a scan of her computer. Susanne will tell you that they were trying all day to get her to slip up so they could avoid promoting her, and maybe even give them enough reason to can her and save a few bucks. She was too good at her job, too by-the-book for them to get away with the shortcuts they wanted. Anyway, they get to Susanne's office and immediately have her log in to her computer. They wanted to see files on other staff members and patients. This, of course, was confidential information they were not authorized or entitled to see.

"They kept pressing her, and despite knowing better, she was ready to give in. Like I said, she wanted the director position bad. And that was when Phil, from his front desk workstation, found a workaround into the system and locked Susanne out, locked every machine in the building out. He suspected something was up when they went to her office at the end of the day. So he did what he does best. He turned on a few speakers in her office, reversed the feed to use them as microphones, and heard verbatim the rock-and-a-hard-place position Susanne was in."

I admit, at this point, I was impressed with Phil's selflessness. I wasn't sure what could have been in it for him, but doing a good deed is a good deed done.

Fuck, Phil. Why is this story triggering Stockholm syndrome?

"Long story short, Phil shut down the entire system, so even if Susanne had wanted to show them the files, which, of course, she didn't, there was no possible way it was happening. And it turns out this was a good thing too. None of us were aware, but in those files were business cases for buying out the Springs and taking control of their share of the operation. There was intel, if you will, like the kind you do on political opponents. What's it called? Oh yeah, opposition research."

Wow. I was surprised, impressed even, and despite the conclusion of the story taking twenty minutes to arrive, I was slightly enthralled by the favourable attributes of some people I had perhaps hastily and unfairly passed initial judgment on.

"So how did Susanne find out it was Phil that pulled the hack?" I asked.

"Well, for as smart as he is, once he saw the Springs kids leave, he celebrated his successful mission and unknowingly toggled the speakers' microphone function—Susanne could hear him instead of the other way around."

Smart idiot indeed.

"Well, how about that," I said, eyeing Phil from across the short expanse of the garden. "I mean, he's still kind of a dick though, right?" I wasn't yet of a mind to let one redeeming story about my sworn enemy sway me to the ranks of Team Phil.

"Oh, absolutely. He's got the personality of a hockey puck, but he means well and he's family here. Craziest part of the whole thing, he doesn't know Susanne knows, still to this day. He's totally clueless. We all know, but she never told him. She offers him thanks for that day, and others, in different ways, such as her trying to get you to ease up on him."

Now I felt a little bad. Shit. "I suppose I could ease off that gas pedal," I acknowledged. "But not always. I've still got an axe to grind with him."

"Fair enough, man," said Fred. "That's your business. Just know, there might come a time when you need him to bail you out, so tread lightly."

I hoped it would never come to that.

"But come on, there's time for other stories tonight. Let's go mingle. You can ruffle some feathers, make some new enemies by rubbing it in their faces that you'll be off for the weekend."

So mingle we did. But I made a few more friends than enemies that night. Phil was still not one of them.

I made it back inside just after midnight, ready to retire for the night. When I got to my room, I found Mae rifling through my things and packing what she could.

CHAPTER 12

"Where've you been? Pack your bags; we have a weekend adventure ahead of us," Mae said with her back to me, busily packing *my* duffle bag. "When we're done here, we'll go pack my things. No time to waste, my boy." Her energy was infectious, even if confusion obscured my understanding of what was happening.

"What do you mean *we* have an adventure ahead of us? Fred said you've got a weekend pass coming up, so I'd say *you* have an adventure ahead."

Mae didn't skip a beat, she bounced around the room grabbing clothes, incidentals, whatever she could get her hands on. It was an everything-but-the-kitchen-sink moment. I hadn't the slightest idea what she was packing for or why. Given that our maximum stay away from Silver Springs could only span the weekend, I wondered what more would be needed than a few changes of clothes and a book to pass the time.

"Maybe you do belong with us seniors. You seem to have a hard time hearing like most of us blue hairs," she chided. "We, as in you and me, the both of us, the two people in this room—are you following?—are going on a wee bit of an excursion this weekend. So, like I said, grab your things and pack your bags." She kept repeating the request for me to pack, but in actuality, she was doing it for me. Her barking the order felt more reflexive than mandated.

I floated somewhere between confusion and surprise, feeling an equal pull from each. Sure, Mae and I had developed, at the very least, a tolerable working relationship, but certainly not one that would warrant an invitation to a weekend getaway, and certainly not as the third wheel with whoever was coming to get her—a son or daughter, maybe a grandchild.

"Mae, you can't be serious. I mean, this is *your* weekend with your family or whoever. Do you even like me that much? Where are you going anyway? Why are you packing so much?" My rambling, rapid queries were an effect of the previously mentioned surprise and confusion.

Mae stopped picking up random items like loose change on the street and looked at me, politely and calmly asking if I was in the midst of having a stroke; ever the thoughtful one, that Mae. She said she'd seen plenty of strokes and I was resembling the all-too-familiar lead-up.

Was I having a stroke? No, of course not. But Mae made me wonder. And doubt. But mostly wonder. Maybe I was having a stroke. No, definitely not. Maybe?

"Mae, listen," I said, sitting on the edge of the bed and speaking clearly and calmly as if I had to prove to her that I was not suffering from any type of medical episode. "It's very kind of you to invite me to wherever it is you're going. And I'd like to join you, I would, but I'm not sure it's the best idea. And besides, what would Susanne say? I'm already on pretty thin ice with her, as you know. She says she believes me, but I'm pretty sure she still thinks I've been the cause of some of your recent medical oddities, which we both know is bullshit."

Mae laughed at my mention of her performances, content and pleased with her routines to date. It was becoming apparent, if only to me, that she harboured a deeply hidden secret, and I suspected her behavioural escapades were nothing more than cleverly choreographed theatrics to keep her here. As this notion permeated my thoughts, its saturation soon gave way to a series of questions: Was I to try to uncover it? Why would I even want to? What could I possibly gain from befriending this woman? Would going on a two-day trip propel us not just to, but past the threshold of hell?

The faded permanent ink on Mae's forearm that had peeked out of her sweater on my first day meeting her flashed before my mind's eye, and I knew the answers to my questions. I needed to uncover this mystery as assuredly as she needed to excavate it from the catacombs of her history and deal with it.

As I took over packing my belongings, Mae reclined in the chair near the window, stretching her legs in the cool of the night's breeze. Unbeknownst to us, the upcoming weekend would catapult what we both wanted to keep hidden onto the map of discovery—personal plot points that, once charted, could never be erased. Thankfully, we didn't know it yet, otherwise we would have never agreed on what time to leave. Which turned out to be within the hour.

We stood out front of Silver Springs, hugged by the darkness and the quiet that sweetly danced with the midnight hours, waiting for her friend to arrive. It was just after two in the morning, and to my surprise, we were permitted to be outside. Apparently, weekend passes aren't bound by the place's structured operating hours and literally begin Saturdays at 12:01 a.m.

Each year, Dolores would come pick up Mae and they would have a girl's weekend. This is how it was told to me, and I accepted it with a grapefruit-size grain of salt. The story, albeit brief, was advertised as a nice, natural bond between longtime friends who rarely got to see each other anymore. This year, however, I would be the third wheel to whatever mischief Mae and Dolores would undoubtedly get into. Mae didn't share any information about the happenings of their previous excursions, but if Dolores was anything remotely like Mae, I knew the next forty-eight hours would exceed my initial fears and anxieties, which, of course, did nothing to soothe my current fears and anxieties. As soon as I spied a car rolling into view, the hairs on the back of my neck erupted to attention. The vehicle rumbled down the drive, audibly sloshing the pools of water in the weathered potholes, freshly refilled from the recent deluge of rain.

Upon seeing the car, approaching at an acceptable speed for a jetliner at cruising altitude, Mae giddily told me to grab the luggage, instructing with excitement in her words that we had better move as quickly as the vehicle coming to scoop us up. In near pitch-black darkness, we made our trek across the front lawn, now damp with early morning dew, to the parking lot. Approaching the vehicle, the silhouette of Dolores revealed features I was not prepared for. As we got closer to the car's illuminating interior light, I couldn't believe what I was seeing amplified against the blackened backdrop of night.

"Mae, are you sure this is who you were expecting?" I asked, digesting the pink-and-blue Harley Quinn hair, cigarette smoke billowing out the driver's side window, and what I can best describe as God-awful thrash metal music thundering from the speakers.

"Yep. Now get in."

I did as I was told. I found that employing this tactic with Mae resulted in fewer kicks, screams, and vernacular assaults.

I hoisted Mae's suitcase—an old, cracked Samsonite—and tossed it in the trunk of the light-blue Buick LeSabre, circa 1990. Had we been in the light of day, I doubt very much I would have climbed inside. The creeping rust, bent antenna, and cracked rear window initiated strong reservations we would not make it off the property, let alone the two hundred kilometres we would be travelling to Pineton, a small, isolated town known mostly for its remote cottages and summer vacation rentals.

But Mae assured me, and convincingly so, that the last weekend of September was the best time to visit Pineton, and Dolores owned property there. I was skeptical of Mae's assertions, but again, she was convincing. I packed the last of our things in the trunk and looked around to make sure I hadn't missed anything. As far as I could tell, it was all there—all, perhaps, except my best judgment. What the hell was I doing? There was that question again.

Before I could slam the trunk, Mae was getting into the passenger seat, announcing shotgun with a gleeful, youthful thrill. I couldn't help but smile at her child-like exhilaration. I suppose when you reach Mae's age and don't have a lot of people left in your life, the little things become so much more relishable.

I opened the rear passenger door, and upon doing so, was certain I felt it come off its hinges ever so slightly. I didn't dare test my discovery. Instead, I opted to put it out of my mind, telling myself I wouldn't die in this vehicle, and settled into the plush, velvety backseat. Instinctively, I reached for my seatbelt only to find that where one should have been, there was an unevenly sawed-off strap of fabric, chewed through by what had to be strong, sharp teeth. There was little comfort when Dolores craned her neck and declared it was her dog that had gnawed through the once-functioning safety requirement. Thankfully, the beast wasn't here now, but I wondered if it was waiting for us at the cottage. I had an irrational fear of large dogs and was intent on eventually allaying it, but my current capacity for life improvements meant tackling them one at a time. We hadn't yet shifted into drive, but I could feel my stomach lodged in my throat, having ascended from my depths to make an escape at the first and likely sign of certain destruction as we travelled farther north.

"All set?" asked Dolores, adjusting the rearview mirror and making eye contact with her backseat passenger. I opened my mouth, but no words came out. I gulped and nodded, lying to myself, and everyone else, that I was indeed all set. Mae, on the other hand, was forcefully ready, commanding Dolores to "get this bitch on the road!"

As we drove opposite Silver Springs, I couldn't help but glance back at the safety and serenity that was inching further and further away, quickly disappearing into the dark grasp of night. I felt like a child in a movie, watching my friends disappear as Mom and Dad drove away from the place we grew up, the one family that left while all the others stayed.

Before I managed to swing my vision back to facing forward, our speed was decelerating; we were stopping. I inched to the edge of my seat, about to ask the obvious question. We had just reached the point where Silver Springs was no longer in view. What was in view was Mae counting twenties, peeling off five or six bills and handing them to Dolores, who promptly shoved them into her purse and exited the car, getting into another that was idling on the other side of the road. I felt an uneasy lurch and tightening in my chest, an army of anxious soldiers scattering in every direction at the realization that something wasn't as it should be.

"Uh, Mae, what's going on?" It was the obvious question, of course, but now it was two-pronged: why did we stop, and what was with the money?

"You're riding shotgun, Sonny, let's go." Mae also exited the car and walked around the front to take her position behind the wheel. If Dolores driving two hundred kilometres of highway at night was terrifying, this new development was downright apocalyptic. But I did as I was told, fear preventing me from uttering any defiance.

Mae gripped the blue, cracked rubber steering wheel, rubbing her hands on it as if she was revving the throttle on a motorcycle or feeling the softness of an old lover—both equally unnerving. I looked at the dashboard and was relieved to see that the gas tank's needle was on the reassuring side of half full. The odometer read 146,090 km. This was clearly faulty and a bit concerning. I talked myself into subscribing to the fact that the gas tank needle was more important and pulled my seatbelt across my chest, letting a thankful sigh escape as I heard it click.

"Mae, are you sure you should be driving? Do you even have a—"

Mae cranked the gearshift into drive and peeled away from the shoulder, spitting up loogies of wet gravel and spewing the rocky shrapnel in all directions as we fishtailed into the northbound lane.

Jolted, as if I was experiencing g-force in a flight simulator, my neck whipped back over the top of my seat, which was inconveniently missing a headrest.

The interior of the vehicle smelled about as clean as it looked, the dim lights from the instrument panel offering a peek unseen from the dark shadows of the backseat. I could feel cigarette burns in the fabric of my seat and see an ashtray full of butts, many smudged with lipstick. The salt stains decorating the passenger footwell were rough under my feet—something easily preventable with floor mats, of which there were none. There was a waxy film across the dash that extended up the lower part of the windshield and windows. The motor for the automatic window hummed sickly as I pressed it down, hoping to coax some fresh air inside. It refused to budge more than a couple centimetres.

The engine moaned as Mae's foot routinely forgot that consistent pressure was required to maintain speed. As she drove, she smiled. It was nice to see Mae smile, but given the circumstances, it was like we were playing out the ending of *Thelma and Louise*. I think they were smiling, maybe not. In this moment, I know I wasn't.

"Mae, I have some questions," I said nervously. "I have a lot of questions actually. But let's start with this one: What the actual fuck is going on here? And who was the woman you paid a hundred or so bucks to get out of the car?"

"We're getting an early start to our weekend. And that was Dolores, I already told you that. Next."

"Yes, I know her name, but who the hell is she? She looked like an angry teenager experimenting with some twisted cosplay character who also happened to offer chauffer services for meth money."

"Well done, young Alex. Bang on!" exclaimed Mae. "She is almost exactly all those things. Her hired name is Dolores. The money was absolutely for whatever drugs that little harlot is going to purchase. What's next?"

"Wait, what? You *hired* her? You don't *know* her?"

"Her actual name is Chandra of the Midnight Sun. What more is there to know? She needed money; I needed a service. It's a clean transaction. We've had this arrangement running for the last six years."

Despite the many fresh questions this new information now demanded, I needed a moment to appreciate what I had just heard and what it could mean, if anything.

Five, ten minutes must have passed before another word was spoken by either of us. I was the one to break the silence.

"Mae, I've got to use the facilities. Can you pull over?" As soon as I said it, I heard it and immediately regretted it.

"Use the facilities? Need some privacy to pull your panties down, do you? If you've gotta piss, hit the bushes like a man and find a nice tree to water."

"I've got to go to the bathroom, okay? Can you just pull over? Anywhere is fine."

Mae kept driving. And driving. And driving.

"Mae, are you going to pull over or what?"

"Oh, right, the liquid evacuation thing. Let me find a safe spot."

The whole highway was a safe spot at this hour; we hadn't passed a single car since we'd started driving. Mae drove. And drove. And drove.

"Mae! Please pull over!" My urgency was driven by the pressure building in my bladder and the utter and complete fear that was stoking my nervously spiralling thoughts.

Mae, giving a laugh, jerked the car onto the shoulder with the finesse of a sumo wrestler auditioning for *Swan Lake*. I didn't know if she was laughing at me or the road sign she'd pulled in front of: Hardwood Road. She quickly confirmed the latter, repeating the road's name, shaking her head, and chuckling like a teenage boy.

"Well, get moving, I don't want you making a mess in my car."

I couldn't help but think the acidity from my urine might actually clean some of the grime I was currently sitting in. I was looking at Mae like a deer in the headlights. Take me now, Lord.

Pulling the door handle and launching my elbow into the door to get it to open, I clambered out onto the side of the road. The treeline was close, about three metres at most, and the brush was dense. I wouldn't have to venture too far in for some privacy. I didn't need to be the star in another one of Mae's peep shows.

"Better hurry up, or I'll leave you here to experience your own moment of *Deliverance*."

I stopped dead in my tracks when I heard Mae squeal like a pig in her best mountain man impression. After that alarming sound, it was miraculous I was able to squeeze even a drop out, but I worked as quickly as I could, emptying my tank and hustling back to the car. It wasn't so much that I believed Mae would leave me at the side of the road, it was that she was wildly unpredictable and sometimes took things too far. But more than that, I didn't trust her as far as I could throw her.

Despite her age and the fact that she sat far too close to the wheel than would normally be comfortable, Mae, surprisingly, wasn't a terrible driver. It's a little prejudiced, I suppose, to assume that because she was old, she would be a bad driver. Don't get me wrong: she wasn't a good driver—no, not by any stretch—but she wasn't terrible.

The signs on the side of the road indicating the distance to Pineton incrementally counted down. There wasn't much to look at outside of nature itself—at least whatever you could see when the moon shone its spotlight between the clouds. Though Silver Springs was surrounded by tall trees and rolling hills—with stunningly picturesque views from nearly every window—being on the open road amid the vast forest was heartening, even if it was in the middle of the night with a maniacal senior.

The first establishment I recall us passing was a motel with a small diner attached to it, its lights flickering just strongly enough to glimpse the Hardwood Motel and Café's NO VACANCY sign. Out front stood a battered road sign that read: PRETTY GOOD FISH & CHIPS, BUT NOT ON MONDAYS. REASONABLE RATES, USUALLY.

I internally applauded the honesty. Moreover, it made me curious as to what pretty good fish and chips tasted like in comparison to other restaurants that boasted the best fish and chips.

The rates must have been reasonable on this day, as the parking lot appeared full. I had no idea if this was a popular rest stop or just some place perfectly positioned in between nowhere and beyond nowhere. As quickly as these thoughts manifested, they dissolved.

"Must be in Hardwood country," I said to Mae as I shifted in my seat to get more comfortable.

My forehead met the faux wooden dash of the LeSabre as Mae slammed the brakes.

"Now you listen here," said Mae. "You keep your wood, hard or otherwise, right where it belongs in those skinny jeans of yours. Do you understand me?"

"Mae, Jesus. What are you talking about? First of all, I was just saying that between the road sign and the motel, the name Hardwood must be popular around here. And second, gross. And third, these jeans aren't skinny. Sure, they're a little snug in the leg, but I don't wear skinny jeans."

In what almost seemed like one fluid motion, Mae stepped on the pedal and had us moving forward again. This time I braced my neck for whiplash.

After another twenty minutes or so of silence, Mae announced that we had arrived. She pulled into a barely defined driveway and followed it towards a cottage that looked like it belonged in the movies. The car was a piece of shit, but this abode in the woods was fucking magnificent.

CHAPTER 13

"Mae, this place is amazing," I gushed, exiting the LeSabre with a degree of effort, which was required after a few hours' drive and cramped muscles.

The trees loomed like stately giants, swallowing any evidence of activity among their expansive branches and ample foliage. The trunks were thick and strong, demanding you take notice and appreciate their stable bulk. The liveliness of animals was heard, not seen: a rustling of bushes on the ground and tweets, chitters, and squawks from above. Nature was all-consuming here, and it was humbling and enchanting, if not marginally daunting, in dawn's early light. The sun, gradually making its ascent in the day's infant sky, offered a glimpse of the few red, yellow, and orange leaves—which would soon number in the thousands—among the green, preparing for their annual and inevitable descent to the ground. Those that had made the plunge already were not yet crunching beneath our feet but instead paved a smooth, slippery path leading towards the three-storey A-frame cabin.

A soaring silver chimney rose from the right side of a metal roof, the sun glinting slightly off both and casting short shadows on the natural carpet we stood upon. I had no clue of the roof's actual material, but it looked like tin and fit the vision in my mind of rain tapping on a tin roof. The porch boasted a wrap-around wooden deck featuring several planters of greenery, long since expired, and seating arrangements courtesy of a pair of Adirondack chairs. Softly glowing lanterns hung from either side of the front door, a metal bear-paw door knocker fixed to its centre. Two more, halfway up the A-frame, illuminated the windows of the second floor; whoever lit them must have known we were on our way. The third floor remained dark.

Mae smiled quietly as she drank in her oasis. My observations of these surroundings weren't anything she didn't already know. Though I was hesitant at first, the edifice that stood before me had completely transformed my thinking, and I too would have gladly paid someone to transport me from Silver Springs to this sanctuary, even an unmitigated wackadoo like Dolores, a.k.a. Chandra of the Midnight Sun.

The air was sweet but earthy, and I opened my lungs to it, welcoming in as much of the fresh forest aroma as I could. I closed my eyes, trying to remain present in the moment. The moment didn't last long. As I took in my third deep breath, a sharp elbow popped me in the ribs right at the completion of my inhale.

"Grab my bags," ordered Mae. "Let's get settled. We only have two days, so quit wasting time standing here taking breaths you still could have taken while being productive. Boy, the work ethic just isn't what it used to be."

"You know, Mae, sometimes it's good to take a little time to enjoy the moment and what's around you," I said, gently rubbing my ribcage. "It's called mindfulness."

"I'm ninety-one years old," said Mae, walking towards the front door. "I don't have time to be mindful, and I sure as shit don't have time for your tai chi breathing bullshit either."

A crass interpretation, but she had a point. At her age, thinking of your mortality must be a dark, depressive slope. Mae mumbled something about kicking my ass, but I couldn't make it out precisely, which was probably for the best.

Much like using the Buick's other features, opening the trunk was no simple task. After some jimmying and exerting more strength than should have been necessary, it popped open, almost striking me square in the jaw. With much annoyance, I grabbed our bags and slammed the trunk closed harder than I needed to. It immediately flew back open, this time succeeding in catching me in the forehead. Twice now, the Buick had launched a full-scale attack on my face. I couldn't help but start to take it personally.

Entering the cabin, I was awestruck by the live-edge wood beams lining the ceiling. The stone fireplace at the far end of the main room was cozy and inviting, and the wall-to-wall windows offered an uninterrupted view of the lake. The still-rising sun sparkled off the water's ripples, reflecting a warmth towards the shore and tricking this onlooker into thinking the water might not be as cold as I knew it must be given the time of year.

Next to the fireplace was a stack of wood, a crate of kindling, a pile of aged newspapers, and a box of quick-strike matches. They were long and thin; a worn strike pad was glued to the brass holder. The mantle hosted no photos, no mementos, nothing to signal any memory that was worth preserving, at least not here. In fact, the walls were also bare, not a single decorative item was visible. I tried to quickly decipher whether this was due to the fact that Mae visited so infrequently or if there were other demons at play. Knowing what I did of Mae, I knew it'd be best to leave it alone and just keep my mouth shut.

"So, Mae, why are there no photos, art, or decorations on the walls or, you know, anywhere?" I couldn't help myself.

Mae had disappeared to the main-floor bedroom, either not hearing me or ignoring me all together. I gave her space and did not follow, instead opting to acquaint myself with the indoor surroundings. I was quite confident there was an unwelcome surprise lying in wait for me somewhere, and it would be best if I could determine its whereabouts now.

I sat down in one of the armchairs near the fireplace and gazed with curiosity at the empty bookshelf. What books must have lived there at one time, I pondered. There must have been copies of Dickens or Brontë, Kerouac or Hemingway. An empty bookshelf was a sad sight.

I ran my hands along the worn, brittle surface of the chair, its feel offering subtle indications that it was once fine leather. Now, however, it was weathered to the point of being stripped to its last layer of life before cracking. In the safety of solitude, I closed my eyes again and took a few more deep breaths, taking in the distinct scent of stale cabin. On my third breath I felt another sharp jolt, only this time, it was on the back of my head. The culprit was a book Mae had thrown at me. She was now telling me to put it on the bookshelf. I picked up the book, turning it over in my hands: *Robinson Crusoe*.

"There, now you've got something to look at," she said, confirming that she had caught my initial question. I placed the book on the shelf in what I thought was the prime spot. It looked lonely but appropriate, and given the tale's theme, it felt almost like art. Two birds and all that.

"I'm going to get organized," said Mae, standing in the spot from which she had launched the classic novel.

"No problem," I said. "I'm going to take a walk around and check things out."

"Do whatever you want."

There were a number of man-made trails to choose from, all leading away from the property and into the woods. In addition to those cultivated by steady, repetitive treading, there were inviting interruptions in the brush beseeching an intrepid explorer to create something of their own, to chart a new course. From their openings, some appeared to be a straight shot down to the lake, others a labyrinth of conjoining trails that would send you on a long loop, if you were lucky. I opted for the one I could see tip to toe that pointed to the lake.

Exiting the trees, a small boardwalk, maybe one metre wide, offered safe passage towards a dock that appeared to be in rather good standing. Leaves had begun to litter the pathway, wild grasses growing high on either side, but otherwise, the wood was solid, and neither sight nor sound provided any indication of decay. The coolness of the path's shade was quickly erased by the warmth of the sun. The water lapped gently on the shore, crystal-clear waves crashing softly.

Small rocks and pebbles littered the lake floor, resembling the depths of a wishing well you'd find in the mall—hopeful dreams cast on the backs of nickels, dimes, and quarters. As I reached the end of the dock, I dipped my fingers just below the crest of the water. It was cold and refreshing, confirming my earlier suspicion of its temperature.

Looking across the bay, I noticed a few docks scattered about. One had a boat tied to it; the others were empty, waiting patiently to welcome their visitors. The dock with a boat soon produced the recognizable shapes of people. They were too distant to discern anything more than the fact that other travellers were present in Pineton, but with confirmed life on the lake, my chances of having a witness to Mae murdering me had just gone up. Squinting with a hand visor, I watched as they emptied their vessel and carried their belongings towards the trees before disappearing, presumably to their cabin.

I skipped a few of the flat rocks I had picked up on my way down to the water, requiring a few tries to get my form. Once muscle memory kicked in, I managed a couple successful tosses at just the right angle, sending stones jetting along the water's surface like a hovercraft before sinking to a final resting place on the bottom of the lake.

As I pondered the rock's watery fate, I thought of Mae and her army tattoo. I knew Mae wouldn't have served—women weren't allowed to do so when she'd have been of age for active duty. Whoever she knew that had served must have been important enough to permanently inscribe their memory onto her body.

This consideration was interrupted by a motorboat's engine roaring to life, the body of a wakeboarder standing erect several metres behind it coming into view shortly thereafter. Whoever it was seemed to be experienced, bouncing over the wake with ease and possessing the skills necessary to perform a trick or two. I watched the boat make its rounds, cutting hard in all directions, initiating the cat-and-mouse game with the boarder behind who deftly matched every move.

Everything about Pineton so far was perfect. The water stretched across the horizon as if it were the ocean, limitless in both beauty and expansiveness. The sky was becoming a brighter blue than the city could ever manufacture, and the clouds exploded like pure, fluffy white marshmallows.

Nature's saccharine opus played at the perfect volume. It was easy to lose track of time in such an idyllic place, and I had managed to do exactly that. Between the daydreaming, dock watching, and stone skipping, I had failed to notice the passage of a couple hours. If Mae was ready and waiting for whatever was next, her concern for my whereabouts was non-existent.

I checked my phone once more for the time, making sure I hadn't unwittingly misread it, but the digital numerals corroborated that I hadn't. I did an about-face and headed back to the path that led back to the cabin. I was equal parts curious and scared as to what would take place this weekend. Mae hadn't let me in on her plans—if she even had any. Certainly, we weren't just going to quietly sit by the fire for two days. Knowing Mae, that would never be an option.

In the opposite direction, the path to the cabin seemed completely different. Maybe it was the way the light slashed through the tree branches from behind instead of in front. Or perhaps it was the angles at which the inclines and declines were reversed. A mild anxiousness settled in my stomach. Hoping I hadn't accidently wound up on the wrong path, a wave of relief overcame me when I exited the trees and saw the A-frame cabin. I spied Mae standing on the porch, holding a cup of some hot beverage. As I raised a hand to wave, I was struck with a pinecone from above.

"Even the squirrels think you're an easy target." Mae laughed, then turned around and walked back into the cabin. "Come on in. Coffee's on, and you look like you could use some."

CHAPTER 14

Mae and I sat in the mahogany-and-leather armchairs by the stone fireplace, Mae sipping coffee from a rustic tin camping mug while I drank from a water bottle, now half empty. Mae had started a fire, the smell of burning timber infusing the room. The crackling wood and glowing embers below reminded me of my youth and time spent at camp, sitting around a campfire telling ghost stories and making fleeting eye contact with whichever girl I had developed a crush on that week. Not to sound overly cliché, but sparks flew every time that campfire roared.

There was a set of wooden oars high above the mantle that I hadn't noticed until just now. They crossed in the middle, forming an X. Sunshine filtered in through the drawn curtains on the windows, casting shadows on the floor on the far side of the room. The air was noticeably chilly despite the warmth radiating from the fire. Mae had a blanket draped over her shoulders. She looked content as she gazed with deep concentration into the flames, as if trying to solve a puzzle.

It had been hours since I'd eaten anything, and I asked Mae if there was any food in the kitchen. She simply nodded, indicating there was sustenance to be found but I was on my own to discover what it was and to uncover its whereabouts.

"Don't eat too much," hollered Mae as I entered the kitchen area and rummaged through the cupboards. "There'll be plenty of food later at Plymouth Rock."

"Mae, just once it would be nice if you explained what you were talking about instead of waiting for me to ask the hundred follow up questions I usually have after you make a vague statement," I shouted back.

I poured a bowl of granola and added almond milk that I wasn't certain was anywhere near the right side of its expiry date, but still went for after a quick smell test—I hoped I wouldn't pay dearly later. I then returned to Mae by the fire. Scooping spoonfuls into my mouth, I asked Mae what Plymouth Rock was and if she knew who I might have spotted when I was on the dock. I did my best to offer coordinates and descriptive landmarks that might make it clear where I'd been looking, but I apparently failed.

"Lewis and Clark you are not," she said, though I had a feeling she knew what I was talking about. "But despite your feeble attempt at painting a picture of my humble surroundings, I can, in fact, answer your questions, as they are one and the same."

Mae explained that the people I saw on the dock earlier unloading their things were a group of college kids who came up here at the end of every September. The dock had been dubbed Plymouth Rock due to its connection, albeit loose, to the landing point of a new group of settlers each year. After a month of studies, the group, which changed with the ebb and flow of enrolments and graduations, came to party and let loose. Recalling my own days at university, this seemed a natural course of action and one that I was envious of; I had never taken part in anything exceptionally fun while getting my degree. I studied hard, got the grades I thought I needed to be successful upon graduation, and stayed away from the excesses that can quickly derail one's plans. That, and I was busy trying to forget the years leading up to post-secondary education. There were plenty of reminders in the dorms, the hallways, and everywhere else on campus, and I figured adding any other diversions would only make things more difficult.

"We'll be joining them tonight for their party, which is themed, by the way," concluded Mae.

"Themed? As in, like, a toga party? Are we going to wrap ourselves up in bed sheets and do keg stands? TOGA!" I laughed after bellowing the frat-boy mantra.

"No, it's not like a toga party," said Mae, clearly unamused with my impression. "So don't worry, no one will see your skinny little arms." This moderately offended me, though any mass in the bicep area would have been a result of me pushing up the sinewy flesh on my upper arm to give the appearance of a medium-size potato.

"Okay, so what kind of theme are we talking about here? And moreover, are you sure you want to be going to a party? It's already getting a little cool, and the temperature will only continue to drop as the day goes on."

"Are you sure *you're* not the ninety-one-year-old?" asked Mae with a hint of disgust. "You always have an excuse, or the beginning of an excuse, to never do anything fun. Let loose for a change. You're young and you won't stay that way forever. You're currently spending all your time at Silver Springs, for God knows what reason, and now you're here, in the almighty Father's slice of heaven on earth, and you're ready to pack it in and read a book at the first sign of fun and the mercury dropping."

I was afraid to argue. Not because confrontation with Mae was intimidating—though it certainly was—but because she had a point. She had more than a point. She was not just hitting the nail on the head, she was annihilating it past the flush point.

What I wasn't going to tell her, at least not yet, was that I hadn't really had *fun* since I was about seventeen years old. You wouldn't think the path you travel at that age would have a profound effect on the years that follow, especially sixteen years later, but for me it did. It wasn't necessarily that first year, no, it was when I turned eighteen and could choose my own path. I chose poorly. And that choice had resounding consequences I still hadn't forgiven myself for, and I probably never would. But I wasn't going to tell Mae that, even if it permitted me a small reprieve from her relentless mockery.

"Well, enough chitchat. Let's go. It's time for a walk." Mae rose from her chair like a spring and made her way to get changed for a walk in the woods.

I followed suit without argument or question.

Though I hadn't fully packed my bags myself—Mae had taken care of most of that in our flurry to leave Silver Springs—I found myself in possession of a pair of sweatpants, a hoodie, and some comfortable, if not slightly worn, sneakers. The few items I had gathered for myself prior to my arrival at Casa de Mae were comfort themed. Almost everything I had with me was non-restrictive, so I was all but guaranteed to remain swathed in a state of relaxation while we were in Pineton.

I was outside tying my shoes on the deck when Mae joined me to do the same. She sat on the top step and dexterously tied her laces into a knot that would not come undone. She wore what I will politely refer to as a leisure suit. It was a shade of dusty rose, a colour I had never imagined ever having to describe. The pants were cuffed and looked to be made of velvet. The top half was similar, zipped to the base of her neck and void of cuffs on the sleeves.

With white earmuffs and sunglasses to complement the ensemble, Mae could have appeared in a Northern Reflections catalogue.

We headed off in the opposite direction I had travelled earlier that morning. I trusted Mae knew where she was going—after all, there were trail entrances everywhere. I followed in tow as we began our hike, the path not wide enough for side-by-side strolling. Mae never looked behind her but talked to me anyway, her words never fully making their way back to me in an audible manner I could understand.

"Here we are," she finally said as we reached the opening of the trail at the other end. "You wouldn't know it's here unless you explored a little bit. The trees are a good fortress, and this place needs protecting."

She wasn't kidding. The sun was still high in the sky and penetrated the forest canopy, and there was no comparison for the sunlit expanse of meadow that revealed itself before us. The grasses were tall and unkempt, dwarfing what remained of the season's wildflowers. It seemed like every turn I made here took my breath away.

"Wow." It was about all I could muster as I tried to appreciate the organic beauty that only nature could offer. "This is amazing."

Mae stood silently, smiling. I did too.

The meadow must have been the size of a dozen football fields. It was like Central Park in the sense that only an aerial view could really do justice to the full spread of this hidden gem. The wind sighed through the openness, gently bending the tips of the tall grass as we wandered through it.

"So, what do you think of your new adopted home?" Mae asked me, the two of us now walking side by side.

"It's great," I replied. "I mean, it's a little dated inside and out, but I was expecting that. The people are decent too, present company excluded."

"Watch it, young man," snapped Mae, trying to hide a wry smile. We were beginning to connect, and we could both sense it.

"But seriously, everyone on staff seems to be genuinely there for the right reasons. They're dedicated to making sure health and well-being are top priorities and those who need the place are taken care of. That's not all that common, you know," I said with sincerity. "And you know what else, Mae? Even though you break my balls on a daily basis, I think we're more alike than you'd ever admit. Like it or not, I think we're kindred spirits."

"Kindred or otherwise, we still don't know if you're here for the right reasons," she pried. "And you've got Phil and Susanne to deal with if you're not."

"Don't get me started on Phil," I scoffed. "And Susanne, yeah, she means well even if she isn't exactly sure how to show it all the time. She watches me like a hawk."

Somewhere in the distance, the feet of thunder danced in the clouds. I looked up to a still-clear sky, white puffy clouds skittering off as if spooked by the coming storm. I was no meteorologist but was fairly certain rain would be coming our way soon. The breeze had picked up and the volume of the leaves rustling went up a notch.

"We'd better head back soon," I said to Mae. She ignored me.

We continued walking the expansive field, soaking up the afternoon and one another's company, even if most of it was spent in silence. It might have been what we both needed—who knows. All I know is that I was enjoying it until the rain I'd forecasted arrived.

"Okay, now we'd better get moving back to the cabin," I said to Mae as drops pelted the back of my neck and shoulders.

"Put your arms out," was her curious reply.

"What do you mean, put my arms out?" I said, eyebrows raised.

"Well, I don't know if I can dumb it down any more for you, but I can try saying it slower."

"Come on, Mae, let's go. It won't do either of us any good if we get soaked out here and you get sick. Susanne will have my ass if I bring you back in even a slightly poorer state than you left in."

Mae instantly gave up on her instructions to me and opted for a visual demonstration. With arms wide open, she tilted her head back and opened her mouth. And then she began to twirl. It was an awkward, arthritic twirl, but it was a twirl nonetheless. The raindrops gathering in Mae's mouth caused her smile to widen, but thankfully, she didn't choke. After the moment had consumed Mae in an embrace of joy, she crumpled onto the soft, damp grass.

Fearing the worst, I knelt beside her to ask if she was okay. Mae just laughed and told me to do exactly as she had just done.

"Mae, there's no time for games. We need to get you back," I pleaded.

"Alex, my boy, let me put it to you this way. I'm not moving until you put your arms out, catch raindrops on your tongue, and spin around until you collapse, got it?"

With a harrumph, I obliged. I spun twice and sat beside her.

"Not good enough," she said. "Enjoy this moment. Enjoy one moment of your time in my presence. I know you're afraid of life's happier moments, that you feel like you don't deserve them, but you need to open up. You're too young to be so despondent about simple pleasures. You've got a dark spot on your soul."

How this clairvoyant continued to channel her sorcery to dissect my persona was beyond me, but she would have been worth every dollar at the local fair.

Before I could ask her how she knew I had a dark spot on my soul, she looked at me with genuine sadness and said, "I know because I have one too."

Feeling our link strengthening, I forfeited my inhibitions and spread my arms as wide as I could possibly reach them, my fingertips stretching to meet a wall that didn't exist. I cocked my head back and began to spin, carefree and embracing of the open space around me. Rain filled my mouth, splatted my face, and assaulted my eyelids, which were tightly shut. When I finally opened them, I was ass down in the grass about six metres from Mae, who had since risen to her feet and was giving me a slow round of applause.

I smiled. Maybe at her, maybe just to myself, but both were deserving of praise in this moment. I got to my feet, took a small bow, and made my way to her. I wanted to give her a bear hug but feared she would interpret my gesture as a threat and thus cause me physical harm in the name of self-defence. Heeding that instinct, I told her, instead, that she was beginning to grow on me.

Mae agreed that it was now time to head back. I followed her lead, somewhat less certain about her sense of direction than before given the tornado she had just turned herself into.

Our walk back to the cabin was mostly wordless, but not because we didn't want to speak to one another. It was as if we both knew we didn't need to say anything about the moment that was just shared. Silence can sometimes be an incredibly loud sound.

By the time we reached the cabin, we were both soaked through, though now I wasn't nearly as concerned about the consequences. I had enjoyed a small moment in time that, if not for Mae, I never would have experienced. It was starting to make sense, what she was saying about enjoying the little things while I could.

Entering the cabin, I peeled off my soaked-through hoodie and socks. Mae took her time, sitting on a chair near the entrance, slowly untying her shoes. As with everything Mae did, I wondered whether it was her age that slowed her down or if she was just enjoying the moment by moving a little slower, a little more deliberately.

As I walked up the stairs to change clothes, Mae hollered up at me.

"You're starting to grow on me, too."

I didn't look back or respond. I gave Mae a taste of her own silent medicine and made my way to the bathroom to get cleaned up.

After taking a shower and drying off, I was still riding high from the afternoon's impromptu rain dance and the minor, yet significant, step of opening myself up to the world, even if it was just with an audience of one.

I had nearly forgotten about the fact that the party we were going to was themed. Mae assured me that she had me covered as far as a costume went. I had reservations about this, but they quickly vanished as I recounted the affection Mae had shown me today.

As I lay reading a book, *Breakfast with Buddha*, a knock landed on my door.

"Come on in," I said.

Mae entered the room, shielding her eyes as if she were interrupting a naked yoga practice.

"Very funny, Mae," I said, tucking my bookmark between pages 124 and 125. "What's going on?"

"I brought you your costume for this evening," she said, passing me a hanger covered in the type of milky plastic that hides just enough of what's underneath to keep you from betting the farm on what it actually is.

I studied the garment, unsure what it could be, but given the red-and-white colouring, I thought maybe something Christmas themed. Mae watched me, as if she had just handed me a birthday gift and was eager for me to unwrap it.

"I'll give you a hint," she said. "It'll show off your guns."

"What is it with you making fun of my arms? They're not *that* small," I retorted.

Mae left without saying a word. I guess she didn't want to watch me open the present after all. Once she was gone, I flexed in the mirror, taking in my upper arms and chest from various angles. I wasn't Thor or The Rock, but so what? It's not all about brawn. Brains have to count for something. Either way, Mae was giving me a complex. I made a mental note to hit the gym at Silver Springs when we got back.

I picked up the hanger and removed the plastic. As I did, I noticed that where the pants should have started, there was nothing. Maybe it was just a shirt?

"You've got to be kidding me," I said to the empty room. "Not a chance in hell."

Another knock at the door. "You dressed yet?" giggled Mae, who wore a white lab coat with a stethoscope around her neck.

"Mae, I'm not wearing this. I can't wear this. This won't even fit."

Mae, nearly buckled over in laughter, offered nothing but neglect to my undeniable shame.

The sexy candy-striper outfit left little to the imagination, on a man or a woman. I was absolutely, under no circumstances, going to put this on, let alone go to a party wearing it.

CHAPTER 15

Night was falling in Pineton, and in the distance, you could hear the clamour of the party we were headed towards. The noise ruffled through the forest, a natural sound barrier of trees and bush allowing slight permeations of commotion in the quiet evening.

We set out on a path at the rear of the cabin, not the same one I took to the lake but one that was close in proximity. With flashlights in hand, the darkness that multiplied in the woods was less frightening. As we walked, I repeatedly tugged the bottom of my dress down so I could maintain a shred of dignity; Mae's powers of persuasion were unmatched. I was able to negotiate not wearing the garters, and thankfully, the sleeves included as an add-on would at least provide a modicum of warmth.

"You look good," said Mae. "Maybe some young stud will need taking care of tonight."

"Mae, for the thousandth time, I'm not gay. And if I was, who cares? The stereotypes are trite and the less we use them, the more accepting we'll all be. So what do you say we drop it?"

Our trail's conclusion was within sight, orange-yellow glows from not one, not two, but five bonfires lit up the upcoming property. Bodies floated in front of us, only visible by the neon lights on necklaces and bracelets. Did Mae bring me to a rave?

Mae, always in the lead, broke through the bush first and promptly dropped her lab coat and stethoscope on the ground. My gut twisted. I didn't need to know what would happen next to know what would happen next. Just as the scenery in front of me was becoming clear—college kids in branded hoodies and sweatpants of their soon-to-be alma mater—so too was the wool that Mae had expertly pulled over my eyes. This was not a themed party, unless you consider getting hammered in as little time as possible a theme: the three youths puking in the nearby bushes were evidence this might be the case.

A few girls walked past, looking at me and smiling, but for all the wrong reasons.

"Mae, what the fuck?" I demanded. "Are you kidding me?" I was bordering on furious.

"Oh, would you relax," said Mae. "How many times do I need to tell you to loosen up? This is part of your journey. You've probably never been hazed in your life. In fact, I guarantee it. And if you can look me in the eye and honestly tell me you have, we'll go home and change."

I couldn't. Shit.

"Now, you have two choices. You can tuck tail, or whatever it is that keeps poking out from between your legs, and go home, pick up that Buddha book of yours, and lose another night of your youthful life, another night that you could look back on in thirty years and laugh and spin tales about, or you can stay, get a drink, have several of them, and let yourself go. Have fun for one night. Forget all the shit that blackens that spot on your soul and have fun. It's your choice. But if you choose the former, you'll have to remember which path we just came from."

Mae pointed her flashlight to the entry of six different routes back into the woods. We had walked far enough away from them that I couldn't confidently settle on which would be the most reasonable selection. Apparently, I didn't have a choice. I was here, dressed in drag, with kids ten years my junior and Mae, a crazy, loveable pain in the ass who was actually trying to help me, despite her sadistic way of doing so.

"Okay," I mumbled.

"Okay what?"

"Let's get a drink. Let's get, as these kids might say, lit. Well, maybe not you, but certainly me. Only an abundance of whatever booze is here can drown some of this shame."

"You sound like an idiot. Don't pretend to know what lingo these kids are using these days. It changes as often as your sexuality."

"Mae, I'm not—forget it. Where's the keg?"

It wasn't difficult to find a drink. They were stationed at every corner of the property and, seemingly, every handful of metres in between. A keg on ice here, a row of hard liquors there, and coolers scattered about, every one of them filled with beer, wine, and premixed beverages. Thankfully, I realized as I surveyed the area, I would pretty much always be within reaching distance of the great liquid memory eraser.

There were tree trunks that had been split in half forming benches around the various bonfires. Most had a fluid residency, as everyone was on the move, whether to puke in the bushes, hook up in the bushes, piss in the bushes, or do whatever else one might need to take care of in the bushes. The bushes, it seemed, were as popular as the bonfires.

The trees were even more impressive in the advancing dark than the daylight, extending into the sky past the point of being able to see where they ended. It was as if they reached the heavens above, tips darkened by night's black brushstroke. The stars popped and constellations revealed themselves, none of us knowing what they were or what they meant. The sheer number of them was impressive enough without considering they were an astral puzzle that someone had once put together.

The temperature was dropping; I could feel it on my very exposed bare legs. It was the end of September, and the weather was a real crapshoot. Thankfully, we were still in a warm spell and the evening air, though turning chilly, wasn't entirely debilitating in such a skimpy outfit.

Mae had scampered off somewhere in the darkness. Under any other circumstance, my concern for the sudden disappearance of a senior citizen in the woods at night would ignite a fire of panic as big as the flames dancing before me in what had to be the biggest bonfire going.

"You look like you could use a drink." The voice, accompanied by a beer in an outstretched hand, belonged to a young woman, though not as young as the majority of the other partygoers.

I gladly accepted the proffered can of Molson Canadian and cracked the tab, pushing the tin with my thumb just beneath the mouth; it helps with the flow out of the can, trust me.

"You have no idea," I said and took a generous sip. "I'm Alex." I thrust my hand forward in reflex of meeting someone new.

The handshake was always a formality I never quite understood. Why do I need to touch you in any fashion when we meet? What additional connection is forged other than the feel of my clammy palm on yours? And how often are the weak-wristed crumpled by those with handshakes firmer than a caveman's bed? But we did this. Get on board or get off the train, I suppose.

"Erica. Nice to meet you, Nurse Alex," she said with a Cheshire-Cat grin that sent a newfound warmth through my otherwise cooling extremities. There was a familiarity about her, but I couldn't place it.

"Yeah, about this," I said, modelling my costume, "it's actually a candy striper, but we can move beyond that and get right to the point where I'm on the receiving end of a cruel joke."

"So you're here with Mae?"

"Yes! How did you know? Wait, *you* know Mae?"

"She has done this to everyone who has ever come with her to this party. My family owns the cottage here, and we've known Mae for as long as I can remember. I'd say you're probably the fourth or fifth person to wear this particular getup."

I cringed—not trying to hide my discomfort in the facial expression I made—at the thought of multiple others wearing this costume. I doubted very much that a thorough cleaning had ever been performed.

"I will say this, though: you're probably the one who has pulled it off the best."

Erica flashed a smile that could have lit up the night sky. My knees literally buckled, but they didn't betray me, at least not as much as my short skirt, which I again realized was showing far more than I had ever intended.

"If you head into the cabin, there's a change of clothes you can put on. My brother is about your size, and my Mom always does his laundry, so they're legitimately clean. Second door on the left once you're inside. It was nice to meet you, Alex."

As simply as that, Erica walked off into the darkness. She reappeared some distance away, lit by the warm light of a fire, hugging a group of people and exchanging pleasantries. Letting my gaze linger for a few additional seconds, I completely forgot what I looked like until someone bumped into me, spilled their beer, and erupted into wicked gales of laughter. I made a beeline for the cabin and a change of clothes.

It wouldn't have been my first choice, but the black sweatpants, grey T-shirt, and charcoal hoodie—with the vulgar suggestion that "ALMOST EVERY HAND YOU'VE EVER SHAKEN

HAS HAD A DICK IN IT," were a welcome reprieve from my former attire. If I had been unsure about handshakes before, I was definitely ready to rethink them permanently now.

Erica was right, though; the clothes were fresh and clean, smelling as if they had just come out of the dryer. I didn't stay inside long enough to get much of a take on the cabin Erica grew up visiting. I wanted to find her again to thank her for the clothes and to continue talking to her. I was also beginning, very slightly, to wonder about Mae's whereabouts.

I exited the cabin through a different door than I entered, and I met the reflection of the moon making the ripples of the lake sparkle like diamonds. There were fewer bonfires on this side of the cabin, but there were a couple, one in particular vaguely illuminating a set of chairs on the dock. A solitary shadowed outline could be seen there, raising a drink to their mouth, no doubt enjoying the majestic beauty that nature was offering at no cost. I hoped, but held mild confidence, the person on the dock was Erica. There was only one way to find out.

I descended the stairs and grabbed a pair of drinks from the cooler at the head of the dirt path leading towards the lake, the ground beneath my feet still spongy from the day's earlier rainstorm.

As the shadowed outline came into clarity, my heart skipped a beat. It had been a long time since I had felt that. There sat Erica, a blanket on her lap and a glass of white wine resting in her hand. I don't know what I would have done had it not been her, but I was relieved I wouldn't have to come up with a plan B.

At the crunching of a twig under my foot, Erica turned around to see who had come to invade her solitude. Seeing it was me, she smiled. That smile was really starting to wear me down. It could have been the same response had I been anyone else, but I was keeping it for me.

She offered me the seat next to her and I gladly accepted.

Erica told me how her family had owned this piece of property for decades and had handed it down through the years, renovating, updating, and changing it to meet the desires of the generation of the day. In the past ten years or so, she had established the tradition of welcoming the incoming class of post-secondary partiers on the last weekend of September. Since then, all six of her siblings had followed suit.

I had no traditions, neither did my family. In that department, we did what we were supposed to: get together for birthdays and anniversaries, holidays and funerals. We did it all by the Hallmark playbook.

"The crowd here looks pretty young," I said, offering my observation of the group I'd first encountered on my arrival. "Present company excluded, of course."

"Are you suggesting that I'm *old*?" she asked.

"What? No, of course not. I was just saying—what I meant to say was—"

"I'm fucking with you, Alex. Relax," she said, sipping her wine. "My younger brother, Brandon, it's his senior year of college. This is mostly his group of friends and tagalongs. I'm the designated chaperone, I guess you could say, though I have little interest in doing anything outside of making sure this place doesn't become a crime scene of some sort."

"Well, if anyone commits a crime tonight, I think it'll be Mae."

She laughed as sweetly as she smiled. Who was this woman? "She's quite the character, isn't she?" asked Erica.

It was my turn to laugh. "That would be an understatement, don't you think? There is absolutely nothing about that woman that isn't a surprise. I haven't known her as long as you have, but I know enough to never underestimate her capabilities."

"How do you know Mae, by the way?" asked Erica, pulling her feet up and the blanket closer.

"I volunteer at Silver Springs. Do you know the place? I've been there about a month now. There was a mix-up in my placement, and I ended up with Mae."

"That's nice—that you volunteer there, not necessarily that you ended up with Mae. I don't know if I'd wish that upon anyone," she said with jest in her voice. "What made you want to volunteer there? From what I hear, most of their non-paid staff are people looking to fill some hours for this or that. Are you court-ordered to be there, Alex? Should I be nervous for my safety right now?"

"No, no. God no. I'm there of my own accord, really," I explained frantically before realizing that a wide grin had crept across Erica's face. "Ah, you're kidding. But yeah, I just wanted to give back, I guess. And look what it got me: Mae Seasons."

I felt compelled to tell Erica about my true intentions at Silver Springs but couldn't pull the trigger. Maybe another day—if there was another day. For now, I was actually heeding Mae's advice to have fun and enjoy the moment. And this moment was about Erica.

The small talk evaporated after about a half hour. We went to find Mae upon Erica's suggestion, leaving the silence and seclusion of the dock. Erica folded the blanket and placed it back on her chair for her eventual return at the end of the night. Before departing, we grabbed a few drinks from the cooler in preparation for our search.

"You have these strategically placed, don't you?" I said of the seemingly always-full coolers.

"We've perfected a system over the years. And it keeps people outside instead of in. We've had a few instances we'd rather not talk about in terms of interlopers and their indoor renovations to the old cabin."

Cracking our drinks in unison, we touched cans—a wet, tinny handshake—to initiate our mission. Seems cans can't escape the moist palm either.

"Hope that doesn't concuss them," I said.

Erica gave me a quizzical look, before catching on to my poorly told joke. "Because we knocked their noggins?" she said. "Alex, I'm sure you're a funny guy when you're not trying so hard. Most people are. Just be you, okay? It's the best advice I've ever received and can ever give back."

I thought about something to say but came up empty. After a second, Erica laughed. "Let's go, dummy."

Dummy. It shouldn't have sounded so nice, but it did. I was smitten.

Our search to find Mae didn't take long. Our attention was immediately seized by a throng of partygoers congregating at the largest bonfire. Cries of "chug, chug, chug" were accompanied by various hoots and hollers, cheers and chants.

Erica and I looked at each other, knowing our search was over as quickly as it had started. I was relieved to have located Mae but equally full of self-pity for the lost time with Erica.

As we weaved through bodies like two concertgoers trying to get a better view of the stage at Coachella, the outline of an energized ninety-one-year-old woman on top of a small table came into view. Mae had one hand above her head, holding the bottom of a funnel. The other was holding a hose pressed to her lips. A soon-to-be graduate cracked a beer and, because kids seem to be grown larger these days, extended his six-foot-nine, Viking-size frame, which required no chair to reach the top of the funnel, filling the blue plastic contraption.

Within seconds, Mae slammed the funnel to the ground and raised her arms in the air. The crowd cheered as if they'd just witnessed a game-winning homerun in the bottom of the ninth in the seventh game of the World Series. Mae relished the attention.

And why not? How many more chances would she get to receive such an ovation?

"Mae, are you doing alright?" I shouted at her, grabbing hold of her arm to get her attention, praying her answer would be yes.

"Hey there, Sonny. Where you been? You missed the show. That was number four!"

The crowd cheered at Mae's count.

"Four?! Mae, you should sit down." I'd never used a beer bong, but I've been witness to those who have, and four beers going down that fast isn't good for anyone, let alone Mae.

Mae moved towards an empty spot on one of the log seats and sat down. Erica and I followed, flanking her in our seating arrangement, hoping we could contain Hurricane Mae.

"Erica, honey, how are you? It's been a long year since I saw you last. Who knew time could go by so slowly? Isn't time supposed to go by quicker as you get older? And don't you look good. Time is not withering that body in the manner it is mine. Damn, girl."

"I'm good, Miss Seasons, thank you." You could sense that Erica took Mae's evaluation as a compliment, her growing smile giving away her humility.

"Cut this Miss Seasons shit, honey. It's Mae. And I see you've met our sexy candy striper—or at least he was. Why are you in different clothes?"

"Erica here felt sorry for me. I was the victim of a cruel joke, and she took mercy. You should try it some time, Mae."

"Oh, jog off with that pity shit. It was fun. And besides, had you not been wearing that saucy little number, you and this young lady—who is out of your league, by the way—likely wouldn't have crossed paths. She likes a good charity case, don't you, honey? Now, go ahead and tell me you'd have preferred missing out on this beauty."

I couldn't, and Mae knew it. I was realizing that Mae had an uncanny gift for reading people. Whether it was me, the others on the fourth floor at Silver Springs, Susanne, or anyone else, Mae could read them like a large-print book through a telescope.

"Well, I'm going to give the people what they want," announced Mae, rising to her feet. "I'm going for five!" The crowd, within earshot, erupted in a chorus of cheers.

Erica and I looked at each other and figured we'd have no chance of talking her down, so we let her go. After all, she was showing no signs of actually being intoxicated. What was she up to?

Taking her place on the log was a young kid, no more than seventeen, I guessed. He reeked of weed and beer. He asked me if I could believe "that old bat is crushing beers like a champ." To some extent, yes, I could. Mae seemed to defy the definitions and rules of the universe. Why should chugging beer be any different? But again, it seemed wildly improbable—I just hadn't figured out how she was doing it yet.

With a slight assist from someone standing nearby, Mae clambered up the table once more, flapping her arms up and down, pumping up the crowd as if she were a WWE star about to finish her opponent with her signature move. The same Viking who had filled the beer bong the first time was back at it, filling it up for lucky number five.

The kid next to me sparked up a joint, confirming one half of his pungent cologne. Although I had never tried weed, I've always enjoyed the smell of anything freshly lit, whether a joint, cigarette, cigar, or even incense. Mae, in another few seconds, had completed her task and high-fived the adoring teenagers who would go back to school telling stories of this magnificent, crazy old woman.

"Dude, you want to hit that?" said the kid sitting next to me.

"What?! Are you serious? First off, let's be honest, there comes a time when all wells run dry, if you know what I mean. Second, she's in her nineties. That's a guaranteed broken hip or worse. And third—"

"Third," said Mae, who I hadn't realized was within earshot, "is that he was talking about hitting the joint, not me. Fourth, *boys*, let's not pretend we know much about female physiology. Besides, neither one of you could handle this."

Mae took the joint from the scrawny teenager and inhaled a long drag. She grabbed the young gent by his collar, stood him up, and blew the smoke right back into his gaping mouth. In a near instant, the kid collapsed to the ground in a splutter of coughs. Mae winked at me, as if to say "I told you." She didn't need to tell me. I believed her. No one could handle Mae Seasons.

Erica, who had hung around to watch Mae's theatrics, shook her head with a laugh and came to share a quick word.

"Have another drink, enjoy the night, and come say goodbye before you leave tomorrow. I've got a date with the solitude of a quiet dock and a glass of white wine. I keep the good stuff reserved for the end of the night when I know it won't get poached. It's time for my reward for chaperoning this shitshow. It was nice to meet you, Alex Chambers."

She leaned in, lightly kissed me on the cheek, and gave me a hug that lasted just a little longer than it should have considering tonight was our first time meeting. But I wasn't going to complain. Then, just like that, our encounter was over.

As she stepped back, I couldn't separate my eyes from hers. They were ocean blue, and the dancing flames reflected clearly in them, captivating me in a manner I didn't know was possible.

"Come on, honey, it's time to put this one to bed," said Mae, reaching her arm out for Erica to guide her home through the deep, dark woods. "And you, dummy, stay right here and have some fun tonight."

It was the second time a woman had called me dummy tonight, and for different reasons, they both felt right.

Erica had shuffled off to grab a flashlight, and while she was gone, Mae nudged me, giving me a look that indicated time was of the essence.

"Before she gets back, hit this," said Mae.

This time, I knew she was talking about the smoldering joint she held in front of my face.

"Fuck it, gimmie that."

I immediately regretted it.

CHAPTER 16

I had assumed Mae would have wanted me to accompany her home, providing safe travel through the darkness of the woods, but as we stood at the edge of the bush, she informed me that my night was far from over, and that under no circumstances would she allow me to call it quits so early. I was feeling something. I was tired but wired, an odd combination given everything that had occurred not just tonight, but over the last few weeks.

Despite how the night had started—with great shame and transitory self-respect—I was now falling victim to an inflated and misguided sense of confidence. As Mae's words pumped me up, I told her I was going to make this night last forever. It's not something I would normally say or reasonably expect someone in their thirties to ever utter or think, but there I was, feeling like a teenager again—an invincible, stupid teenager. The booze was definitely taking effect.

Mae, of course, had encouraged this burgeoning machismo, and she firmly planted her lab coat on a stick near the entrance to the forest path that would lead me back to the cabin. After a very one-sided conversation, I said goodnight to her as she and Erica departed into the bush, assuring me they both knew the place like the backs of their hands and that Erica would have no problem finding her way back safely. The mixture of alcohol and weed in my system more than derailed my train of good judgment and responsible decision-making and compelled me to let them go. In hindsight, I never should have done that. I wonder how many people think that after a night of drinking or getting high or overindulging—*I never should have done that.* Mae made it home without issue, as I'd find out early the next morning, but still, what kind of person lets people walk through the woods in the pitch-black of a cool September night? Or had we reached October?

Finding myself solo at the party, I rummaged through the closest cooler I could find, grabbing a pair of beers, cracking them both, and openly declaring to anyone within earshot that I would double-fist the rest of the night. A couple of young ladies walked by as I did this and left with the completely wrong impression of my spirited avowal. I knew this because of the look they gave me and the "eww gross" they uttered in unison.

I ambled aimlessly around the property, taking in my surroundings and trying to figure out exactly how I was going to make the most of the rest of the night. My brain continuously urged me to go to the dock, but my other brain—and I should note that by this point, my growing intoxication had convinced me I had two—provided thoughtful counsel that I was in no condition to speak to Erica. Surprisingly, this second brain was the smarter one, and I listened to it. Maybe I wasn't quite doing this right. I was supposed to be making poor decisions tonight, not good ones. Epiphany established, I drank the two cans as fast as I could.

My wandering landed me near a large card table where seats were starting to fill up with bodies. I walked closer to see what was going on. The Viking, who had been fueling Mae's rise to stardom earlier, was confidently calling the shots.

"Okay, we've got thumper, followed by boat races, followed by chandeliers. Any questions?"

"Yeah, I got one," I said at an unnecessarily loud volume for my proximity to the table.

"What's up, my guy?" asked the Viking as the many other heads whipped around to see who had chimed in.

"Can I get in on this?"

"If there's an open seat, it's fair game. And look here, an open seat." The Viking pointed to one at the end of the table. "Okay, let's get to it," he said, ready for the games to begin.

"I have another question," I interrupted, even louder than the first time.

"My guy, what's up?"

"Why do you keep saying 'my guy'? And more importantly, what is thumper? And two more, if I may. What, since I'm on a roll, are boat races and chandeliers? I'm not interested in going in the lake or doing any type of electrical work tonight."

The crowd at the table erupted with laughter, though I can truthfully say I wasn't joking. Hand to God, I had no idea what was going on or what any of the things the Viking had said were.

"Don't worry, my guy, you won't be in the water tonight, at least not with these games. Now, who's ready to get fucked up?!"

He never did answer my question about calling me 'my guy'.

Everyone at the table started thumping their hands on the tabletop. I followed suit. Fake it till you make it, right?

Thumper turned out to be a simple game—in theory. We went around the table choosing a hand gesture that would be unique to us for the duration of the game. Some of the gestures were simple and polite—a thumbs up or a peace sign—while others were a little more sexual in nature. I opted for voguing. This was literally the first thing that came to my mind.

Once all the gestures had been established, the Viking started thumping his hands on the table. Everyone joined in.

"What's the name of the game?" he yelled.

"Thumper!" replied everyone at the table but me. I didn't know that was a requirement.

"And why do we play the game?"

"To get fucked up!" And it was on.

The Viking started us off with his gesture, which was running his hands through his hair. The players to his left followed suit. Hands through hair, peace sign, fellatio—male and female. When it got to me, I only did my hand gesture, even though I knew I was supposed to do everyone else's first.

Everyone cheered and chanted for me to drink. I did so willingly. I was indeed here to get fucked up, my earlier proclamation unfolding. Because I was the violator of the round, I got to start the next round, making it likely I could somewhat pace myself. This assumption was immediately negated, as I joined the other violators each time they drank, not by rule but of my own volition.

Thumper petered out and the Viking declared it was time for boat races, a much more straightforward game. The Viking instructed someone to grab a cooler of beer and distribute two cans to each person at the table. There were six of us seated on each side of the table, forming our respective teams. The Viking was on my side, so I liked our chances. With our drinks at the ready, the Viking yelled "Go!" and started chugging his beer. Once he was done, he slammed it down, and the next teammate followed. As this was happening, I realized I was at the end of the table and would have to pull back-to-back chugs; I did so with the ease of a seasoned drunk, because in that moment, I most certainly was one. Our team was victorious. We rejoiced with high-fives and hugs. It was exhilarating and it felt like winning the World Series.

Finally, we arrived at the third of the aforementioned drinking games: chandeliers. This would be the night's closing ceremony, the coup de grâce, not because of the hour, but because by the game's conclusion, the field would be decimated, wounded soldiers sprawled on the battlefield of booze.

If you were skilled, it was possible to remain relatively sober during chandeliers. But if you lacked the proficiency to bounce a quarter into a shot glass or had slow reflexes, you were, by all accounts, doomed to drink. Each player was given a shot glass to fill with whatever alcoholic beverage was at their disposal and then place around a community cup. After filling up your personal glass, a contribution was made to this community cup. It didn't matter if more than one variety of booze was in play, it still went in the cup. Thankfully, tonight, it was just beer.

The game was simple. If a quarter bounced into your shot glass, you drank. If it landed on the table, everyone drank their shot; the last person to put their glass down on the table then had to drink the community cup.

After a handful of rounds, and a few downed community cups, I called it a night. I was proud of my showing despite the fact that binge drinking was not something my liver was particularly used to.

"My guy, nice work tonight," said the Viking, who was showing little to no indication of being drunk. "By the way, who the fuck are you? I don't recognize you." He asked this jovially, not out of suspicion or disagreeableness.

"Yeah, I didn't meet the requirements of boarding your warship," I slurred, forgetting he was completely unaware I had dubbed him the Viking.

"Well, you're good people, I'll give you that. And you're still standing, unlike the rest of these lightweights." He pointed around at the diminishing number of upright bodies on the property.

Somewhere along the way, amidst thumper, boat races, and chandeliers, people had pitched their tents and zipped themselves inside, ready to sleep off as much of their hangover as possible before morning hit and they were forced to endure the bright light with eyes open. It hadn't occurred to me before that all these bodies would need a resting place and the cabin was not nearly large enough to house them all.

"And seeing as how you're still with us, there's one more thing for the survivors," he whispered, as if inviting me to participate in a secret Masonic ritual.

"Let's do it," I said without hesitating or thinking.

I stumbled along, following my new Hagrid-size friend. We ended up in a dark corner of the property where three or four other people had congregated. I wasn't exactly sure on the number, mostly due to the darkness but partially due to not trusting my blurred vision.

"Okay, my guy, last feat of the night: a man shot."

A man shot? Whatever the hell that was, I could handle it. "What's a man shot?" I asked.

"A cup of whisky," said the Viking.

That's it? A cup of whisky? No problem, let me have it, I thought. *All whisky comes in cups, after all.* "Easy-peasy, the queen may please me," I garbled, giggling to myself.

"Are you sure, man? He looks pretty fucked up already," said a voice from a face I couldn't discern in the darkness. "We're talking about a cup of whisky, a metric cup of whisky. That's eight shots in one cup, down in one chug."

None of this made sense to me. He was talking gibberish. The Viking handed me a measuring cup of the golden liquid, and I held it up.

"To night's we'll most certainly forget!" he roared.

I chugged the whisky and woke up the next morning in a tent with three other people, having forgotten most of the night.

CHAPTER 17

I awoke with a foot in my face. It could have been worse, I suppose. Thankfully, it belonged to a woman. I abhor feet, but if I had to choose which kind of foot I would want in my face as I woke up to the worst hangover of my life, it would be a woman's. At least they take care of their feet. For the most part, men clip toenails only when necessary or if one becomes bothersome, not because of any general manicuring principles.

Pushing the painted little piggies away from my face, I wished for a quick death, but any death would do. My head pounded like a jackhammer in a prison cell, and my mouth tasted of ash and copper. I wasn't yet able to relish in my success of acting like an irresponsible idiot. That would come later. I was, however, capable of devising several mental plans in my mind's eye on how to murder an entire forest of chirruping birds. It wasn't pretty, and I wasn't proud of it, but they had to go. Sorry, birds.

I had no recollection of how I ended up in a two-person tent with four other people but was thankful I was spared the overnight elements of the great outdoors. The tent had an odour that was repugnant at best and vomit-inducing at worst.

Though I had no desire to get upright—and to be honest, wasn't confident I even possessed the dexterity to do so—the fresh air was a bracing consolation for my efforts. Escaping the tent, though not bothering to zip it up after I left—my tent mates would thank me for airing it out—I vigorously rubbed my eyes, slowly letting them adjust to the increasing brightness of a new day. They burned from the sting of the air and sight of the light.

Yawning and stretching more audibly than one should, I looked around, wincing in pain each time I moved my head too fast in any one direction. It was rapidly becoming evident why I never drank to this extent.

"Well, good morning, sailor," came a zestful voice from behind.

Between my blurry vision from my still-present, but slowly waning, state of inebriation and the pale morning light, it took a moment before I clearly saw the face that accompanied the familiar voice. Wrapped in a woodland-themed fleece blanket, Erica offered me a bottle of lemon-lime Gatorade. My saviour.

"Thank you," I said, twisting off the cap and consuming the electrolytes like a rescued castaway, gulping down as much as possible in one breath.

"You, Mr. Alex, had quite the night," she said, a tone of sympathy, and perhaps mild scorn, in her voice. It was a polite way of letting me know I was in rough shape—looking like shit and smelling like death. Of course, I knew these things already.

"Well, uh, yeah, I guess." I rubbed my head, tussling the knots in my hair. Bits of pinecones and twigs had somehow nested near the roots. "I'm not terribly proud of myself at the moment, but I have no idea what happened last night."

"Well, things went a little south for you after playing chandeliers with Jacoby and his friends," she said, offering one missing piece to the puzzle that was the night prior. Like the good chaperone she was, she had kept a vigilant eye on me after returning from getting Mae squared away.

"Jacoby?" The name was foreign to me.

"I think you kept referring to him as the Viking," she said.

The Viking. Yes, the vague recollection of a giant kid who was always around doing some sort of ringleading was embedded in my slowly returning memory. I thought I remembered him with Mae at one point but couldn't fully grasp the memory.

"Well, I appreciate the pity you're showing to a college-aged wannabe," I said, finishing my Gatorade. "Do you happen to have any more of these kicking around?"

Like a well-oiled machine, the coolers that were once full of assorted alcohol were now well stocked with bottles of Gatorade, water, and juice. It was like there was a stage crew who had transformed the set while the actors were in a costume change. How this sorcery had been seamlessly performed, I wasn't sure, but I certainly wasn't complaining.

"Here, take a couple of these too," said Erica, handing me two nondescript white tablets, pills that I assumed were Tylenol. I popped them in my mouth without hesitation, trusting she was keeping my best interests at heart and not dosing me with a psychedelic.

"What time is it?" I asked instead of just checking my phone.

"It's six, maybe a few minutes after," she answered, checking the clock on her Fitbit to confirm. "Why don't you head back to Mae's and get some rest? And because I very much doubt you remember from last night, I'll remind you again: come say goodbye before you leave. But this is your last warning."

I had forgotten, but I wouldn't this time.

It was quiet when I tottered into Mae's cabin, which meant Mae was sleeping it off or was already up and about somewhere, neither of which would have been surprising. I was becoming uncomfortably self-aware of the booze-soaked stench emanating from my body and fought off the urge to throw up. Adding in the various smoke smells on my clothing, a blind person would have been justified in mistaking me for a dumpster.

Doing anything hungover is an exercise in determination and total focus, and climbing the stairs to the second-floor bedroom took everything I had. I mustered enough energy, the last of it, to shed my borrowed clothes and crawl into my single bed in just my boxers. The sheets were soothingly cool on my skin, a prescription my body needed filled. The pillow had the same effect, and I was edging towards a deep slumber.

Just as I was about to drift off, a tiny winged demon buzzed near my ear, landing briefly on my forehead before taking flight again. I brushed my hands wildly in front of my face, shooing the insect to anywhere but here, but to no avail. The little bugger kept buzzing my tower—the tower being my face. This felt personal, like the universe was orchestrating punishment for the bevy of suspect decisions I had acted on in such a short time frame.

It finally came to rest on the lampshade that shielded a yellow bulb screwed into a lamp shaped like an acorn; I laid eyes on the black, awful thing, its wings taking a momentary reprieve from buzzing with the volume of a jet engine. I would only get to sleep if I could eliminate the distraction. From a horizontal position, I scanned my nearby environment for my weapon of choice: the book resting on the table hosting the acorn lamp was the only usable option within reach. I calculated the potential outcomes of any decision resulting from Alex versus the fly. Outcome one: kill the fly but break the lamp. Outcome two: the fly lives but the lamp breaks. Either way, I was about to break a lamp and therefore shouldn't proceed with my intended course of action.

After cleaning up the broken pieces of the lamp and watching the fly leisurely make its way to another room in the cabin, I gave up on the idea of sleeping and decided the best tonic would be some fresh air down at the lake. I read somewhere that shocking your body with cold has a sobering effect. This was probably debunked six ways from Sunday and had I just consulted my phone, I would have saved myself undue shock therapy courtesy of Lake Too Fucking Cold.

The true coolness of the morning revealed itself in the form of mist blithely whirling above the water. The blue sky was beginning its emergence from the cocoon of pale pinks and purples as this day's sun rose. The clouds rolled by, and as I looked up, standing in this perfect place, I felt certain I could hear their delicate march across the sky.

I had enough memory stored to recall which path I had taken yesterday to get down to the lake and onto the dock. I made this trek barefoot, which was ill-advised given the path's rocky terrain.

After gingerly venturing through the woods, I made it to the dock, where I stood peering into the water to determine whether or not a dive, of any depth, would cause paralysis or seize me in a wet, hypothermic hug. The latter happened, and when I emerged from the depths of Lake Too Fucking Cold, I screamed at a pitch on par with an under-ten, all-female a cappella group winning a competition. System successfully shocked.

Whether it worked or I was just too damn frigid to realize my headache was still knocking on the walls of my brain, my polar plunge sent my mind elsewhere in terms of pain. My skin, though freezing, somehow also felt like it was on fire. My teeth chattered and my extremities shook beyond control. If I'd had any sense, I would have brought a warm drink or a towel, knowing full well I was going to jump into a cold lake.

For the second time this morning, a voice beckoned from out of eyesight. And for the second time this morning, the voice came from a familiar face holding the exact beverage I required.

"I'll admit, it was fun to watch. That scream made me think the leeches found a new home on your testicles, but then I remembered your testicles would have constricted somewhere up towards your stomach by the time you hit the water," said Mae, holding a cup of steaming hot something. My saviour.

Mae looked rested, spry even. How?

"It never happened," she said, answering the question my open-jawed trout mouth was incapable of asking. "Those beer bongs never had an ounce of liquid in them, let alone booze."

I just stared at her.

"It was all a show," she explained. "You get that many drunk idiots together in near pitch-black, desperate to see something amazing, and they'll see it, even if it never happened. Penn and Teller can kiss my ass. You honestly thought I could have handled that much alcohol? I'd be dead. You, on the other hand, look like the living dead, and methinks it's from more than just your quick little dip. Here, cover up."

Mae threw me the towel that I had neglected to bring. My brain was not processing anything other than a recurring thought: *What if.* It was an all-too-familiar pair of words that ricocheted through my mind, even as I stood on this dock, half naked, with Mae. If I couldn't escape them here, where then? Maybe I was destined to carry a burden of sorrow with me. The bad decisions. The failure to know my heart and follow through. The inescapable plague of what ifs.

"I don't know the details, and trust me, I do want them at some point, but anyone who looks as close to death as you do right now must have had a good night."

"You know what, Mae? I have no idea. I'd like to say I had fun, but I don't remember. Everything is pretty much gone, at least when it comes to the salient details, but I appreciate what you did for me last night. You pushed me, maybe a little too far, but it was the push I needed." I was starting to appreciate my night of blank memories. "Your methods are depraved, but they're effective." I raised my mug in homage.

"I get results, young man," she said. "And sometimes, that's all that matters—the end result being what you want it to be. And I must say, you seemed quite taken with our young chaperone next door. The way you looked at her, well, I have only ever seen one other man look at a woman like that—the only difference being that he knew what he was looking at. I think you're still a little lost."

Oh, Mae, if you only knew. I wasn't just lost; I was dropped in the middle of a desert with amnesia, a blindfold, and overlapping layers of debilitating guilt.

"Reminds me of the way you look at a certain someone at Silver Springs," she said quietly.

My body shot up straight and my head jerked towards Mae.

"I'm perceptive and well-connected, if you hadn't noticed," said Mae, speaking with an uncharacteristic softness, as if she were the first to uncover the incoming sad news. "I did some digging. Her name is Alicia Emerson. I couldn't get the full story, but whatever damage was done, she hasn't spoken a word since she arrived, doesn't get any visitors, and doesn't write letters, read books, or watch TV. She's just there in body. Know anything about that?"

It was instantaneous: my eyes welled with tears. They immediately flooded and streamed down my cheeks without warning. I buried my face in the towel, hiding its sudden wetness and my shame. Somehow my breathing remained calm as Mae listed a few other details, leaving out the one only I knew.

"Her name is Autumn," I said quietly. "Autumn Alicia Emerson. She hated being named after a season and went by her middle name, Alicia. She went so far as to officially change it when she was eighteen. Her name is Autumn, and she's at Silver Springs because of my actions—or, I guess, inactions."

CHAPTER 18

After admitting to Mae that I not only knew Autumn but she resided at Silver Springs because of something I had done, or not done, as the case may be, I felt relieved. A colossal weight lifted from my shoulders, and perhaps there was a partial cleansing of my soul.

I didn't fully explain how I knew Autumn or how I knew why she was there or even the full details of how she got to Silver Springs. There would be time for that, but that time was certainly not now.

I did, however, enlighten Mae on the promise I had made to Erica about seeing her before we departed our forest oasis. This seemed to please Mae in a similar but more affecting manner than parading around in a ridiculous costume, as I had the previous night. This revelation freed me from Mae's hook; she was very tenacious with her insistence that I engage with Erica. If acquiescing to this got me out of sharing a story I wasn't eager to retell in the first place, then so be it.

Having cleaned myself up back at the cabin, I rummaged around the cupboards for whatever food might sit well in a hungover stomach before heading back into the bush and over to Erica's property. Whole-wheat bread with crunchy peanut butter looked to be the best I could forage. I left the bread open-faced and slathered the peanut butter on thick. I paired this with a tall glass of room-temperature water.

"Mae, if you're going to continue this annual trip, you really should stock the shelves with something other than bread and crunchy peanut butter," I said, taking a large bite from my deconstructed sandwich.

"You've probably got a point," she agreed. "But usually, this trip is just me, and I don't need much to keep the engine running. Plus, Erica usually brings me a little something to snack on when I'm on my own. Oh, and I don't have crunchy peanut butter—can't stand it. It's creamy or nothing. The nuts don't play well with the dentures."

I spit out a moist wad of bread, surprised that more from the depths of my guts didn't come sprinting out immediately after. I put my hands out on the counter and hung my head in defeat. Defeat of what, I don't know, but defeat nonetheless.

With last-minute directions from Mae on where I was headed, I stepped back out into the fresh air, taking it in like a drowning victim having just been resuscitated. If this seems an odd way to breath, you're right. I found myself choking on the air that accompanied the fluttering wings and bitter taste of the moth that mistook my yawning, gaping mouth for a cozy place to land.

The peanut butter hadn't induced last night's brew to resurface, but the moth certainly did. As I stood in the brush, hands on my knees, spitting out the sticky, leftover bile that was coating my lips and teeth, I made the sweeping declaration that I would never drink again. This wouldn't last, of course, but it felt good making that teetotaler pledge to myself in the moment.

Rinsing the sour tanginess from my mouth with a bottle of water I'd thankfully had the foresight to carry with me, I continued my journey to bid farewell to the newest enchantment staking claim in the grey matter between my ears. The wetness of the leaves underfoot was slippery like ice, which would probably form in a few short weeks. The sun had not yet dried them back to being a moderately safe surface underfoot. The sun had also not yet penetrated down to the lower twigs of the trees on either side of me, their bare, smooth arms shooting water at me like bullets as I brushed past them.

I emerged from the woods, and the space in front of me looked entirely different in the light of day. The bonfires that had served both as landmarks and lighting last night were now piles of smoky ash, some still home to the last remains of smoldering firewood. Toppled chairs, empty beer cans scattered on the grass, and tents at various stages of assembly painted the picture of a landscape decorated by a tornado—the grim aftermath of a raging party of rowdy youths in the woods. It was appropriate. Oddly, I hadn't noticed any of this when I left the property earlier in the morning.

It didn't take me long to find Erica; she was the only person playing the role of adult, garbage bag in hand, picking up and pouring out cans that varied in their degrees of emptiness.

"The gloves look good on you," I called out.

She looked up from her trove of ten-cent returns and smiled, signalling me to come over and grab a bag. I was more than happy to oblige.

"Sorry, no extra gloves," she said, snapping the blue rubber gloves keeping her hands free from the sticky, stale liquids. "But that doesn't get you a pass from helping me clean this mess up."

"Not a problem. These here hands are working hands, rough and calloused," I said as I held them up for admiration.

"They look like they've been manicured lately," she said with a laugh. "You don't have to admit to it, but you also won't change my mind by denying it."

She had me there. My hands were anything but calloused. They hadn't seen a day of hard labour since I'd pulled a landscaping job the first summer of my freshman year of university. It was a rewarding job, if nine bucks an hour, heavy lifting, and a boss who'd rather watch you dig a hole with a shovel than let you use his backhoe fulfilled you in any manner. I lost some weight that year, gained a few muscles I didn't know I had, and earned a hell of a tan. All in all, I guess it wasn't too bad. But still, my hands were as smooth as silk at the present moment.

Erica had her hair pulled back in a ponytail, enhancing the loveliness of her facial features. If I thought she was attractive last night, shitfaced and in the dark, then she was a goddamn goddess in the here and now.

To avoid shamelessly staring, I looked up, commenting on how the morning's open sky was quickly losing space, now becoming crowded with cumulonimbus clouds, and noting that if grade-ten science had taught me anything, it was that they were ripe with precipitation. In the interest of terribly dull small talk, I said that, if nothing else, they would douse the remaining embers in the various firepits.

"Not only will he take care of you in the hospital, he'll give you the weather report too," Erica said.

"You know, people who invite company and ask for post-party cleanup assistance usually have knives a little duller," I said with what I was certain—or at the very least hoped—was affable charm.

"Don't tell me you can't take a little ribbing," she said. "I mean, the man I watched last night, if he can't laugh at himself—" She trailed off, letting me pick up where she stopped.

"Yes, not a display of me at my finest, as we've already agreed. But hey, I'll never see these people again, so I guess any shame I may have accrued really isn't worth carrying."

"I hope you'll see some of these people again," she said, offering what I took to be an invitation to exchange numbers and some possibility to reconnect after the day concluded and Mae and I returned to Silver Springs.

"Drop your bag, let's go for a swim," she said with the impulsivity of a toddler at a playground.

"What? Are you crazy? It's going to pour any minute. And I don't have a swimsuit. And, most importantly, that lake is way too damn cold. Trust me."

"Live a little, Alex. And besides, after last night's ensemble, there's not much we haven't seen." She said this last bit with a smile I would spend the rest of the day deciphering.

As the last syllable left her lips, raindrops exploded on our shoulders. Erica, having made up her mind, took off towards the dock, shedding her sweatshirt and sweatpants with a fluidity better suited for Cirque du Soleil than the backwoods of Pineton. She glanced back with a hypnotizing look, daring me to join her, and before I knew it, my feet were sprinting in lockstep with my heart, catching me up to Erica at the tip of the dock.

As our gaits synchronized, my hand reflexively reached for hers. Her hand, perhaps reflexively too, interlocked with mine. As we reached the end of the dock, having run out of real estate to change our minds, we committed to the plunge. The water enveloped us, sending tingling waves of shock through our bodies. As we broke the surface, the rain began coming down with greater intensity. The jolt of the water's temperature wore off as I looked into Erica's eyes. They were steady and deep and transfixing, an algorithm you wish could be programmed in your memory's hard drive.

The rain was like holy water, washing over me and cleansing my sins from the night before and possibly beyond. I didn't want this feeling to fade away. More than that, I didn't want to stop treading water with this gorgeous, enlivening woman, who, by all accounts, was still as much of a stranger to me as Jacoby, a.k.a. the Viking.

"Now, Alex," she said through chattering teeth, propelling her body closer to me, "you need to do more of this."

"More of what?" I asked, my breathing becoming shallow and irregular at her closeness.

"Spontaneous fun, whatever that might look like," she said. "It doesn't have to be jumping in a freezing lake with a stranger in the rain, but I observed enough last night to know that you need more of it. And you need to do it more in less impressionable environments. I don't think you should drink as much as you did last night ever again. I mean that. Ever. Again."

Before I could say anything, Erica kissed me on the cheek for the second time in the last twenty-four hours, then she swam away. If I said I didn't watch her every move from that moment to when she left the water and entered the small shack near the dock where dry towels awaited, I would be a liar—a stone-cold liar. Turns out this hypothermic shock thing might be the trick to curing a hangover after all; I was feeling great.

The weekend excursion to Pineton went by in a blur, in some cases literally. Though we had the whole weekend off, when you factored in the early Saturday morning and late Sunday afternoon travel, it really was a small sliver of time that Mae and I had away from Silver Springs. As much as I wanted to stay, mostly because of a newfound crush that had me feeling like I was fifteen again, I needed to return to Silver Springs. I packed our bags and put them in the car, this time wise to the springy trunk and determined to avoid further facial damage.

I had fulfilled my obligation of saying goodbye to Erica, which had proved to be exactly as ambiguous as expected. I didn't want to go. I didn't have to go. But I *had* to go—my penance was not paid, and I was not yet forgiven. Until this was the case, Silver Springs was the only place I could be. Erica and I exchanged numbers and the promise to keep in touch. I reflected on how often people parted with this very intention only to never follow up. I hoped we'd be the rare exception to the rule. Time would tell.

Mae let me drive the return trip, which was a welcome change, if for no other reason than it signalled a relinquishing of control on her part that I had not encountered before. She claimed fatigue, but I sensed otherwise; there was a trust growing between us.

I tried to adjust the seat but made no progress. I was faced with four hours of driving like a sardine crammed in its tinny, cramped casket. I turned the radio dial and settled on the only station that came in; a soft piano-laden melody crackled through the speakers. The lyrics were few, perhaps due to the static, but I caught one line in particular that fixed itself in my brain: I'll see you in my dreams.

We hadn't listened to the radio on the way up—we'd mostly sat in silence and endured a few odd conversations—so I had no idea if it was our current location causing the askew antenna to reject incoming signals or if the LeSabre had lost most of its functionality in the audio department. To be honest, it didn't much matter. Trying to digest all that had happened in Pineton was enough to keep me alert and occupied the entire trip back.

To my surprise, Mae actually dozed off in the seat next to me. The fatigue angle perhaps held a nugget of truth after all. I mean, she was ninety-one. When she woke, she made a few unselfconscious sounds that I concluded were just part of aging. And even if they weren't, she had earned the benefit of the doubt.

"Where are we?" she asked groggily.

"No idea. This isn't my neck of the woods. All I can tell you is that we've been on the road for about two hours, give or take. Good sleep?"

Mae yawned but didn't answer. It was common for her to ignore some of my questions, and I'd learned quickly to just move on. She gave a stretch and rubbed her eyes back to focus, exclaiming that she was famished.

"Hardwood Café, driver," she said with a snicker. "If we can't get filled up there, where else can we?" Mae's double entendres were as frequent as they were juvenile, but I couldn't stifle my laugh.

It was about twenty minutes later, the sun hovering above the horizon as it began its gradual descent, when we pulled into the Hardwood Motel and Café. The gravel parking lot was chewed up and potholes the size of sewer covers proved impossible to manoeuvre around and avoid—the LeSabre was lucky to get in, and eventually out, intact.

We parked in the first spot we could find and made an easier trek on foot. There was a smattering of people inside the diner, and the same sputtered melodies from the car played from overhead speakers, now perceptible with greater clarity. The place looked exactly like what anyone would expect a diner in the middle of nowhere to look like.

Cracked vinyl-covered stools were bolted to the floor, forever evenly spaced along the aluminum-edged laminate countertop that spanned the room. The booths were rigid and cemented in their grid-like placement. The turquoise vinyl that covered all the seating was likely original and had yet to be replaced. On the tables, glass ketchup, mustard, and white-vinegar bottles neatly stood guard beside the plastic salt and pepper shakers, both of which flanked the thinner-than-thin paper napkins packed in their rectangular metal home. Cutlery was wrapped with a pink or blue band of paper. Upon receiving ours, we realized it was handed out based on your gender. Why this was the case was a question probably best left unasked.

The blinds on the windows had years of built-up grease on them, causing dust to congeal and harden, one sediment settling over the other, forming a stratum of the many meals eaten here. The menus were safely secured in plastic, though judging by the looks of the stains, it hadn't prevented various drinks, mostly those of darker liquid, from penetrating the casing and imprinting their presence for eternity.

Said menu included only a handful of options under each of the three headings: breakfast, lunch, and dinner. Large, all-caps text topped the menu: NO SUBSTITUTES. DON'T BOTHER ASKING. It seemed the Hardwood Motel and Café adhered to a very serious no bullshit policy; they kept it simple and said it like it was. A waitress whose nametag read Judy, though she looked more like a Sally, tapped her pen on a notepad as we perused the minuscule list of options.

"So, what'll it be?" she asked.

"Meatloaf with the fries and a glass of water," said Mae in a manner that suggested she didn't need to reference the menu to discern what she desired.

"Are you sure you want the meatloaf, Mae? I mean, Silver Springs food isn't the best, but surely what *they* call meatloaf has to have this place beat?" I had no frame of reference for this statement, and Judy quickly called me out.

"Our meatloaf is a top-seller, I'll have you know," said Judy with a scowl. "But hey, I'm sure your uninformed opinion holds weight. Anything else you care to enlighten us with?" she asked sarcastically.

"Club sandwich for me. Fries and gravy and a Coke." It wasn't so much an order as it was a response to Judy. That is to say, I had nothing to offer, so I gave her my order.

"Don't have Coke. Pepsi okay?" asked Judy.

"Yes, Pepsi is fine."

"We're out. How about diet?"

"Why would you ask me, then—sure, that's fine. Diet."

Judy gathered up our menus and walked towards the kitchen to place the ticket in such a manner that made me certain the mayo on my sandwich would not be just mayo.

The walls of the Hardwood Café were covered with typical diner nostalgia: licence plates from all over the map, black-and-white pictures of The Rat Pack and Marilyn Monroe and Elvis Presley, old tobacco tins, empty glass soda bottles, antique toy trucks and cars, an old gas pump in one corner, and a life-size

Betty Boop in the other. It was a veritable feast for the eyes no matter where you looked.

"Quite the place, isn't it?" I said to Mae, gesturing at the décor.

"It is. It reminds me of when I was younger and the places I would frequent with—friends."

Mae, having afforded me a slightly opened door into who she was, caught herself. She knew I had picked up on this but wasn't going to acknowledge it. There would be a time and place. This was not it.

A few other patrons filtered in, the chiming bell above the door announcing their arrival. To me, it sounded exactly like the kitchen's order-up bell, but the staff here looked to have the years of experience needed to differentiate between the two.

Judy eventually came back with our order, placing Mae's meatloaf—which looked surprisingly appetizing—in front of her gently. Still offended by my questioning the meatloaf's quality, she kind of tossed my plate down, causing a few fries to tumble onto the table. Along with the plate came a glass of white milk.

"Don't have diet either. This'll be good for your bones, especially those arms of yours." This caused Mae to do a spit take of her water, spraying me with its mist.

"I told you that you had little girly arms," she said. "Even with your jacket on, Judy here still knew you had weak little appendages."

I opted to say nothing, wiping my face with a wad of napkins pulled from the dispenser.

"Let's save some for the other customers, shall we?" snarked Judy.

"I'm sorry, Judy, is it?" I said. "My friend here just spit your well water, along with God knows what else that's living in her mouth, directly into my face. I'm covered with whatever germs we brought in and those that have already set up permanent residence here. So you'll excuse me if I use as many napkins as I feel necessary to clean myself up."

Judy huffed and walked away.

"Thank you for that, Mae," I said as she continued laughing. "Please tell me I'm not about to catch any virus from either the water, food, or you."

"Unless you think getting old is something you can catch, you'll get nothing from me. As for anything else, I cannot speak for the quality or level of cleanliness of this establishment."

I wondered, in part, if this was how Mae stayed young: cracking the jokes of a teenager and using inappropriateness to stimulate her adrenaline and serotonin.

Once her laughter subsided, and I was done carefully inspecting my clubhouse sandwich, she asked about Erica.

"I really don't know, Mae," I replied to her question of when I would see her again. "We exchanged numbers, and we'll go from there. We'll just have to see if the timing is right."

"Oh, fuck the timing, Alex," said Mae with a sudden hardness in her voice. "Life isn't about timing, regardless of what those Hallmark pricks make you believe. Life is about taking advantage of the moments that are right in front of you, right now. You can't plan ahead; you don't have that kind of control. All you have is today, this minute, this second. If you remember nothing, remember that."

It was a rare moment of forthright sincerity from Mae. I could tell she wholeheartedly believed the words she was saying to me. Moreover, these words carried a weighty significance—the way she spoke made it clear this was undeniable.

"Well, Mae, you could be right. We aren't all guaranteed ninety-plus years to figure things out." This touched a nerve.

Mae dropped her cutlery on her plate, the cheap steel fork and knife clanging off the diner-issued porcelain.

"You think this is about *age*? If you think that, you're dumber than you look. You have an opportunity in front of you, right now, and you're pushing it aside, and for what? Some mute at Silver Springs that you knew once upon a time? That girl back there likes you. You like her. Anyone with half a brain and a barely open eye could see that."

I had no idea where this blow up had come from or why; all of a sudden, Mae had assumed this passionate determination to play matchmaker. I meant no offense in my response, but she certainly took a dollop or two of it, and I, in turn, received a dollop or two of her misplaced microaggression. I had a feeling that the rest of the drive home would be a quiet one.

It was.

CHAPTER 19

Returning to Silver Springs was a welcome reprieve from the quiet anxiousness of the car ride back. Mae and I had basically spent nearly every day of the last month together, but perhaps the magnitude of the weekend had gotten to both of us, and for different reasons. Maybe? I really didn't know. I was searching for rationales that made sense but came up empty with each attempt.

This thought pattern repeated as I woke Monday morning, back in the comforts of Silver Springs and away from the beguiling haven that was Pineton. The calendar had rolled into October, confirmed by the rapid change in the scenery outside. If the colours were rich in mid-September, what was emerging now was nothing short of wealthy beyond belief.

Mae had a series of appointments today, so I had some free time. Or so I thought. Susanne asked me to touch base with her for a monthly check-in. How wonderfully curious that it was arranged the day after Mae and I returned from forty-eight hours without being scrutinized under her hawkish watch. This morning seemed as good a day as any to do so, or so she indicated. For the most part, Susanne had stayed off my back in the days leading up to my weekend trip, though I think Mae had something to do with that. Despite it all, Mae seemed fond of me. I was told by Fred, upon my return last night, that I was by far the longest relationship Mae had kept since beginning her residency. This made me feel good, though I didn't fully understand why exactly.

I showered and dressed and made my way to Susanne's office. I was expecting to be intercepted by Phil, but he was nowhere to be found. It was strange not seeing Phil at his front-desk post, but I suppose even *he* deserved a day off.

As I walked the hallway to Susanne's office, I deliberated over what I could tell her about the weekend that would put her mind at ease and continue to keep her reprimands and scorn at arm's length. I couldn't tell her about Chandra of the Midnight Sun. I couldn't tell her I had let Mae wander the woods at night while I got blackout drunk. I couldn't tell her about Mae's masterful escapade with smoking weed or my less skillful ingestion for that matter. And I certainly couldn't tell her about how Mae had coerced me into dressing in drag—and that I had reluctantly accepted it.

Between the moments of terror, shame, and frustration, Mae and I did have more than a handful of interactions that could be categorized as meaningful—sentimental even. I settled on our walk in the woods and morning chat on the dock as the benign highlights I could recount to Susanne.

I had my story fairly well rehearsed by the time I reached her office. I told myself that if I got painted into a corner by any line of questioning Susanne threw at me, I would revert back to the drive to Pineton and the breathtaking scenery throughout the weekend.

I knocked on the door. No answer. I knocked again, a little more forceful this time. Still no answer. Customarily, upon receiving no response to a knock on a door, you turn around, walk away, and try again later. This is what I should have done.

I turned the handle of the door instead, not expecting to see anything other than an empty office when I walked in. Nothing could have prepared me for what lay before my eyes.

“Holy shit.” The words escaped my mouth before I could harness them.

Susanne and Phil, in a tornado of motions, none of which could be deemed graceful, desperately grabbed at skirts to pull down, pants to pull up, and anything else that could be used to cover their nearly naked forms.

“Get out!” they screamed simultaneously.

“I’m sorry. I’m sorry. I’m sorry.” I repeated my apology, lowering my eyes and backing out the door. As I was about to close the door, I poked my head back in.

“So, is this a good time to inquire about a spot on the third floor?”

“Get out, Mr. Chambers!” Susanne screeched.

I didn’t know if I should laugh or retch, both seeming more than appropriate. Some things best left unseen are forever unforgettable once seen: Phil’s hairy, pimply ass was now chief among them. Dammit, Phil.

I walked back to my room at a deliberate, disciplined pace, one akin to seeking a restroom after having just eaten some questionable Mexican food. I had no plan for what I should do with the morning, aside from maybe washing my eyes with bleach and inducing a head injury to bring on localized amnesia.

Mae’s advice at the diner about not wasting moments or planning too far ahead popped into my thoughts. This was perhaps due to recently witnessing Phil and Susanne enthusiastically exerting their acceptance of that very ideology, but I was trying to apply it to my situation.

Her snap judgment on my inability to chant and enact her mantra bothered me, perhaps more than I had originally realized. But she didn’t know the full story; she wasn’t playing the game with a full deck of cards but still cast her sharp criticism anyway. I don't blame her for this, but I did feel it was a bit unfair considering our developing bond.

Once inside my room, I kicked off my shoes and flopped on the bed, staring at the stippled ceiling. Without invitation, Erica popped into my head. Her blue eyes, thick, wavy brown hair, and soft smile flooded my vision. Mae was right: I looked at her in a way that I hadn't looked at anyone in a long time. I knew I had done this; I had felt it as it was happening. I just hoped it hadn't been too obvious. And Mae seemed to think that Erica looked at me in a certain way too. I wasn't as sure about this, but then again, I never gave myself much credit or had great confidence when it came to the opposite sex's interest in yours truly. Most of the time I had spent with Erica was lit by the wavering glow of a fire. Aside from our spur-of-the-moment swim and goodbye in the day's morning light, which had only amplified her beauty, I hadn't really *seen* Erica, but I felt her, if that makes any sense.

With this realization, a smile crept across my face, and it felt good. The ephemeral spell was broken, however, by the nagging pull of my conscience, forcing my gaze towards my wrist, noting that it was time to look down upon Autumn.

I tried to convince myself that I should stay in my room to ruminate on what Mae had said, to set the demons aside for just one day, one morning, one moment, but my willpower failed me, and I was out the door.

Once in the cafeteria, I positioned my chair in its familiar voyeuristic location. Sure enough, everyone from the third floor, including Autumn, was out in the fresh air. The sun was shining, providing some warmth to the early October day. Everyone wore their coats, scarves, mittens, and toques. Maybe it wasn't that warm after all.

Autumn sat in her wheelchair, her chaperone standing nearby but not too close, sort of like a bodyguard giving just enough space for a private conversation but near enough to act should a threat arise. She was faced towards a pond filled with climate-suited water plants, all surrounding that customary water feature: a fountain in the shape of an angel.

Fitting, I thought, *an angel looking at an angel.*

Her strawberry-blonde hair flowed from underneath her toque, and I knew her brown eyes were filled with impassive sadness. She was as still as the statue she gazed upon, and I wondered if she was warm enough, comfortable enough. I'm sure she was, but my acute Autumn anxiety was kicking in.

A flood of emotions and memories swirled within me. The dam once keeping them at bay was now fully breached. Unlike the swell of tears that rose and fell at the lake, the sound of Mae's voice made the current excess of moisture swiftly retreat.

"Oh, Jesus. Again? I figured you'd be here, but I hoped you wouldn't be."

"I thought you had a morning full of appointments, Mae. What are you doing here?"

"The good doctor kicked me out. Can you believe it?"

"Actually, yes, I can."

Mae laughed her signature laugh. She pulled up a chair next to me and sat down. Before she spoke again, she looked out the window, taking a long drag of nature's sweet nicotine, swivelling her sightline from east to west.

"Ahh, there she is, in the black coat," she said upon spotting Autumn. "Now, you ready to tell me what's so special about this girl and how and why you think you put her here?"

No. I wasn't. I would never be ready to willingly reveal it. But it was time.

"She was my first love," I said, desperately trying to keep my voice steady.

"Oh, fuck off with that," said Mae in disbelief. "You're what, like, thirty? She's about the same age, and she's been here for the better part of a decade."

"I know she has. Like I said at the diner, it's my fault she's here, that she doesn't speak, that her life is essentially over. But believe it or not, she *was* my first love. And I've never stopped loving her. She would have told you otherwise when we were eighteen, but she would have been wrong."

"Alex, if you want me to listen to this sob story, cut the cryptic shit, would you?"

"Mae, I don't want you to listen to this story. I don't want to tell you this story, but based on your constant insistence, please just let me finish."

"Proceed," said Mae, gesturing with her hand, palm up.

"We were each other's first loves. We were in high school. Classic trope, right? It's funny, there's a lot I don't remember about those days, and even if you asked the right questions, I don't think I could mine my memories for the right answers. Something inside me changed when I met Autumn. Something in her changed too. Our interests were very different. I was into music and the arts, and she liked the sciences. She loved animals—wanted to be a veterinarian one day. Her group of friends back then was different than mine, but it never mattered. She was my Juliet, and I was her Romeo. We were inseparable for two years, and our love seemed to grow exponentially by the day. We talked about the future, a family, a life together. And the crazy thing was that we both believed it at the time; it wasn't just about saying what we thought we were supposed to say, what we thought the other wanted to hear. We believed ours was a long-term love."

"So what happened? Juliet get wise and dump your nerdy ass?"

"First of all, we were both kind of nerds. And second, no, Mae, she didn't dump me—I moved away. My Mom was an exceptionally smart and savvy business executive—she still is.

She was constantly being headhunted, and where better to land a corner office than downtown Toronto? I was seventeen, which meant I just had to make it through one more year before I could make my own decisions, go where I wanted to go, be where and with whom I wanted to be. Despite my best efforts at not moving with my family and staying with Autumn, deference to parental authority fundamentally trounced my wishes. I promised our year apart would go by quickly and that as soon as we both graduated, we would attend the same university and rekindle what we had."

"So you failed high school and had to stay behind another year?"

"No, Mae, I didn't fail high school," I sighed in anguish. I just wanted to get through this. "We graduated on schedule, applied to the same school, both got accepted, and made plans to move in together. Autumn went through the efforts of securing us an apartment near campus. Our year apart was enough to spurn the idea of living in a dorm with other first-year students. We didn't need or want to live on campus; all we wanted was each other. Or so I thought, because when the time came to show up, well, I didn't show up."

The tears I had suppressed upon Mae's arrival betrayed me now, but I continued my story. "I stayed in Toronto. I have no idea why; I had no good reason. Hell, I still can't explain my reasoning. I was about to go back to everything I knew, everything I wanted: the girl I loved, the much-talked-about life with her that awaited. But I didn't leave. During the year I spent in Toronto, I was exposed to a million things I had never experienced before: the arts scene, the music scene, culture and diversity in abundance, the buzz and electricity of a city that runs constantly. It pulled me in close and wouldn't release me when the time came. Ultimately, I left her broken-hearted, holding two apartment keys in Vancouver.

"Okay, so you bailed. Big deal. That's part of growing up, Sonny. People change their minds about things all the time, especially when they're young. You're supposed to have your heart broken, that's how life works. If you've never had your heart broken, you've never known it to be intact."

"Is it, Mae?" I snapped back. I was not in the mood for her preachy, reproachful shit today. "Is that why *you're* here too? Someone break *your* heart? Be thankful you can still spew your sanctimonious bullshit because that girl down there can't say a word about anything."

"Mind your tone with me, Sonny. You don't know what you're talking about. You don't know me."

"And whose fault is that, Mae? You don't share anything. All you do is give me and others shit about everything we do and say." I had no idea why I was becoming this irritated, but I was down the path of defensiveness, latching on to some reverse code-of-honour thing. "You think I couldn't know what love is at fifteen? You think just because I was young and inexperienced, I wasn't capable of feeling something bigger than myself? I know what I felt, and feel, and I won't let you trivialize it."

"Trivialize it?" Mae barked back. "There are few people in this world who can claim, let alone truly believe, to have felt what you did at fifteen. I'm just trying to tell you that life is a big, messy middle finger at times."

This was the most heated Mae and I had ever been with each other. Perhaps our current circumstance was a spillover from the unresolved conversation at the diner. Usually, Mae was in the driver's seat, but this time, I wasn't backing down. We were venting, and we'd later realize it was healthy. In the moment, however, it was an all-out oral war: who could hurt who with the most piercing exclamations of our hastily chosen verbal weapons.

"Right, because you've got that love, Mae? That person who comes to visit you here? The friends you don't have to pay to sneak you out for a weekend? You're the loneliest person I've ever met. The people here aren't nice to you because they like you; it's because they're afraid of you or because they need something from you."

For the first time since I'd arrived at Silver Springs and met Mae Seasons, she didn't cut back with a clever retort. Instead, tears began to form in her eyes.

"Shit, Mae. I'm sorry. The weekend with Erica and seeing Autumn and all this stuff coming up, it just—"

"You're right. I am lonely. I've been lonely since I was fifteen too." Mae got up and walked away.

"Mae, I'm sorry. I didn't mean it. I was upset."

Mae stopped, turned around, and told me that she would be spending the rest of the day in her room. Alone.

Between the encounter with Phil and Susanne a few short hours ago, this blowup with Mae, and the demons of the past starting to surface, I was exhausted. The rest of the day off was exactly what I needed.

After finishing my watch over Autumn, I slogged back to my room for some peace and quiet and, in all likelihood, some over-analyzing of my life as it existed in the present moment.

Halfway down the hall, Fred yelled out for me, telling me to meet him in twenty minutes at the cabbage patch, which I now knew, more than a month into my time here, meant the hidden piece of real estate just beyond the north side's garden.

I didn't want to go, but I knew that wallowing in my room probably wasn't the best idea either.

"See you there," I said.

CHAPTER 20

I met Fred at the agreed-upon time, following the exact directions I had been provided for my first trip to the cabbage patch. I wasn't sure why it had garnered this particular moniker, as there was certainly no cabbage to be found and, as far as I could tell, no plot of earth worthy of growing any vegetables or fruit. I suppose I could have asked someone, but it never really crossed my mind to do anything other than accept it. Some things are better left unasked, trust me.

The area was a well-manicured outdoor space that, through the years, staff had taken time to perfect. So long as the patch was maintained, saving them from added upkeep work, the groundskeepers promised to always keep the place a secret. I wasn't sure from whom since Phil already knew about it and, therefore, so did Susanne. Again, some things are best left unasked.

The bushes that buttressed this safe haven were the sort, I was told, that kept their thistles and leaves year-round; there was no possibility of the private area ever losing its natural cover. Due to the obvious giveaway of footprints, wintertime was the only time of year when accessing the cabbage patch proved difficult and required effort for concealment, as the snow provided a blank canvas for wandering feet. But nobody really wanted to spend any amount of time outdoors when the winter conditions were in full effect anyway.

"Okay, man, out with it," said Fred when I arrived, handing me a cardboard-sleeved to-go cup of coffee.

Fred was unusually chipper, even for a guy who always seemed to be in a good mood, smiling and pleasant. Apparently, he and others on the fourth floor had mused about what might have gone down during my weekend away.

"What do you mean, out with it?" I asked, mostly serious. It was strange for Fred to desire gossip. Usually, it was the residents, not the staff, who staked claim to propelling the chinwagging at Silver Springs.

"I mean just that: out with it," he repeated. "Come on, man, you've got to have some stories from your weekend. You were gone from the watchful eyes of Silver Springs with none other than our floor's—hell, the entire building's—most notorious, unapologetic rebel. Surely you got up to some shenanigans."

Yes. Yes indeed; we did. But I wondered whether sharing any tales of the weekend would be a betrayal of sorts. It felt like it would be. Certainly to Mae and the privacy she cultivates, and possibly even to Erica, despite, presumably, her not knowing anyone here. I wasn't so much worried about betraying myself—I was quite adept at that—but I did want to preserve my place as a confidant to Mae.

"Well, we hitched our ride out with someone named Chandra of the Midnight Sun, if that's any indication as to how the weekend went," I offered.

Fred's eyes doubled in size, his mouth salivating in anticipation of salacious details and more fulsome descriptions. Unfortunately for him, he wasn't getting them. Instead, I danced around the specifics and gave him the same spiel I had prepared for Susanne before interrupting her and Phil's morning calisthenics.

I felt moderately bad for not being completely forthcoming with Fred; he had become my closest friend at Silver Springs other than Mae. But I also remembered the tiny bit of hazing he'd been in on when I first arrived, so I wasn't completely remorseful.

"Well, to be honest, I expected things to be a little wilder," he said, somewhat dejected. "But hey, I guess when you're ninety-one, you're not exactly toking weed and hitting beer bongs, am I right?"

Had the twigs directly behind us not crackled at precisely that moment, I have no doubt my face would have betrayed me. I do not possess a poker face. Thankfully, the audible arrival of an interloper forced both Fred and me to focus our attention elsewhere.

Out of the corner of the patch, which was only accessible through the one hidden entrance, came Phil, skulking in like a dog that had just eaten his owner's breakfast off the table.

"Gentlemen," said Phil, brushing leafy remnants from his coat as he strolled towards us. "What a beautiful day, wouldn't you say?"

Fred and I weren't sure what to make of Phil's arrival, and I took his obvious attempt at using the weather as an icebreaker to be a red flag that he was up to something, fishing for something.

"I *would* say," I replied with, truth be told, a mischievous grin. "It's a great morning for some exercise, something to really get the heart rate up."

Phil's face flushed, turning the colour of a ripe tomato.

"Phil, did you follow us here?" I asked. He was supposed to be manning his post at the front desk, keeping an eye on all things Silver Springs, but had instead opted to play a little hooky; a ballsy move, I thought. If Susanne knew he was gallivanting around the grounds when he should be working, even their affection for one another wouldn't save him; her loyalty was to the job, to the rules. Or was it? Maybe some leeway was granted to lover boy.

Phil nodded, clearly unsure as to what he should say or do next. His face expressed the reality that he hadn't fully thought out his plan, at least not beyond his prepared greeting.

"Come on, Phil, not cool," I said, gently scolding him. "Espionage isn't your thing. Well, it is with your cameras and whatnot, but this watch-and-walk action you're doing right now, not a good look."

"Listen, I know, I shouldn't have followed you, but I, uh, I needed to talk to you, Alex," he said, unable to make consistent eye contact, all confidence he may have carried into the cabbage patch having vanished. "So, maybe, uh, when you're done here, we could just have a quick chat. Maybe pop by the front desk when you have some time. No rush."

Phil was panicking, and who could blame him? I wasn't going to say a word about what I saw this morning, but he didn't need to know that. Phil could be an asshole, but he could also not be. I could be an asshole, but I too could also not be, and in this moment, I was choosing not to be.

"Yeah, sounds good," I said. "In fact, let's head there now."

I had no desire, immediate or otherwise, to engage one-on-one with Phil, but this provided precisely the type of organic exit I needed to brush off Fred and preserve the details of the past weekend. I'm sure stories would come out in due time, and his curiosity would be satisfied. Fred wore a forlorn look at my decision to depart, but his disappointment was not so great that he wouldn't soon recover.

Some of the weight was taken off my decision as two other staff members made their way through the brush where Phil had recently emerged from. Faltering in their tracks at the sight of him, it was clear Phil had an unfavourable reputation as someone who wouldn't waste time reporting malfeasance to Susanne. I waved the duo over and assured them there was nothing to worry about; Phil and I were just leaving, and no reports would be filed, verbal or otherwise. Phil nodded in agreement.

"Thanks, Alex," he said as we made our way back inside Silver Springs. "I mean it, thank you. I just need a few minutes of your time."

"Phil, relax," I offered in as calm and reassuring a voice as I could conjure up. "Let's just get you back to the front so no one sounds the alarm that you're missing again, and we'll get whatever this is squared away."

Phil bowed in silent compliance. The walk back seemed unusually quick, and before I knew it, Phil was nestling his rear end back into the grooves of his station's chair.

"So, Phil, what is so important that you needed to tail me to the one spot where staff here feel comfortable knowing they can speak relatively freely?"

"Well, I guess I should tell you—they are being watched out there. Heard too. For some reason, everyone thinks that area is secluded and off our radar, but we've known about it for years. Ever since we caught a few former staff members using that area to smuggle things in and out of Silver Springs, it's been under surveillance."

This was certainly news to me, but then again, I had not been privy to this private space for more than a few weeks. For others though, this detail would likely be devastating.

"But it's fine," said Phil. "We never turn the audio on. We know who goes back there now. We trust the staff, and we let them have their downtime and space—honest. I only show up every now and then as a deterrent to make sure the past doesn't repeat itself, ya know? Because if it did, the whole place would get shut down. I can't let that happen."

Phil's layers were peeling back with each encounter, and the man who began this chapter of my life as a sworn enemy was unknowingly wearing my defences down—I was starting to appreciate him.

"Okay, well, if that's the truth, there's no point in discussing it any further with anyone else," I said, hanging on to a thread or two of skepticism. "But surveillance aside, what's going on? You're being a hell of a lot stranger than usual."

Phil leaned back in his chair, nearly losing the equilibrium between upright and on the floor but rescuing himself at the last second. Steadied once more, he rubbed his eyes and drew in a long breath.

"Listen, Alex, what you saw earlier, that was, well, unintended to say the least, ya know?"

"To say the least, yes."

"Anyway, that was all my fault, not Susanne's. I made her do it and—"

"What do you mean you *made* her do it?" I instantly challenged, more aggressively than Phil had expected. The idea of abuse was a hair-trigger for me.

"No, no, not like that—I mean it was *my* idea; I pushed for it. I didn't make her do nothing she didn't want to already, I swear. We're in love, really, have been for some time now. We both work so much, and Susanne is so dedicated to everyone here and everything about this place, sometimes it's hard to get some time to ourselves, and, well, ya know, urges and whatnot."

I was surprised at Phil's blatantly straightforward admission but probably shouldn't have been. The two of them, in lightning-fast retrospect, were actually perfect for each other.

"Well, that's great you're in love, but why are you telling me this?"

"So you won't tell anyone else."

"Let me see if I understand this," I said, with more than a hint of confusion in my voice. "You have told me something that, previously, I was not able to tell anyone because it was something I didn't know. But now I know, and the only reason I know is because you don't want me to let anyone else know?"

"Yeah, man, exactly. You got it."

What I had just said barely made sense to me, and it was my rapidly firing neurons that articulated it from thoughts into words before I could take a beat to understand it. Keeping this secret seemed important to Phil, and I guess I was taken by his lovestruck audacity.

"Phil, I'm not going to tell anyone about anything," I said. "It's great that you guys are in love—hopefully she feels the same."

"Oh, man, she totally does. I mean, only a woman in love would let me do—"

"Okay, got it," I interjected before Phil had a chance to wax sexual. "Your secret is safe with me. But for God's sake, man, lock the door next time."

Phil gave an awkward laugh and his face flushed in a way only budding love can produce. "Seriously, man, when you find someone you love, you've got to hang on tight, ya know? Toss everything else aside and just go for it," he said unabashedly. "You ever been in love? It's pretty awesome."

Yes, Phil, it's pretty awesome.

CHAPTER 21

Three weeks had passed since Susanne had said a word to me, let alone made anything that resembled eye contact, but her voice on the other end of the phone that late-October morning was calm and clipped, as if nothing had happened, nothing untoward had been seen or heard. I'm not sure if there was a chapter in her manual that covered getting caught performing the two-person tango in the nude. If one existed, I had some questions, some very specific questions, about the person who wrote that chapter.

"So you will come down for a quick chat, then, would you?" she said. "It would be in everyone's best interests if we could establish an understanding about our current state of affairs."

"Yes, Susanne, I'll come right down," I obliged, curious as to the nature of what she described as a state of affairs. "And, Susanne, I'll be down in about five minutes. So, in five minutes, you'll hear a knock on your door. It'll be me—in five minutes."

"Yes, Mr. Chambers, that will be fine. I appreciate your promptness."

If she got my joke, she refused to entertain it. Kudos to her if that was the case. Surely, she had *that* in her manual: don't take the bait.

Susanne wasn't the only one who hadn't spoken to me in three weeks. Mae had all but shut me out, despite my ongoing efforts to smooth things over. Twice, in very short order, I had not only hit a nerve with her but obliterated one, and all I had deciphered up to this point was that it had to do with love and loss. But shit, *who* hadn't experienced those two things, especially someone her age?

I knew my upcoming conversation with Susanne had to do with my relationship with Mae—or what was left of it. Basically, since the time of my arrival, I'd been assigned solely to Mae, as that was the only manner in which I could be useful. And though I wasn't paid, I was consuming all available resources—occupying a room, eating meals, and drawing on the water and utilities. Without any volunteering efforts, unlimited access to these amenities could not continue, and I'd likely be shown the door. Unbeknownst to me, Mae had requested I not be sent packing or reassigned to another resident on another floor—a topic I later found out was the crux of more than a handful of heated discussions between her and Susanne. But Mae only had so much pull, and even then, how she had it at all was a mystery.

Out of an abundance of caution, I loudly announced my presence as I came into the lobby, thrilled to see Phil at his post. I was met with a snort and a headshake from the burly munchkin. He didn't say a word, just nodded in my direction. I could tell he was appreciative of my discretion, but he was clearly battling his instincts to bust my balls.

Susanne's door was open when I arrived, but I knocked anyway while simultaneously entering.

"So, Susanne, what can I do for you?" I asked, sitting down to face her.

"Well, Mr. Chambers, as you know, for the past several weeks, your duties as a volunteer have all but ceased thanks to a very unfortunate incident with Ms. Seasons," she replied stoically. "She refuses to tell me exactly what occurred, but one only needs a few logical guesses. Though we are not paying you, your compensation comes in the form of us housing you, feeding you, and providing you with unlimited access to all utilities. You are not, as the lack of a paystub may indicate, free."

I wanted to say "great minds think alike," but I wasn't sure that I wanted to share a similar mindset with Susanne, and I didn't want to have to explain what I meant.

"Once again, what happened between you and Ms. Seasons seems to be shrouded in some mystery, and she is unwilling to tell us what transpired despite our best attempts. You have presented your story, and while we do not disbelieve it, we would like to confirm it with Ms. Seasons, but she refuses to confirm or deny anything."

"Susanne, listen—shit happens, okay?" I said involuntarily, forgoing all politeness in making my case for acquittal. "Mae and I had an argument. We both harbour some strong feelings about certain subjects, and given the way they came up, our conversation reached a boiling point. That's it. I was upset and said some things I wish I could take back. But Mae won't talk to me. She won't let me apologize despite my best efforts."

"Well, that brings me to the reason why you are here," said Susanne. "In speaking with Ms. Seasons just this morning, she provided three stipulations for you to complete before this arrangement can get back on track."

I almost immediately agreed to the terms without hearing them, and had it been anyone other than Mae, I likely would have. But Mae being Mae, these three provisions could have literally been anything. Truth be told, I missed her. I missed our conversations because, at times, they had a deeper impact than I think either one of us fully realized.

Susanne slid an envelope across the table, as if we were negotiating a salary. I picked it up, opened it, and read Mae's three conditions:

1. Finish your story
2. Call Erica
3. Candy striper

A smile stretched across my face. Mae's ransom demands were doable—embarrassing but doable.

"I gather from your agreeable reaction that Ms. Seasons's requests are to your satisfaction."

"You can tell Mae that I accept her terms," I said to Susanne as I stood to leave.

"Oh, Mr. Chambers, one more thing," said Susanne with an air of fortified courage. "What you observed a few weeks back, there really is no need to discuss it other than to say nothing in that moment was meant for your eyes. I hope we can maintain some respectful discretion."

"No shit it wasn't meant for my eyes. What I saw wasn't meant to ever be seen in the light of day. But don't worry, Susanne. I have no desire to share that moment with anyone—ever. You can count on me. Honestly, I'd really like to forget it. Oh, how I'd like to forget it."

"That would be just fine if you did, Mr. Chambers. I will notify Ms. Seasons to meet you in the cafeteria in an hour."

"Great, thanks. And just one more thing before I go. About the third floor—"

"Good day, Mr. Chambers."

I left Susanne's office feeling better than I had upon entering, and I took that as a promising sign of things to come.

Mae found me sitting in the exact same spot she had the last time we spoke. I was again peering down at Autumn, desperate to know what she was thinking, if anything at all. It was agonizing to be so close yet so distant.

"Well, dipshit, I'm ready for your apology," said Mae.

"I'm sorry? *My* apology was attempted the last time we spoke. And besides, it wasn't on your little list of demands you had Susanne broker on your behalf."

Mae stared at me with a flicker of irritation in her eyes.

"Okay, okay. Mae, I am sorry. The last time we were here, I got upset and words came out before they could be filtered. I don't know what sadness you carry with you, but the evidence is there. I see it. I have it too."

"Well, isn't that nice of you to say, but I was talking about the coffee in front of you. I'm told you took the last one before they closed up the machine. That, Sonny, is a dick move."

Mae laughed, and I couldn't help but join her. We were slipping back into our accustomed routine, and although it was one that usually involved me receiving physical and verbal abuse, I was ready for it.

"So," said Mae, "how about you finish telling me what happened with that red-haired beauty down there?"

I couldn't argue with Mae's description. Autumn was—and had been since the first day I met her—breathtakingly beautiful in a way that was refreshing, delightful, and unique. I don't know if anyone else ever really saw it, but I did, and that was all that mattered to Autumn. She told me that once, and I never forgot it. I've forgotten a lot of the little details about our relationship all those years ago but never that.

I picked up where I left off in my tale of heartbreak: my regret for leaving Autumn high and dry in Vancouver, and it mostly seemed to satisfy Mae's curiosity.

"But what you haven't told me is why you think it's your fault that Autumn is here," pried Mae.

I knew that once I started this story, I would inevitably reach the end, and I had prolonged unearthing this portion of the sad, gut-wrenching conclusion for as long as I could. I didn't want to relive it but had been told repeatedly by my therapist that I would have to address it if I ever wanted to move on.

"It's my fault because I never showed up in Vancouver, and that one selfish decision caused a ripple effect I never could have imagined. Autumn was heartbroken when I didn't show but not the kind of heartbroken where she stayed in, ate ice cream, ripped up old pictures, and cursed my existence. It was as if, in the moment that I was supposed to be there and suddenly wasn't, something fundamental in her character changed. She went out with her friends a few nights later, met a guy, and figured that making me jealous by flaunting how quickly she had gotten over me would leave a mark. Who's to say why we do things at that age? I realize this somewhat contradicts my belief in young love and how solid ours was—we were kids, and that's just how it goes.

"The jealousy angle worked; mind you, it wasn't jealousy I felt. It was self-shame. And I knew this wasn't who she was. She wasn't vindictive like this. She was guarded with her feelings and generous with her affection for others, so to forfeit all that so quickly was entirely out of character. Anyways, she ended up dating a real asshole, who, according to our remaining mutual friends, was abusive, physically and emotionally. I didn't know any of this until after the fact, and I don't know what I would have done if I had known, but I'd like to think I would have acted and done something, anything, on Autumn's behalf. I didn't fall out of love with her; I just made a self-centred decision.

"Anyway, one night, a particularly awful night, Autumn realized that her condemnation of me wasn't worth the continued mistreatment at the hands of the first prick she'd found on her quest to erase my memory. Story has it that she tore out of the house, hopped in her car, and attempted to get away, likely with the plan to never go back and to break off all contact with him. But she wasn't quick enough. He managed to catch her before she could get the car out of park. The driver's window was down, and this was all the room he needed"—my voice cracked as the images from my words caused a searing pain to radiate through my entire body—"to pull her out of the car by her hair. He proceeded to beat her until she was unconscious, and according to the police report, he kept going. Thankfully, a neighbour, hearing the screams, intervened after calling 911. Had it not been for that neighbour, I am sure Autumn would be dead. She came within an inch of losing her life because I never showed up."

My tears bubbled like an impending volcanic eruption. The very thought of this happening to Autumn was physically sickening, and I could feel the same tightness in my chest and throat as I had when I first heard what happened.

Mae took my hand with both of hers and held it tight. Without realizing my body's movements, I leaned in to cry on her shoulder, and she embraced me like a grandmother would, soft and sweet, a reassuring rub of the back letting me know I was safe, that it would be okay.

"You couldn't have known that's how things would turn out," said Mae softly. "Nobody could have known. People can be shitty. People can do shitty things. Autumn was a victim of a terribly shitty thing done by an even shittier person. But none of that is *your* fault."

Mae and I were locked in an honest moment, and despite its infinite sadness, it was the only place I wanted to be.

I recounted to Mae how I'd flown to Vancouver immediately upon hearing the news and stayed in Autumn's hospital room for three weeks, never leaving. She had no idea I was in the room, and I had no idea what I was doing there. All I knew was that I should be there. Her parents didn't show up even once the entire time I was stationed by her side. I thought it might have been my presence that repulsed them, but in fact, they had abandoned Autumn in the same fashion I had, the only difference being they did so after learning about Autumn's dependency on liquor and drugs to get through the new life she'd designed for herself. I couldn't imagine her parents giving up on her like that—but wasn't that basically what I had done?

Autumn never fully recovered and required constant care, which no one in her life could nor would provide, and thus, she came to reside at Silver Springs. Physically, she slowly healed. Her bones mended; wounds became scars. Mentally, though, she was never the same. She was no longer the Autumn I knew after enduring that harrowing day, and maybe she hadn't been for quite some time leading up to that day. She looked like Autumn Alicia Emerson, but she was no longer that person. She didn't speak, didn't remember, didn't recognize. She was a shell.

"And so, for the second time in the two years since I left her, my heart shattered. Despite my actions of not returning, the initial departure was the most difficult moment of my young life. Nothing prepares you for that anguish, especially at that age. And so, I would never be able to right my wrong. I don't remember exactly when I learned she'd ended up here, or even how, but when I did, I made the decision to come and spend the rest of my days, her days, together, even if she didn't know who I was. From the very start, I was supposed to be volunteering on her floor, but they reassigned me when I got here, giving me some bullshit story about that spot being taken."

Mae was quiet as I spoke, listening to my words and feeling my pain, crafting the type of response that can only come with wisdom through lived experience.

"That, my boy, is a very sad story. What you've just described to me is love of the purest form, despite what you perceive to be your self-inflicted mistake of wanting to grow up in a place that was new and exciting for you. But the depth of your love—that's rare. Moreover, it's beautiful in ways we can't fully comprehend, and maybe we're not supposed to."

We sat in untroubled silence for a while, two guardians now watching over Autumn. Mae was beginning to understand why she hadn't been able to drive me away in the early days, no matter what she'd done or said to me. Being here, even on the wrong floor, was enough to fulfill the promise I had made to myself. Nobody was going to take that away from me.

Mae, still holding my hand, squeezed it one last time, indicating all was right, all was forgiven.

With an understanding established between us, I said to her, "You'll never guess what I caught Susanne and Phil doing a few weeks back."

Sorry, Phil and Susanne, I lied.

CHAPTER 22

Disappearing in a haze of rapidly changing weather, October's colourful leaves, which had once populated the valley's trees, were now nestled on the forest floor. Halloween was upon us, and at Silver Springs, this was a holiday that carried the anticipation and expectation of Christmas. Apparently, it was customary for all residents and staff to dress up for what Fred guaranteed me was the biggest party of the year. I had my reservations about where to set my expectations, as this wasn't exactly Delta Phi.

In my efforts to live up to my promises to Mae, I acted on the second item on her list of demands and called Erica. The call actually checked off two requests, as contacting Erica was the only feasible way for me to get the candy-striper costume I was none too eager to don again.

With minimal cajoling, Erica graciously agreed to deliver the costume to Silver Springs, despite the roundabout trip she would have to make from the city to her cabin to the facility. I hoped that most of her willingness came from wanting to see me, but in all likelihood, any opportunity to have a laugh at my expense was the driving factor.

When she arrived, I met Erica outside in the parking lot, as far away as possible from the prying eyes and eavesdropping ears of Phil, who was still under the impression his amorous secret was safe, despite my disclosure to Mae. The truth was, with Mae, it could go one of two ways: it could remain locked in Fort Knox, or it would be spilled the second she saw him. Only time and Mae's temperament would tell.

As I opened Erica's door for her, Norah Jones emanated from the speakers, and my hands began to sweat. I tried to hide this by stuffing them in my jacket pockets, which only made things worse.

"Well, who would have thought you'd have an encore with this particular number?" said Erica as she got out of the car and opened the back door to grab the all-too-familiar frock of embarrassment.

"Yes, well, I liked how my legs looked in it, so I figured I'd take this chance to show them off again. After all, it is a *sexy* candy-striper costume."

Her hair was windswept and somehow fell in all the right places. She tucked a few strands behind her ear in that cute rom-com kind of way and smiled at me. Her ocean-blue scarf pulled the blue in her eyes to a prominence otherwise only found in the digital editing world of Photoshop. Her beauty was indisputable, but there were hints aplenty that her intellectual depth trumped what could be seen by the naked eye—most notably, a copy of *Thinking, Fast and Slow* on the passenger seat.

We walked together to the front doors of Silver Springs and milled about out front, awkward in our attempt to figure out what to do or say next. It felt like a date walking me to my door.

"Thanks for bringing this, I really appreciate it, I think," I offered with an anxious laugh. "It's kind of like a gift to Mae, and I couldn't think of any other way of getting my hands on it."

"It's cool. I'm glad you called, glad I could help," she said, kicking an invisible stone on the ground. "Listen, I don't know what your schedule is like here, but if you're ever free, we should maybe grab a coffee or something." She said this shyly, which was both adorable and emasculating. I was supposed to be the one taking the lead, making the move, putting myself out there.

"Yeah, that'd be cool. It'd be fun. Let's do that. I'll call you for sure." I sounded like a bumbling idiot. Erica was clearly reading my signs, though they were unintentional. I did like her, but I couldn't allow myself to fully delve into that until I had righted my wrong, which may never happen.

"Well, Alex, whenever that is, and I hope it's not too far off, I look forward to it."

She made the return trek across the lawn by herself, insisting it would be silly for me to have walked there and back twice. I watched her every departing step, offering a weak wave when she pulled away. I doubt she saw it across the distance.

The one benefit of my Halloween costume being as scant as it was, I could fold it up and keep it out of Phil's view on my way back in. The night would hold plenty of ridicule; I didn't need it starting now.

The day's regular schedule was thrown out on Halloween, and I do mean completely tossed in the shredder. Instead of regimented mealtimes, a continuous buffet of themed treats and savoury dishes was available throughout the day, continuously refilled whenever an item ran low. Residents were permitted to roam reasonably free across their respective floors; quiet time, reading time, and game time all dissolved into a fluidity that excited the senses for the evening's main event.

It was nearing four in the afternoon—two hours until the first portion of the party would begin. Fred had mentioned earlier that on Halloween everyone got together in the main-floor conference room, or at least those residents who posed no threat of disrupting the party. If there was ever an argument for revoking Autumn's invitation, it was not that. For the first time since I'd arrived, I was going to be able to see her up close. Cue the heart palpitations, which occurred for the second time that day, and not because of what I would be wearing. It seemed the women in my life, old and new, had a similar effect on me.

As I unwrapped the costume in the seclusion of my room, I noticed some twine and a tiny bottle. With them—a note.

Here are some fishnets to complement those killer legs and some liquid courage to get you through the dress rehearsal.

A hand-drawn heart stood beside Erica's name. Thankfully, she hadn't dotted the *i* with it, but I wouldn't have counted that as a point against her.

Her comment about my legs ignited the idea that there was a connection between us, one that I simultaneously wanted and feared. I contemplated the fishnets, wondering if they'd be too porn adjacent for this type of party. This thought quickly evaporated as I remembered the rest of the costume; fishnets would actually lend an added degree of modesty. The tiny bottle of booze was most welcome.

I got dressed at a vigorous pace, despite the good-natured mockery and awkward glances awaiting me downstairs. I was getting closer, second by second, to seeing and talking to Autumn. But is this how I wanted her to see me? Fuck it; now or never.

I downed the miniature-size bottle of whisky, feeling the burn in my throat as it descended to that special area in the bottom of my belly. Once settled, the whisky calmed all nerves. There wasn't nearly enough of it to make me not give a shit, but every drop helped. I had no idea what type of beverages would be at the party but doubted any of the alcoholic variety would be available.

Once dressed, I stared at myself in the mirror. I looked like a fool but didn't care. Maybe the booze was working better than anticipated. I straightened my collar and tugged down my skirt, ready to take on whatever was waiting for me on the main floor.

I was about to head down to the lobby when the phone rang. What was it about this phone? Why did it always seem to ring with news guaranteed to pull me away from whatever I was looking forward to doing? I could have left, letting it ring, but I didn't.

"Hello?"

"Alex, thank God you're there." It was Phil. "You've gotta help me, man. Something happened. I—I—I—"

"Whoa, Phil, relax. What happened? What are you talking about?"

"Just get down here, man. Something bad—there's been a—just hurry up." With that, he hung up.

Fuck. What could it possibly be now?

I hurried to the elevator and made my way down, heart rate rising with each passing floor, imagination running wild. The ride to the ground level passed in slow motion, but eventually, the elevator sang its familiar tone of arrival, and the door slowly opened, leaving me to gaze upon—Susanne dressed as a car and Phil dressed in black with a sash that said *Oops*.

"Thank God you're here, Alex," said Phil. "There's been a—holy shit, what are you wearing? Never mind, we'll get to that. Back to this."

I stared at him. Then at Susanne. Then back at Phil. "What?"

"Come on, man." Phil winked, excitedly gesturing back and forth between Susanne and himself. "You're here just in time to save us from a—"

"Awkward encounter? I couldn't agree more."

"A car accident," said Susanne in a singsong voice. At this, she and Phil broke into outrageous laughter, clutching each other's arms in gleeful cahoots.

"You two belong together, you know that?" I said as I brushed by them. "That was bullshit. How dare you."

"Nice legs," they said in unison, immediately turning towards one another to administer an awkward, uncoordinated high-five, causing them to once again break into laughter. Dammit if they weren't starting to grow on me as a couple.

The music issuing from the conference room was distinct from the elevator's standard melodies. "Monster Mash" was currently playing. It would be played at least fifteen times throughout the party. People were shuffling in and out of the room dressed as everything from witches to ghosts to princes and princesses. No one was wearing a *sexy* anything, which was refreshing for Halloween. I was the sole exception, if I do say so myself.

The conference room was appropriately dark, the only light coming from numerous jack-o'-lanterns with flickering battery-powered candles, faux cauldrons in the corners, and some streaming lights positioned on the stage. I had to admit, it was pretty impressive for the venue. Fred told me this was the one day of the year when all the stops were pulled out; I could see he hadn't been exaggerating. Take that Delta Phi, you've got nothing on Silver Springs.

Despite the darkness, it was obvious the room was quite crowded. While my eyes adjusted to the lack of light, I would bide my time before surveying the landscape to find Autumn.

"There you are, and you've completed your apology with this slinky little number," said Mae, coming up alongside me and slapping me on the back.

She wore a red sweater with a white collar, a black skirt with yellow trim, big brown shoes, a black wig, and a—beard?

"I'm Oliver Oil."

"Jesus, Mae," I said, laughing. "Game over. You win Halloween. We can all go home."

Mae was pleased with herself; how could she not be? She'd pulled it off. "I couldn't let you be the only one dressed in drag tonight," she said with a smile of solidarity. "Now, we have a mission, Sonny. First, take a swig of this."

She pulled a flask from her skirt, unscrewed the cap, and passed it my way. I didn't say a word, not even thank you, I just took the flask and let a hot shot of I don't even know what rifle down my throat. My eyes twitched, my body seized, and I needed to shake it all out.

"Holy shit, Mae. What is this, turpentine?"

"Close; it's toilet whisky. You've heard of toilet wine. Well, this is better, patent pending."

"Please tell me that this wasn't actually made in a toilet."

Mae didn't answer but began scanning the room for Autumn, which was helpful because I wasn't sure my vision would remain clear for much longer after consuming that swill.

"There." She pointed across the room, past a couple of witches and wizards doing some kind of robot dance. "There she is, your sleeping beauty."

In this case, she literally was, except she was awake; that is to say, she was dressed as Sleeping Beauty. She sat in her wheelchair, just kind of there. I didn't know if she was capable of walking and chose not to or if she was confined to the chair. I had never seen her out of it and resigned myself to the latter, despite some faded memories of a doctor telling me it was likely she'd recover physically and could regain most, if not all, of her motor functions.

My vision, thankfully, did not fail me. In fact, it went tunnel, and I became unaware of anything else in the room. I felt like we were at a high-school dance, my nerves mixing with the cement in my feet before the long, slow walk across the floor.

My thoughts were interrupted by Michael Jackson's "Thriller," the creepy werewolves howling behind the beat piercing the momentary silence between songs. Breaking my line of sight was the car accident of Susanne and Phil performing the pop hit's choreography in the middle of the dance floor. A crowd of people began to form as if witnessing a dance-off.

I refocused only to notice that Autumn had been moved. To where, I wasn't sure. Shit.

"Mae, I lost her, where'd she go?" I said to no one apparently, as Mae had also disappeared. Great. I hoped this wasn't a sign.

The room was becoming increasingly lively; seemingly everyone in the building was now here. The music pumped, bodies gyrated, and no one really seemed to pay any mind to what I was wearing, the room's dimness helping my cause. The lights pulsing in a strobe effect made it difficult to differentiate anything, let alone single out a familiar face in a sea of costumes. Add to that the many people here in wheelchairs, and I was working through a real-life *Where's Waldo* scenario.

I caught a glimpse of a chair headed towards the elevator as the big wooden door to the conference room swung open. I also caught a glimpse of a reddish head above a blue dress. It was her.

I bolted for the elevator, running into a handful of people and knocking them back like I was blocking for Barry Sanders. As I got to the elevator, the door began closing while Autumn stared outward.

"Autumn!" It's all I was able to get out before the door slid shut and the lighted numbers above began their ascending count. I silently watched until they stopped at three.

The only saving grace of this moment was we had both gotten a clear look at one another. Whether she knew who she was looking at, I didn't know. I did know that I felt a piercing heat in my heart, a potent blend of anguish and hope, a conflicting cardiac conundrum.

"I'm here, Autumn. I'm here. I'm here for you now," I whispered to myself and the cold steel of the shuttered elevator door.

I didn't go back to the party but instead went to my room, anguishing in what felt like a small victory but also a colossal defeat.

CHAPTER 23

Fred was the first person to greet me at breakfast the next morning, making a few quips about my costume but none I hadn't heard before. It seemed like he felt obligated to make a joke or two—I mean, how could you not?—but they were half-hearted and kind of fell flat. What did I care? The costume was a thing of the past. Everything was now in front of me, and no amount of residual embarrassment from that outfit would dampen my resolve.

"You missed quite the show after you ran out last night," he said as I set down my cinnamon raisin bagel with cream cheese and cup of black coffee filled to the brim.

"What do you mean? What happened?" I asked, settling into my chair and arranging my cutlery.

"Well, for one, Susanne and Phil went from dancing like extras in "Thriller" to starring in *Dirty Dancing*," he said, smiling. I couldn't tell if it was because he found it laughable or, like me, thought Susanne and Phil seemed weirdly perfect together. "It was awkward, even for them, I think. I'm not sure they'd ever shared a kiss with someone before. It was hard to look away. I guess they lived up to their costumes."

"Well, hey, good for them. If you can't let yourself go on Halloween of all days, when can you?" I said with a carefreeness that hadn't existed twenty-four hours earlier—hell, not even twelve hours earlier.

I fussed with the cream cheese on my bagel, as it refused to soften from the heat of its circular carriage, maintaining its form and stubbornly remaining as nothing more than a moveable chunk that would not be spread into submission. The coffee tasted better today. I didn't think it was possible, but that was the reality according to my taste buds. There was a dark, rich boldness to it. Everything seemed to taste a little better, smell a little sweeter today.

"I've got to give Mae credit too," said Fred. "Her costume was fantastic, and who knew she had those dance moves in her. In all my years working here, she's never hit the dance floor—barely even put effort into dressing up. You must be having some effect on her."

I am, I thought. *And her on me. Funny how things work out.*

"I'm sorry I missed the dancing. That must have been quite the sight," I said, though I couldn't fathom any dance moves good enough to really make me miss them.

Staff members shuffled in and out of the cafeteria, many carrying leftover Halloween-themed plates and napkins. They moved a little slower today, zombie-like, which was appropriate given the recently concluded festivities. Fred told me this was common and that most of the year, staff don't get a chance to really let loose or stay up late in the common areas. Silver Springs ran a fairly tight ship when it came to this sort of unrestrained behaviour. I could appreciate that protocol given the nature of the business conducted here.

The clock on the wall above us ticked away. I had never noticed it before. Today it seemed like it was talking to me. It whispered a tick here, a tock there, straining for my attention.

"Has that always been there?" I asked Fred, pointing to the clock, shovelling bagel into my mouth.

"Yep, I think so. Maybe not? You know what, I don't know. Everything seems to blend in here. I can't say I've ever really noticed the décor or anything of the sort for years now."

I counted in unison with the second hand on the clock, though I wasn't entirely sure what I was counting to, as there was no immediate opportunity to see Autumn again. As the hands moved, I felt the clock mocking me with indications that time was the double-edged sword I would die by; I had all of it, but I didn't have nearly enough of it.

"Let me ask you something," said Fred.

"Fire away."

"I heard Mae talking to Susanne about someone here named Autumn. I don't think I've ever heard anyone go by that name in the building and definitely not on our floor. Mae said something about getting you and Autumn together on the trip to the cemetery for Remembrance Day."

"And your question is?" I asked, unsure of where Fred was taking this.

"Do you know who this Autumn is? And why is Mae lobbying on your behalf? She's not really in the business of doing pro bono work."

This news was interesting and made me smile. Mae, who only thought of herself more often than not, was spending some of her Silver Springs political capital on me. Interesting news indeed.

"First of all, that was two questions, but I'm feeling generous today, so I'll answer them both. I'm not sure who Autumn is. Maybe you misheard and she was talking about the season. And I haven't heard anything about a trip to the cemetery. Besides, that scenario seems a little macabre for a set-up with an unknown person, don't you think?"

"Yeah, I guess so. Maybe I didn't fully hear her right. Anyways, thought I'd ask. Seems you and Mae are back to getting along these days, so at least there's that."

Yeah, there's that.

"You won't believe what Susanne and Phil did on the dance floor last night," said Mae as I arrived at her suite.

"Yes, I heard they put on quite the show. Fred told me."

"Oh, he would have watered down what happened. He's never been comfortable with the idea of sex, let alone the sight of it."

"They had sex on the dance floor?!"

"No, you pervert, but they might as well have given the way they were dry-humping each other, two twigs—well, Phil is more of a tree trunk—rubbing together, trying to start a fire. Repulsively beautiful!"

Mae carried on for the next five minutes with very descriptive details of what had transpired last night, and on several occasions, she insisted a baby would be on the way. To her credit, her version was much more entertaining than Fred's, and for that, I was thankful. I thought about asking her what she'd said to Susanne about Autumn and me but opted to keep that in my pocket for now.

I couldn't help but notice, as she related stories from the party, that Mae looked drawn and tired this morning. Her eyes didn't have quite the same twinkle of mirthful life as most other days, and her movements were a few gears slower. This could have been just one of the realities of advancing in age: you have those days where things just don't feel quite as good as they usually do. But moreover, there was a bit of sadness to everything about her when she wasn't spinning a tale from the previous night. The stories, it seemed, were being used as a distraction. I had a feeling I knew what was bothering her but, again, best not to press. The time would come.

It was November 11—Remembrance Day. Every year on this day, Silver Springs residents went to the cenotaph at the nearby cemetery to pay their respects to all the valiant men and women who had participated in the war effort, regardless of the conflict. For those who wanted to attend, which, as it turned out, was mostly everyone who had some measure of mobility, a caravan of minibuses was rented, shuttling people to and from. The majority of residents were going for the eleven o'clock ceremony, while a few others were going later in the day.

There were no parameters for who could attend. If you wanted to get on the bus, you could, simple as that. I was told that the entire third floor usually attended, which meant Autumn would be there. And if Autumn was there, I was there. Also simple as that.

After breakfast, people assembled in the lobby, waiting for the caravan. It was about an hour's drive to the cemetery, and apparently, prime seating was important, hence the early lineups. I milled about the lobby looking for Autumn. I hadn't seen her up close since that brief, fleeting encounter on Halloween. Each day, I continued to watch her from above, but I hadn't been close. And now, with the information from Fred about Mae advocating on my behalf to get one-on-one time with Autumn, I felt more hopeful than any other day I'd been here. I wasn't sure if Mae's idea would bear fruit, but I held on to the hope that it would.

The lobby steadily filled like water rising from a crack in the hull of an ocean liner, and given enough time, it would be full. Based on the numbers in the room, Phil all too happily placed a call on Susanne's behalf to request another bus. They were magnificently and imperfectly perfect for each other, and despite the constant shit Phil gave me—which had resumed in recent days—and the characterless corporate cosplay Susanne dished out, I was happy for them. Life's too short, I suppose, to get caught up in the things that don't bring you happiness.

I was standing near one of the many fake plants housed in inordinately tall pots when Mae arrived and nudged my ribs with her boney finger.

"I'm sorry for this, but you'll understand later and thank me," she said.

In the split second afterward, Mae lined up to my lower half like a placekicker lining up a field goal, took a step back, and let her leg fly, her sturdy orthopedic shoe solidly connecting with my shin and delivering quite the crack.

"Jesus Christ, Mae, what the hell?" I bawled in unforced reaction. "Are those steel toe?"

"You scum bag," screeched Mae, her saliva spraying me as she screamed.

In short order, a couple of staff members came over to escort Mae away from me. Susanne ran over too, Phil in tow.

"Mr. Chambers, what is the meaning of this commotion?" asked Susanne.

"Look, Susanne, I have no idea. I'm out of ideas. Every time I think Mae and I are starting to really come together and figure it out, something like this happens."

"Well, I just do not know how many more of these outbursts we must endure or these conversations we can keep having," said Susanne, shaking her head, "but we are certainly nearing the end of the line. I cannot have you antagonizing our residents."

"Yeah, you're taking up a lot of Ms. Rogers's valuable time with your shenanigans," said Phil with a supportive, overeager bluster. It was clear our little secret would have no bearing on his displaying public support for his soulmate.

"Spare me, Phil, okay? Let me talk to her. I'm sure it was just some misunderstanding."

"I am afraid there is no time for that, Mr. Chambers," said Susanne. "The buses are here. I think it is best if the two of you take separate transportation or if one of you does not go. But in good conscience, given the significance of today, I cannot force anyone who wants to go to stay behind. So, you can join the second and third floor residents on the first bus, and we will have Ms. Seasons on the next bus with everyone else from your floor."

Taking a beat to digest what I'd just heard, I was pleased, though still confused and in pain. Then it hit me. What Fred had said was true—somewhat. If Mae had indeed asked Susanne for this arrangement, this isn't how it would have played out. Unless Susanne said no for whatever presumably uptight, corporate-policy reason she had. And if that was the case, Mae would not be deterred, and therefore manufactured a—

As the realization struck me and we were ushered out the doors and onto the bus, I turned back to look at Mae, who was giving me a wink and a smile.

CHAPTER 24

Based on my position in line prior to exiting the building, I ended up sitting near the back of the bus. Volunteers were seated furthest away from those requiring the necessary space and safety only available at the front, where extra room was provided for wheelchairs and other assistive devices. I was further away than I liked, but that goes without saying. If I couldn't be seated next to Autumn, I was too far away, simple as that. This yearning to be closer tugged harder when I realized I couldn't even catch a glimpse of her between the heads in the seats ahead of me.

Staring out from the bus, I revisited the mental snapshots taken in the lobby, replaying every detail I could recall as we made our way down the road. Autumn wore a red coat with black buttons; she was a living, breathing incarnation of a poppy flower. Her white scarf hugged her neck, fastened in such a way as to keep the warmth in without restricting airflow. A checkered blanket lay across her lap, where her gloved, clasped hands rested atop the folds of the woolly fabric.

Mae's bus tailed us the entire way, and I often glanced back, thinking of what she did for me and whether I could do anything to return such a favour. I feared there was nothing I could offer her, that whatever she would consider a want would be unobtainable.

As part of my plan to get time with Autumn—which was developing as we drove—I figured my best option would be to wander over to her once we were all settled and maybe get a few words in, a glance or two at the very least. Nothing excessive, just small, simple steps that wouldn't raise any alarm bells or create a scene that looked out of place, causing Autumn's handlers to intercede with concern. Just thinking of it gave me pause, an anxious blip interrupting my otherwise steady heart rate.

Making small talk with the other staff members relegated to the rear of the bus, I came to learn that the cemetery we were headed towards was the resting place of many World War II veterans, most of them infantry division, with several from the navy. This seemed a salient detail, as it came up in more than a few different conversations. I'm ashamed to admit that my mind was not with those men and women who courageously served for my freedom but with Autumn.

We pulled onto a gravel roadway in a sprawling cemetery, the path meandering through the immaculate grounds like a lazy river. The tires crunched over the loose stones under their worn treads, casting errant pebbles behind us.

Wreaths, adorned with ribbons and poppies and names of people I didn't know, were placed around the cenotaph in a tasteful manner, guarding the monument, and propped up at an angle that drew an onlooker's attention to the scores of names etched on the smooth stone.

As I stepped off the bus, the day's coolness washed over me in a cleansing manner, fresh and invigorating. I pulled my jacket close and adjusted my toque, drawing it over my ears as far as it would go. My eyes were trained on Autumn; I was not going to lose her like I had a few short days ago on Halloween. Out of the corner of my eye, however, I caught the movement of a lone figure heading in the opposite direction of everyone else. I tried to dismiss it, not wanting to fully look, but I couldn't help myself. An unwarranted feeling deep within forced my sight to break from Autumn and focus on the solitary skulking figure of none other than Mae.

No one seemed to be stopping her, which struck me as odd given that if you wandered off course at Silver Springs, staff quickly prompted you back like an invisible electric fence giving warning to a roaming dog. Did they know she was wandering away? I tried to keep an eye on her and Autumn at the same time, but it became impossible as Mae moved farther away. I had to make a choice.

Fuck.

Once again, my time with Autumn would have to be put on hold. As the masses marched to the cenotaph, I spun on a heel and travelled in the same direction as Mae, my steps taking me towards a far corner of the cemetery.

I maintained my distance but kept her in my view. There were wooden markers staked in the ground, identifying specific areas by date and surname. I read them as I passed, gradually letting the magnitude of the lives remembered on this hallowed ground sink in. Shuffling past marker after marker, I stopped and stared at the one confirming my previous suspicion upon first seeing Mae's tattoo.

A black-and-bronze plaque with WWII etched on it prominently shimmered in stark contrast to its freshly painted white post. Mae knew someone here, and I suspected I knew who.

A light mist began to fall, seemingly out of nowhere since the peaceful drive here had been complemented by clear skies and sunshine. Now, however, thickening clouds were rolling in over the hills, turning the formerly blue sky to slate grey and bringing reminders of the season on sporadic gusts of chilling wind.

Some visitors had come prepared for any weather eventuality with umbrellas and shawls and a variety of other clothing that would keep them dry should the skies suddenly open up. I, on the other hand, was limited to a zip-up hoodie; it wicked the softer precipitation but would surely not withstand a downpour. Fingers crossed it wouldn't come to the latter.

Mae never broke stride, unaware, or simply not caring, that she had a tail. She carved her way down a row of crosses that had been beautified with flags and flowers and photos: heartfelt tokens from grateful descendants. The men and women who lay in these graves were very much alive in spirit, palpable in the presence of pain, suffering, and pride that could not be ignored. I had never had anyone close to me pass away before, so being in a graveyard was a completely new experience. I wasn't sure where to tread, which direction I should walk, or if passing between headstones was a faux pas, so I followed Mae, hoping that she practised appropriate cemetery etiquette.

It seemed as though we walked for a while, but in reality, Mae was just moving slowly, and given the day's weather and her age, this pace was in her best interest. Her steps were even and assured as she navigated white cross after white cross. She'd made this solemn walk before. She could do it with her eyes closed.

"You're about to get a history lesson, Sonny," said Mae, stopping in her tracks. I was close enough now to know she had said something, but with her facing the other way and the wind picking up, I couldn't precisely make it out.

I guess she sensed it was me following her, though how she knew was beyond me; she hadn't turned around once.

"I'm sorry, Mae, what did you say?" I asked, lightly jogging to get within earshot.

"I said you're about to get a history lesson."

We arrived at a white cross with the name John Douglas Seasons on it. Beneath that were the years 1928-1945. Seventeen years old. Seventeen fucking years old. Jesus.

"I'm sorry, Mae." I said.

I didn't ask, but she voluntarily answered. "My husband."

I let that sink in. Suddenly, everything felt immensely heavy, and not just because of my slowly soaking clothes.

Eyeing the gravestone, the dates jumped out at me, and I tried to do some quick math, despite it never being my best subject.

"Don't bother doing the math," she said. "It won't add up. We both lied about our ages: John to serve, me to get married. I was two years younger than him, but none of that mattered. Somehow, two kids fell so deeply in love that nothing else mattered. Well, almost nothing. Sound familiar?"

Mae had yet to look in my direction. I could tell she was in the present, but not entirely.

"Mae, I'm so sorry," I repeated, unable to think of any other offering that would be apt under the circumstance.

"We were married for eight months before he was deployed. I remember he was scared. He was eager and brave, but even the bravest of soldiers get scared. How could he not be? He was just a boy. But he felt it was his steadfast duty. I remember him saying to me that he couldn't live in a world where he had knowingly turned his back on the profound injustices taking place, that he didn't want to raise his family in a household that had a father, a supposed role model, who didn't raise his hand and say, 'Yes, I will serve,' even if he had to lie to do it."

Mae's words were soft and eloquent, a lifetime of quietly rehearsed lines finally spoken aloud to an audience.

"He was so naïve," Mae said with a laugh. "What teenager thinks that way? But that was John. He had his code, and he would change it for no one, not even me, and Lord knows I tried." She spoke of him with such fondness, even after all these years.

"Mae, I had no idea you were married. Why didn't you tell me?"

"Would it have made a difference? Does it matter?"

"Yeah, I think it does," I said. "Given our recent discussion about young love and finding a way back to it, I would have thought you'd be a little more empathetic."

I felt my chest seize as I realized my candor was not appropriate given what Mae had just shared with me. I started to speak but caught myself, realizing I had nothing to say.

Mae said nothing for a long span of seconds. We stood there in silence, pelted by raindrops that were growing in thickness.

"This cross, it's empty underneath," she said, breaking the silence. "John's not here. Most of these people aren't here. It's a place where we can visit the memory of them, nothing more. John was killed in France. Just like that. Never came home. One day there's a knock at his parents' door. I spent a lot of time near that house, hoping to stay close and learn any new information as it arrived because they didn't know about our marriage. They would get the news, not me. One day, I saw a man in uniform deliver a letter. I didn't need to know what the news was; I could feel it. I didn't wait in that moment to find out for certain, but when I did, it wasn't any less bearable."

In the distance, we could hear a trumpet sound, and Mae instinctively bowed her head. Following her cue, I did the same. Whoever was behind the instrument began playing "The Last Post." The sound filled the air, carried on the breath of the wind, on the memories of the soldiers whose graves surrounded us.

Mae put her hand to her heart. Once again, I followed suit. I could not take my eyes off her. There was a raw and powerful moment happening before me, and I had no idea how to embrace it, how to appreciate it.

As the trumpet's final mournful notes wafted past us, Mae raised her head and finally looked at me. "You said I should be more empathetic to your situation."

"I only meant that—"

"You've dated since you and Autumn parted ways?"

"Yes."

"Had your fun with casual flings or semi-serious relationships?"

"Yes."

"Told anyone else you loved them?"

"Yes."

"Had someone else tell you they loved you?"

"Yes."

With each question and response, my shame compounded. I knew Mae's line of questioning was leading somewhere, but I wasn't prepared for its final destination.

"That's wonderful to hear. I'm sure your parents tell you they love you too?"

"They do. Maybe not as much anymore as I get older, but yeah, they tell me."

"I've only ever said I love you to one person: John. Only one person has ever said they loved me: John. My parents—they didn't want a girl. I'm surprised they even kept me, to be honest. My father had no use for me, nor did my mother. My mother didn't even teach me how to cook or sew or do anything you would expect a woman of the early 1900s to do. They left me to raise myself, to fend for and feed myself. It's been a long and lonely life. My one true love was taken by the war. I was a teenager, and I knew there would never be another man for me. You have no idea what that feels like. No one does."

Mae's confessions staggered me, saddened me to my core. I was without words, which was okay because Mae had more to say.

"I've listened to you talk about Autumn, and it reminds me of the way I would think about John and he about me. I understand it. I understand why you're convinced you need to do what you're planning—sticking around here to take care of her. But Alex, she's gone, just as gone as John. Your solace and your anguish now come from the same place. You can see Autumn, be next to her, remember her with your own eyes. But at the end of the day, it's all gone, and you can't get her back. I've spent most of my life trying to get John back. I'm not entirely sure I can explain how, but I've tried. I've looked for traces of him in just about everyone I've ever met. It didn't work. It *doesn't* work. Love is a fucking kick in the balls, let me tell you. And the whole idea of better to have lost love than to not know love at all? Well, as far as I'm concerned, the jury is still out."

The rain diminished during Mae's soliloquy, urged away by the breaking sun. At this point, Mae and I were fairly soaked through, but if we noticed, we gave no indication. The gravity of the scene playing out was all-consuming.

"Mae, I don't even know where to begin." I wanted to console her, but I didn't know how.

"There's nowhere to begin," she said. "This is my reality. I come here each Remembrance Day and remember my John. I take a day off from the eccentric character I play at Silver Springs and return to my younger self. And you know what? I feel it. When I'm here, I feel young again. Staring at his name on this cross is just like staring at his name on the love letters he would write me in his terrible penmanship. Still have them too, you know."

"So the tattoo? That's for John?" I asked.

"It is," she said. "You weren't supposed to see it, no one is, save for the doctors who have to fully check me over, but they don't ask. It's for me and John. He's on me, with me, always."

This unguarded, sincere version of Mae Seasons was a complete one-eighty from the person I'd been around nearly every day for the past few months. It was welcome, but it confused me as to who the real Mae was. Was it this version in front of me or the cursing, screaming, kicking wild card at Silver Springs?

"That's enough therapy for today. We'd better get back," said Mae, brushing past me. "Pick it up, Nancy, or the bus will leave your sorry ass here, and I won't think twice about failing to remind them they're light one passenger."

There she was, rounding back into form. But what Mae had just shared with me connected us in ways that were nearly impossible to grasp.

CHAPTER 25

It was mid-afternoon when we arrived back at Silver Springs, everyone going their separate ways, and I, once again, frustratingly forced to wait for the next opportunity to be around Autumn. Though I had already mentally committed to a lifetime here by her side, the difficulty in starting this journey was becoming irritating, if not a little telling. I tried to practise as much patience as possible, but it wasn't always easy, and doubts sneakily crept in.

The damp and cold from the day's field trip had seeped into my bones, and my body was eager to absorb the warmth of a hot shower and the comfort of a fresh set of clothes. Nearly everyone had been suitably dressed for the outdoor excursion, but when the wind picks up and finds a crack in your armour, it doesn't relent, and it plays to win.

Mae successfully convinced the staff she was tired and simply wanted to retire to her room for the day and was permitted to do so. I got the sense that some staff members knew today was somewhat special for Mae, but I was certain none of them knew exactly why. And based off her personality and predilection for physical and verbal outbursts, there was little guesswork as to why she was rarely questioned on any matter, trivial or not. This day, of course, was anything but trivial for Mae.

As a result of Mae's afternoon of solitude, I too could retire to my room for the day, taking full advantage of the downtime to read and relax and, of course, think about Autumn and how we were closer to reuniting but with much work still to be done.

I ended up showering for far longer than was necessary, but I wasn't worried about the water bill, and the hot-water tank lasted longer than I needed it to. I dried off and rifled through my drawers for the most comfortable clothing I could find. I laughed when I came upon the candy-striper outfit and took a few minutes to reminisce about the times it was worn and how it was a connection to blissful memories of the women I'd lately taken a shine to.

Tossing it back in the drawer, I threw on a pair of salt-and-pepper sweatpants, a grey Harvard T-shirt (no, I didn't attend), and a full-zip red hoodie. I flopped on the bed, atop the covers, and rearranged the pillows so that I was propped up in just the right position to read without straining my neck and, should I doze off, not wake up with a knot in my muscles that would make a sailor proud.

As soon as I opened my book, the phone rang. As was my customary thought process, I immediately debated letting it ring and go to voicemail or answering. Curiosity getting the best of me, I picked up.

"Come to my room; your history lesson isn't over just yet." That was all Mae said before hanging up.

Feeling no need to change my outfit, I slipped on a pair of slides that I used primarily while in my room; the colour of the carpet was far from its original hue, and who knows what was alive between its matted fibres.

I made the trek to Mae's room with no sense of urgency or delay, just a steady pace. This actually crossed my mind, my pace. I can't tell you why. I can't say I'd ever taken it into consideration before when travelling from one room to another, but today, I was aware of each step. And each step had me counting my lefts and rights like a soldier. The tenor of the day had clearly grabbed hold of my subconscious.

Mae's door was open when I arrived, and as was becoming routine, I tapped my knuckles on the door as I pushed it forward. I found Mae seated in her armchair, a small TV dinner tray in front of her with papers spread across its surface. By the looks of them, the pages were old, their age distinguished by their colour and apparent fragility.

"What are those, love letters?" I asked incredulously.

"Yes, they are. From John. He was a beautiful writer, even at his young age. Penmanship aside, his calling was with a pen, not a rifle."

Foot meet mouth; hope you taste swell. "I was—you have quite a few." I tried to save some face. "He must have really loved you."

"I didn't ask you here for your commentary," Mae replied. "I wanted you to see these. I wanted to show you that you and John are remarkably similar people. That's partly why you're still here, you know. You remind me of him."

Mae might as well have been speaking in code, as I had no idea what she was referring to. Did I dare ask? I was already off to quite the shoddy start. What the hell; what was there to lose?

"I do? How so, exactly? Did he have sturdy shins for when you were acting like Diego Maradona?"

"Diego who?"

"He's a soccer player—never mind."

"Anyways," said Mae, "your commitment to love is as strong and unwavering as his, and despite yours being much more misguided, it is still, I dare say, admirable. He would have done anything for me. If you think about it, that's pretty remarkable considering how young we were. I doubted it for many years after, you know. How could two people that young actually have what I thought we had? There were some days it never made sense. Other days, it was completely clear."

I hung on her every word as she shuffled through the letters, appearing to be looking for one in particular.

"Here, read this one." She handed me a letter of integrity, both physically and in content.

My Dearest Mae,

It is but my second day here in France, and I am not ashamed to admit that fear has gripped my soul like vices to a table in my father's workshop. In my platoon, I am outmatched in size, stamina, and wit, but I remain committed to the mission of securing our freedom. The moon hangs lower here. Why that is so, I am unsure. I look to the stars each night and think of you, only you. I do not regret joining the cause, but I miss you terribly and wonder, perhaps too often, what could have been had my truth reached the tip of my pen as I signed my birth year.

The men here talk about women as if they were nothing but a prize, something to be won and owned. I do not know if they truly mean it or if the machismo is simply part of the mental tactics to repress the deep-rooted fear we all carry. I take comfort in the constant thought of you. When I am scared, I think of you. When I am happy, it is because I have thought of you. When I think of death, I think of you. I apologize for the morbidity of that last statement, but it is nonetheless the truth. My love for you will propel me to the end of this great war, and we will have stories to tell our children and grandchildren.

We will be deployed tomorrow. To where, we have not yet been informed. The lack of details has created a buzz among the men, and not for the better, I am afraid. I will be home one day, and when I arrive, I will never spend another day away from you. This much I promise. We will be together forever, no matter the circumstance. Nothing will keep me from you, Mae.

My love is sent across the ocean on the gentle breath of the wind. I know you will feel it, even though I am not there to speak it. I know you hear me as I hear you.

With eternal love and a wishful heart,

John D. Seasons

As I lowered the note from my gaze, Mae asked if those words reminded me of anyone; I sheepishly smiled—of course they did.

Mae rose to her feet and invited me to do the same, moving over to her radio and turning up the volume. What happened next was nothing short of astonishing, for this was not the Mae Seasons I had ever known.

Mae took my hand and engaged me in a slow, thoughtful dance. The lyrics of the song, broadcast through her radio, took me back to the '30s, despite only having experienced them across the silver screen. The singer, with his low, velvety voice, sang about seeing someone in his dreams, holding someone in his dreams. It was tender and altogether appropriate.

As we swayed to the soft tune, accompanied by the stirring sounds of a piano and trumpet, I felt Mae relax. The entire moment was surreal. For the time being, I wasn't thinking of Autumn. I wasn't thinking of myself. I was thinking about Mae and John and life lost—not just John's but the one they would have shared.

When the song ended, Mae sat and I joined her.

"You know, there's not actually anything wrong with me," she said. "I'm completely fine. I don't need to be here." This sounded like every addict who was in deep denial.

"Mae, everyone is here for a reason," I said, trying not to come off as superior. "They may not have been able to identify exactly what it is—"

"There is *nothing* wrong with me." She was calm but stern. "I've been here of my own volition for fourteen years. These people, as sad as some of them are, they're my family, and that includes that oaf Phil and his queen, Susanne. I've made this place my home because there is no other home for me. I get three square meals a day and all the necessary little checkups from a bunch of sexy doctors," she said with a smirk. "The profanity, the kicking, all the antics—it's an act to keep me here. If they knew the truth, I'd be out on my keister. As long as they continue to try to sort me out, I have a place here. But you can't solve a riddle that has no answer."

"Wait a second," I said with growing confusion. "So there was never any good reason to kick me all those times or tell me I'm the vermin of the earth playing hide the pickle with the devil?"

Laughing, Mae nodded in agreement. "Don't get me wrong, I do enjoy the ability to get creative and let loose my tasteless thoughts without a care in the world, but I am rather more reserved than my charade suggests. I still don't give a damn about most things, so don't be too fooled. But these people, as agonizing as they can be, are my family. My little act has allowed me to look out for them as I did for you today, even though you let your own self-righteousness sabotage an opportunity to spend time with Autumn."

"Mae, I don't know what to say." I really didn't. I was as at a loss for words as I'd ever been in my entire life.

"I've done my research; I know what will keep me here. I'm set up. I'm okay. You, on the other hand, you need some guidance, young man."

Preach, Mae, preach.

"You need to understand something," she told me, gripping my hands, her pale-blue eyes staring into mine. "You love Autumn, I get that. But who you love is *gone*. This hasn't changed since the last time I said it. You don't know it yet, but you also love Erica. This too hasn't changed since I told you about the way you looked at her. You need to move on. You need to find love, find your place, live your life. I missed out on my life. I take responsibility for that happening, but I missed out on it nonetheless. I miss John every day. I think about what could have been every day. It's a terrible cross to bear, but it's the choice I made, and I bear it nonetheless. But it's not worth the pain or the sadness. And it's definitely not worth the energy it takes to tell yourself you're okay, let alone convince yourself of it. I've been doing it for so long, it's a part of me now, and heeding my own advice is fruitless, but it's not too late for you. It took me a long time to learn that memories are okay to carry with you if they make you smile, but the ones that don't, you need to clear them out of your mind."

In many ways, everything she was saying made sense. But I was here for Autumn. Only Autumn. Admittedly, something had shifted within when I met Erica, but I'd be hard-pressed to categorize it as Mae did, as love. But there was something: a spark.

"You mentioned a coffee date," said Mae. "Make *that* happen. Make *life* happen. It's not often we have that power or authority. Don't make my same mistake."

If my jaw wasn't on the floor, it wasn't far off. I had no way to process what I had just heard, but Mae provided some help.

"Oh, and if you say a word to anyone about anything you've heard today, well, the kicks will get harder and the insults fiercer—I've got more in this old leg than you know. And besides, who will believe you?" With that, Mae stood, walked over to me, and kissed my cheek. "You're a good man, Alex. Caring. Noble. Committed.

You deserve love. Go get it. And get out of my room before I start kicking and screaming."

CHAPTER 26

It took a couple weeks, but eventually, I called Erica to schedule a coffee date. If I didn't know any better, I'd swear there was real excitement in her voice when we confirmed a day and time: November 30, one o'clock.

The plan was to meet at an artisanal coffee shop called The Oak Bean. It was roughly forty minutes from Silver Springs, and not wanting to risk being late, I left at noon. With my daily duties exhausted, and at the insistence of Mae covering for me—she and Dr. Green were scheduled to meet again, as devised by Mae, of course—I essentially had the afternoon off.

I was always one for being early. If I was on time, I was late. If I was five to ten minutes early, I was on time. I'm not exactly sure what made me this way, but punctuality was as near a thing to religion as I had, and being late was utter blasphemy. Screaming "Jesus fucking Christ" at an asshole in a Toyota Corolla who cut me off on the highway was not. Corolla drivers were—are—the worst.

Driving to The Oak Bean, I watched the trees, now bare of leaves, slowly collecting the first dustings of the season's snow. We had received a light scattering of flurries earlier that morning, and now, as I drove, the wintery flecks returned, falling a little thicker, a little heavier. The black asphalt of the highway glistened, highlighting the slickness caused by the melted flakes, patches of black ice undoubtedly hidden somewhere along these quiet roads. I still had my all-season tires on, but thankfully, they were relatively unused.

All my preset radio stations had been reformatted to play only Christmas music—there was no escaping it. I wasn't opposed to Christmas; in fact, I quite enjoyed it, but I did so on my own terms. I wasn't a fan of having it shoved down my throat.

The Oak Bean, as I should have expected but paid no mind to during my drive, was decked out in celebration of Christmas. The outer brick façade was lined with garland and string lights of warm white woven throughout the crevices in the stone and travelling around four windows, all artfully frosted in the corners with some type of white substance. Fronting the street, where I did my best to parallel park—and succeeded after my third attempt, thank you very much—was the welcoming front door, solid wood and home to a bright-red wreath with silver and gold bows, tied with ribbon.

The chalkboard sign sitting on the cobblestone sidewalk was scripted in some employee's festive font. I wondered if this employee was on the payroll simply for their exceptional calligraphy skills.

Bells above me jingled as I entered, a merry yet practical touch. As a result of being early, I had a chance to survey my surroundings and find a comfortable seating arrangement appropriate for what I was mostly certain was an official first date, though I was still somewhat unsure.

I had spent the last few weeks with Mae discussing my situation with Autumn and once more going over the penance I was forcing myself to pay. Mae understood, she said, as she too had self-imposed her own penalty of spurning any future chances of love after John was killed in the war. She was adamant that I not repeat her beleaguered history.

Partly to absolve Mae's resolute stubbornness and partly to quench my own curiosity's thirst, I made the call and scheduled the date. I was still very much on the fence, perhaps with one leg leaning heavily towards Autumn, but figured there was no harm in a cup of coffee.

The ceiling speakers in The Oak Bean played the same jazzy Christmas songs that had drifted through my car's speakers. The dulcet voices of the singers, combined with the low and smooth tune of the acoustic instruments accompanying them, were the quintessential sounds of a coffeehouse soundtrack.

A series of high-top cruiser tables was scattered throughout the café, situated precisely for those looking to rest a drink for a minute as they put change away in their purse, enjoy a quick catch-up with an acquaintance in line, or finish the text message started pre-order. I decided at once that these would be unsuitable for Erica and me. My nerves insisted I needed to sit with some relative comfort for this encounter. There were wooden chairs at round wooden tables that looked more uncomfortable than I'm sure they were, but these also didn't present an ideal seating option.

Finally, my eyes landed upon a pair of olive-green armchairs near the far window and close to a wood-burning fireplace. How the fireplace met code, I wasn't exactly sure, but then again, what the hell did I know about fire codes? There was a small circular table that separated the two chairs, which, at the present time, were without patrons. It was perfect.

I made my way over to the chairs and took off my jacket, hanging it on the coatrack next to the fireplace. The warmth of the fire would certainly dry any dampness absorbed during my walk from the car to the establishment.

The front wall—composed of exposed red and brown brick and home to the windows I'd observed from the curb—hosted a litany of what I assumed were rotating seasonal posters in antique frames. The armchairs were flanked by Norman Rockwell-like images of Mr. and Mrs. Claus bent at the hips with necks out and lips pursed, as if going in for a kiss, but they were about four metres apart. Above the table was the strategically placed mistletoe that accompanied the photos. I didn't notice it but would be introduced to later. If I had paid it any attention, I would have taken it for holly anyways.

The ledge of the window prominently displayed used books. Nestled close to the varied literary spines was a small sign that read: *take a book, leave a book*. I hoped the honour system was respected. No one should have to endure book thieving assholes.

It was 12:50 p.m. when Erica walked in. In my books, she'd beat the cutoff for on time and was early. As it turns out, punctuality is astonishingly attractive.

"Hey, Alex!" she said with a wide smile as she made her way to where I sat. "Good spot—it's usually taken."

Turns out, Erica was a frequent visitor to The Oak Bean. One of her good friends owned the place—handed down to her through generations of coffee roasters. Though the interior and décor had changed a few times, the quality of the product and service remained constant.

"Erica, hi," I intoned, more like a seventh grader at his first school dance than an adult meeting someone not entirely new for a drink.

I stood to greet her and help with her coat. As she turned her back to me to assist in the de-coating, her perfume nearly knocked me out, not because it was overpowering or offensive, no, just the opposite. It was subtle, sublime, and intoxicating, so much so that I was momentarily paralyzed. She craned her neck slightly to check if I was still there. She slid her arms out of her coat and removed her Kelly-green scarf with tiny white snowflakes delicately stitched into it—something I noticed after closer inspection. She gracefully took off her black leather driving gloves and placed them inside her pockets. Once all items for warmth were tucked away, I hung her coat up.

She wore a cream sweater that hugged her body without being tight. In other words, it accentuated her figure but did not draw immediate attention to it. Her dark-blue jeans ended at the top of her black suede boots. I was going to ask if they were treated so as not to become damaged from the excessive amount of sidewalk salt out front but figured that would be a horrible opening.

So, of course, I started with that.

"Did you treat your boots with anything to prevent the wet and salt from eating away at them?" My brain had just explicitly suggested that this was an ill-advised opening line, and here I was letting the words tumble out of my mouth.

Erica looked at me with a deadpan expression for a second before breaking into a slight giggle, which, at no extra cost, came with a gentle caress of my arm.

"You don't need to worry about my boots, Alex. They are well taken care of. But thank you for asking," she replied.

I am certain I was blushing but had no way of knowing for sure, other than the scorching heat I felt in my cheeks.

"Right, yeah," I stammered. "So, shall we order?" I asked, moving away from suede treatments as quickly as possible.

"What's your preference?" she asked, taking the lead. "I know their menu very well and have something in mind for you, but if you aren't a fan of vanilla, I'll have to rethink this whole date."

That last word hung in the air. I thought it was a date and apparently so did Erica, but neither of us were confident enough in our assessment to fully lean into it.

I gave her a confirming smile and told her that I loved vanilla. This was indeed true; however, she could have asked if I liked the flavour of sewer water and I would have given the same response.

"Great, I'll be right back." And with that, she was off to the counter to place the order. She appeared to float as the distance between us grew. Her gait was a glide, not a plod, smooth and with purpose.

As Erica stood in line, she glanced back every so often to give a smile and a nod, as if checking to see that the toddler she'd left waiting at the table was still there and behaving. Her enjoyment of being here, or what I perceived to be as such, was increasing my own, which was already in generous abundance.

I couldn't help but think that when I was in Erica's presence, I was where I needed to be, but when I was not, when I was with Autumn, I also felt I was where I needed to be. Was I incapable of being on my own? Was I nothing more than a serial crusher?

When it was her turn to order, Erica chatted and stepped around the side of the counter to hug the employee behind it. She placed our order, and the worker, a woman about Erica's age, grabbed a pair of mugs from the hooks lining the wall, some playing host to candy canes, others to sprigs of greenery.

With logs popping without warning, the fire next to me caused me to jump a time or two during this span of waiting. The crackle of the fire, the music, the atmosphere—everything about this place was charming, quaint, and seasonally perfect. It hadn't hit me at first, but as I watched Erica, the spirit of Christmas filled me up inside. That, or my hormones were reverting back to my teenage years. It was probably the latter, but the former was no less true.

Erica returned with two steaming mugs that she gently placed on the table. I had prearranged the coasters to welcome them.

"You'll love this," she said. "But give it a second to cool down. They sometimes put whipped cream in to help with the heat, but it takes away from the flavour, if you ask me."

"Thank you—I will heed your advice, m'lady." *M'lady? Who am I?* Thankfully, my awkwardness was assuaged by Erica's sweet nature.

"I'm glad you called," she said, holding her mug with both hands, warming them on the heated ceramic. "I know you said you would, but you know how it goes sometimes—someone says they're going to call, and then they don't."

I was about to respond that it would be impossible for anyone not to call her if they said they would, but I had done just that not so long ago. It had nothing to do with her; it was my own fucked-up rationale for what I was doing. Or at least, that's how Mae put it. This time, I kept my mouth shut and revised my response.

"Well, it's nice to keep your word when you can," is what I came up with as I too cradled my mug and felt the warmth radiate through my fingers.

"Take a small—"

I gulped and nearly launched a vanilla-laden spit take right in Erica's face. "Shit!" I garbled a few unintelligible words while trying to cool the inside of my scorched mouth.

Erica laughed. "I was going to say a small one; it's still very hot."

Everything about the person in front of me made sense in this very moment: her laugh at my misfortune, the way she passed a napkin so I could wipe vanilla mocha froth off my sleeve, and the soft, kind gaze of her eyes assessing me in a moment of embarrassment and foolish pain.

"You say that now," I said, "but it didn't seem like you were too eager or swift to share the tail end of that recommendation."

"Alex Chambers, are you accusing me of something?" she said playfully.

As I prepared my response, I couldn't ignore a sudden pang of guilt. I was only here with Erica because of the weekend getaway to Mae's cottage, which I had only visited because I was volunteering at Silver Springs, which was only happening because of Autumn. Always Autumn. Here goes that pendulum.

"I would never," I said, reeling it in. If Erica noticed my abrupt change in repartee, she didn't show it.

We chatted for about an hour: where we came from, how we got to where we were, and what we thought might lie ahead. I debated how to tell her about Autumn, knowing full well that I had to be forthcoming if we could ever begin a relationship of any kind. The truth was that I liked Erica; I felt a connection with her. There was something here that was more than a jump into a cold lake or a warm cup of coffee.

"Listen, Erica," I finally said, pushing all my chips to the middle of the table and betting on openness. "I'm at Silver Springs with Mae because of a colossal screw up in administrative functionality on their part, but moreover, I'm at Silver Springs in the first place because of someone named Autumn."

I told Erica the story, the whole story, without hesitation or withholding any detail. I kept my emotions in check during this retelling, which reminded me of the first conversation I'd had with Phil as I sat in the parking lot, when I'd been reluctant to disclose any trace of the truth. But here, with Erica—I wanted her to know that what was keeping me from pursuing her was something threaded into the very depths of me.

Erica was kind and listened, not seeming to feign interest—it was a pretty riveting story, if you ask me. It was sad but compelling. It had love and heartbreak, heroes and villains, and a quest for reconciliation and redemption.

When I finally recounted the last part of the tale, which had led me to the very seat I was currently in, thanks in large part to Mae, Erica smiled. We had finished our drinks during this time, and all that was left was to accept whatever reaction Erica was about to have.

"Alex, that's beautiful."

I was expecting an understanding response, but not this one. "Thank you?" I said uncertainly.

"Was that a question?" Erica laughed.

"No, I—well, I wasn't sure how this would be received."

"Quite well," she said. "I can see Mae's side of things, of course, and I'd be lying if I said I wasn't on her side just a little bit, but I also understand that the things we do for love can often trump all else, right or wrong, and I'm not saying you're either. I don't think it's possible for anyone other than you to know. But what I do know is that life moves forward with or without us."

I wondered if Mae had forewarned Erica and shared some speaking notes.

"I like you, Alex. I think you like me too. I'm not saying I'll stick around and wait for you because that's not fair to anyone, but I wanted you to at least know that much. You are a kind, sweet soul, and Autumn is fortunate to have you watching over her."

Sensing the date had reached its end, we both stood to gather our coats and exchange goodbyes. I helped Erica into her coat, and once she was buttoned up and ready to go, she grabbed the lapels of my jacket and placed her hands flat on my chest, looking up, drawing attention to the mistletoe.

She gave me a kind, tender kiss on the lips. It was romantic without being over-the-top romantic, which made it all the more romantic.

"Do what you need to do, Alex. I hope you call again." And with that, she turned and headed out the door, the ringing bell marking her exit.

I stood motionless by the fire—a fire I might as well jump in because what the hell else was I supposed to do now?

CHAPTER 27

On the drive back, I thought about what I would tell Mae. I feared she would be disappointed in me for returning without so much as a commitment to a second date with Erica, but she would have to live with it.

The highway was emptier in the early evening hours, though that wasn't saying much considering what lay at either end of it. The snow had continued to fall, covering the blacktop in a blanket of white, plows not yet clearing this section of the road.

Silver Springs looked like a ski resort as it came into view—not one of those manmade places that took advantage of convenient proximity to tourists but a legitimate retreat that required dedication and planning to get to. The snowcapped rooftop and accompanying pine trees with the same powdery dressing gave it a Swiss mountain-town vibe. Although the parking lot had been plowed and the spaces made visible, the drivers of the few cars in it were still guilty of centring their vehicles on the lines and parking haphazardly.

I made the trek from the parking lot to the front doors and thought of my initial arrival, only now I was trading raindrops for snowflakes. The latter was certainly preferable. Christmas decorations were beginning to occupy the exterior; white lights were netted on bushes, wrapped around trees, and secured around windows and doorframes.

Brushing the snow off my jacket as I entered the lobby, Phil greeted me with a grin and an unsolicited, "Ho Ho Ho."

"Little early for the big man in red to make an appearance, isn't it Phil?"

"Oh, Alex, get in the festive spirit, would ya? It's a great day."

I moved past him with tepid curiosity and figured it best to just keep going. Phil let out another round of "Ho Ho Hos" and slapped his belly in sheer enjoyment of whatever moment he was relishing. As I continued my way in, I couldn't help laughing a little in a what-a-day-this-has-been kind of way.

Once in my room, I hung my jacket on the hanger in the tiny closet closest to the door. It was still damp with remnants of snow. I noticed the flashing red light on my phone and took my time before checking the message. I changed my clothes, grabbed a granola bar from the Costco-size box on the table near the window, and slowly chomped on the dark-chocolate-and-cranberry brick.

After my snack and several glasses of water, I plopped down on the bed and picked the receiver up from its cradle, pushing the button to retrieve messages.

"Alex, when you get back, come see me. I'd like to hear about your little rendezvous."

Mae sure seemed to have taken a strong interest in my fledgling romantic life, though calling it romantic might be a stretch. The most Erica and I had done was hold hands while jumping in the lake. The friendly pecks on my cheek barely counted. Sure, she'd kissed me on the lips at the coffee shop, but that was more likely out of pity and kindness than attraction. Sabotaging my own gains seemed the best way to temper expectations.

I took my time getting to Mae's room, figuring I'd let her stew as long as I could. It was about the only form of payback I could reasonably get away with for all the shit she'd given me up to this point.

To my surprise, Mae was waiting for me outside her room, ready to usher me in, a couple of mugs at the ready for whatever beverage she was about to prepare.

"Wow, Mae, you've gone all out here," I joked, looking at the cups.

"Oh, shut up, it's how you like it," she said. "Now, let's hear how it went."

I regaled Mae with the story of my afternoon outing with Erica, finally admitting that I'd told her everything about Autumn.

"Oh, you idiot. You spectacular idiot!" She slammed her teacup down on the porcelain saucer that had caught its fair share of liquid from Mae's shaky hands, causing the spilled coffee to spray outward. "What's wrong with you? You might as well have told her you'd prefer to have your balls cracked like Christmas nuts with one of those little metal tools than spend more time with her."

Painful visual aside, I winced at Mae's stern condemnation of my decision. It wasn't the reaction I had braced for.

"Mae, I had to tell her," I said, feeling a strong sense of my side of the story needing to be heard. "She had to know the truth about why I'm here, why I'm incapable of committing to anything more than a cup of coffee with someone who is undoubtedly a great match for me."

Mae just looked at me. Disapproving. Disappointed. Disgusted. "What did she say?" Mae finally asked.

"She was understanding of it, said that what I'm doing is a beautiful thing."

Mae rolled her eyes. I sipped my coffee.

"Listen, Mae, none of this is how I planned it. Absolutely none of it. From day one, I was supposed to be working on a different floor. We've been over this. What does it matter?" I was getting tired of having to explain myself, my decisions. There were times when I didn't mind engaging with Mae about this topic, like when she'd recently disclosed her adamance of pushing me towards one decision over another. But for every pleasant—and I use that term very loosely—conversation about it, there were a far greater number of irritating exchanges that made me feel like I was a berated child, something I took to be incredibly unfair.

Mae didn't say anything as I glared at her. She seemed at the same loss for words I was. What *did* any of it matter? Autumn, Erica, Mae, me. Who gives a shit?

"Well, Sonny, you'll have another chance to think about love tomorrow morning. I suggest you take the night to figure out which path you'd like to eventually go down."

"Tomorrow morning? What are you talking about, Mae?"

"I'll see you at breakfast. The whole place will be there. Turns out you were absent on the wrong afternoon—there's big news brewing at Silver Springs."

Morning came, and my expectations of Mae's set-up were low. I had, however, spent a great deal of time the night before lying in bed, staring at the ceiling, and ruminating. I even went so far as to get a legal pad out and develop a comparative list of pros and cons for Autumn and Erica. Ridiculous, right?

The list got me nowhere, of course, because I was incapable of committing to either column in any fashion beyond putting pen to paper; it was a hollow diversion and would never amount to anything else. I refused to let my mind go where it needed to in order to make the exercise fruitful in any capacity. The piece of paper still sat on the table, taunting me. I wished there was an easy answer, a door that would somehow magically open and lead me to the right place. Deep down, I wanted someone to make the decision for me, but I knew this was not possible. Nevertheless, it didn't prevent me from perpetually wishing for it.

It was drawing near to eight in the morning, and the foot traffic in the hallway was picking up, a low murmur of voices doing their best to solve the mystery of what was going on. As it turned out, Mae was one of the few who already knew what was on the docket. Everyone else was left to speculation, or at least, so said Fred when I tried to pry it out of him. He was as genuinely in the dark as I was.

I gathered what I needed and joined the herd making their way to the conference room on the main floor. I asked a few of the white coats if they knew what was going on, but every answer was an invariable variation of no.

Once downstairs, it was clear that word had spread like wildfire. It seemed like everyone was here, Autumn included. All floors had descended upon the conference room, which, I was learning, doubled as the feature showroom for whatever might be happening at Silver Springs.

I weaved through the bodies to be as close to Autumn as possible, but I wasn't able to get much closer than six metres, give or take. The bodies were starting to pack together tightly, like a mosh pit at a metal concert.

Mae tugged my sleeve to announce her presence. "Look at all this hullabaloo, would you?" she said with a smirk. "I wonder what we're here for?"

Mae knew what was happening, of course, and was more than pleased to keep that little grain of information close to the vest. I didn't bother asking what we were doing here, opting instead to keep an eye on Autumn, determined to get to her today.

When we were all crammed in the conference room, the buzz of competing conversations subsided, and whatever announcement or jaw-dropping news we were about to receive was now upon us as Susanne came into the room.

As she made her way to the stage, it was impossible to dismiss her appearance; she looked magnificent. She had ditched her standard corporate uniform, swapping it out for a flowing purple dress. And, if I wasn't mistaken, her makeup was fully done. She manoeuvred to the front of the room with a nervous grace. The whispers that had momentarily died down now picked up around me, most of them commenting on Susanne's atypical appearance.

"Ex—excuse me, everyone, may I have your attention, please?" she asked, barely audible to those in the back of the room, even with a microphone. Clearly, she was nervous, which sent an anxious ripple throughout the audience.

"Hey! Shut up!" Phil's voice boomed as he took his place beside Susanne. This was enough to get everyone's attention, not so much because of the demand but because of the shock of Phil's chutzpah.

"Thank you, hon—Phil. Thank you, Phil," said Susanne. "I have invited you all here this morning to share some momentous Silver Springs news. As you know, I have been here a long time. Many of you know me very well, and as you are all my family, I felt it important that you all hear this at the same time."

Nervous, confused, and excited faces were hanging on every word of Susanne's awkward announcement. Was she leaving? Was she dying? Was she wanting feedback on her new look? None of these would have surprised me, but no, it was none of those things, and the surprise was coming in mere seconds.

"You also know that Phil has worked here a long time. He has been the face that greets us every day in the lobby. He is the face that greets *me* every day," she said with a smile containing more warmth than I had ever seen from her.

Phil stood by, smug and a little flushed in the face.

"Well, our Silver Springs family is growing a little tighter today. I announce to all of you that Phil and I are getting married!"

There was no applause at first, just an awkward, cricket-filled silence. It was Mae who began the slow clap that picked up steam and eventually turned into an eruption of cheers and whistles.

People flocked towards the couple to offer congratulations in the form of hugs, handshakes, and slaps on the back.

"You look perplexed," said Mae.

I wasn't, not completely. I knew about their feelings for one another, and although I wouldn't have ever bet money on this being the announcement this morning, I was still somewhat unsurprised.

"They've been in love since I got here," confessed Mae, as if sharing this lifted some weight off her tiny shoulders. "While everyone else was busy putting themselves first, oblivious to what was going on around them, I watched. I watched these two kids fall in love. None of this surprises me. Although, I'm surprised making it official has taken this long. They're actually perfect together, if you ask me."

This may have been true, and who was I, or anyone else to cast any doubts on another relationship? After all, look at the messy clusterfuck I'd created for myself.

"These announcements always come with food, you know," said Mae. "The good kind. This morning will be catered to the nines—hope you're hungry."

Mae proceeded to tell me how announcements such as this within the Silver Springs family were grand, booming exclamations. As Susanne had said, the people here were family, and heeding the advice of my seasoned counterpart, I put myself second and observed the room. I mean really observed it. Everyone was engaged with one another, laughing, smiling, beaming. The well-wishes poured in from around the room, and Phil and Susanne were occasionally moved to tears. This was a celebration—a true, undeniable celebration. It could have been anyone—save me, perhaps—and the people here would have opened their arms in the same joyful way. That's what family does.

"These people here, for many of them, if not all, this is it; this is everyone we have," said Mae. "Hardly anyone comes to visit. No one sends cards or emails on the regular or even picks up the phone. Do you remember our weekend getaway? I'm one of the only ones who ever leaves, and even then, I must do so with a monetary transaction to some drug-addled tramp. What you see here is the only family we have left. Other than you, it's rare that anyone new comes and stays for any meaningful length of time and bothers to get to know us and really give a damn about us."

I was speechless. As Mae spoke, the pieces began falling into place. I could see them dancing in the air like I was John Nash in *A Beautiful Mind.*

It was at this moment I took my own action—a long-overdue action that I would not be denied.

I made a beeline for Autumn.

CHAPTER 28

Autumn sat in her wheelchair near the back of the room. Her caregiver had made his way to the line of people waiting to congratulate the happy couple. There was no trepidation in leaving her where she was; she wasn't going anywhere. Besides, there were enough staff members here to quell any and all unexpected situations.

As I approached her, I was stunned, as always, by her beauty. At times I felt like I could never forget it, but seeing it so close again gave me pause. She was so familiar to me, but in many ways, she was as foreign as an uncharted world. I was nervous but not for any of the same reasons she'd made me nervous in my youth. There was no fear of rejection, of saying the wrong thing. The version of Autumn seated before me had no idea who I was, or so I had been told. I believed, though, that I could reach her somehow—that maybe, just maybe, my voice, my eyes, or my touch would trigger some hardwired memory and she would acknowledge me, my sorrow, my atonement, my love.

It didn't seem as though Autumn knew I had arrived. I stood beside her and couldn't be sure whether or not she registered awareness of my form in her peripheral view. She stared straight ahead as she always did. I was closer to her now than I had been in sixteen years. My body began to betray me: knees buckling, breath labouring, beads of sweat running down my neck.

"Autumn?" I said haltingly, as if approaching someone I wasn't sure was who I thought they were. "It's me, Alex. Alex Chambers." I had moved around to the front of her, squatting down so that we were at eye level.

"There are a million things I want to tell you, *need* to say to you, but I have to start with—I'm sorry. I'm sorry for not showing up. I'm sorry for the selfishness that sent you down the path that put you here. I'm sorry for, well, pretty much everything that happened the day after I moved away until now."

As I spoke, my eyes welled with tears. I wiped one away, hoping she wouldn't notice, but her placid expression suggested I could have full-on sobbed and she wouldn't have reacted.

"Autumn, I fucked up. I was young and dumb, which, isn't an excuse for anything. I wasn't sure how to approach my life. I thought I'd come back to you, I really did. I have no good reason for why I didn't."

I felt a strange frustration beginning to take hold. Not so much with Autumn's lack of acknowledgement regarding what I was saying—that was to be expected—but with myself for believing I could find a way to connect with her through this impenetrable barrier, the way true love in the scripted land of movies and television suggests you can. I kept on anyway.

"I wasn't there for you when you needed me, but that's going to change. I'm here now, at Silver Springs, and I'm not going anywhere. We have so much life left. New treatments will become available. New therapies will be developed. We'll get you back, Autumn. And I'll be here when we do. I owe you that much. I love you. I always have. I always will."

My knees, which had been in suspect physical condition prior to my Johnny Bench squat, were now veritably on fire. I persisted through the throbbing strain.

"My actions, my decisions, took your life away, and now I am giving you mine. I want to be here with you for the rest of our days. I can't say for certain that I'll be with you on the third floor tomorrow or even next week, but I'm working on it. I promise you I am working on it. Autumn, if you can hear me, I mean really hear me, show me something, anything."

I was met with the same blank look the conversation had started with. I dropped my head with a heavy sigh. I didn't know why I was expecting a miracle, but perhaps grasping at divine agency made the encounter easier.

"From this point forward, there is nothing that will take me away from you again," I said, raising my head to look at her once more. "This is my solemn promise to you."

I was unaware that I had taken both her hands in mine. Familiar or fearful, my touch registered nothing. I wasn't sure which one carried a bigger sting.

"Sir?" came a voice from behind me.

I stood up to face Autumn's caregiver, back from the receiving line.

"Hi, I'm Alex." I extended my hand. "Autumn—Alicia and I go back a long way. I was hoping that, despite everything with her condition, there might be a flicker of familiarity in my voice or my appearance. No such luck, I'm afraid." Saying this out loud stung.

"No, that doesn't surprise me," said the caregiver. "Alicia hasn't spoken a word, recognized a photo, or shown any sign of interest in anything since she arrived here. It's sad, but unfortunately, her story is all too familiar at Silver Springs."

The caregiver said this with an exhausted tone; it was not the first conversation he'd had with someone trying to squeeze blood from a stone. I was slightly put out by the fatalistic intonation of his voice but quickly realized he had no reason whatsoever to care about my plight or my mission.

"Okay, Alicia, let's get you outside for some fresh air, shall we?" he said as he wheeled her away.

I stood perfectly still for as long as it took Autumn to be shuttled from the conference room and through the side doors to the outdoors. I'll be damned if I didn't stand there another five minutes and cry silently, as invisible to the room as I was to Autumn.

A few nights later, I found myself milling about the lobby. I had no reason to be there, but the festive feeling supplied by the rich green garland, accented with red and gold bows and pinecones artfully scattered throughout, was comforting in a homey way. I tried to remember a holiday I had spent with Autumn but was having trouble conjuring up anything. I shook this off; it meant nothing more than my memory was a little less than spectacular. What was important, or at least what I told myself was important, was that even if past holidays weren't readily available in the memory bank, the future ones would be more than enough.

Bulbs encircled the windows and the four-metre trimmed tree in the corner, and there had to be no fewer than thirty poinsettias adorning every available flat surface. I thought of the animated *Frosty the Snowman* cartoon from my youth. Something about poinsettias seemed to be ringing familiar, but the recollection was murky. "Silver Bells" played from the speakers, and Phil, nestled behind his station, was the model of contentment, leaning back in his chair with his feet up on the desk.

"Hey Phil," I said. "Congratulations, that's really wonderful news about you and Susanne." It was the first time I had run into him since the day of their announcement. I hadn't spoken with them when the engagement news was shared and I had not come into contact with either of them since.

"Wunderkind making the concession to his superior, is he?" Phil replied, absolutely befuddling me as to what the hell he was talking about. I wasn't going to get into it; this was his moment.

"I guess so, man," I said. "Anyway, here's to a life of happiness." I raised an imaginary glass and received a look of perplexity in return.

Under normal circumstances, residents of Silver Springs were not permitted in the lobby after their dinner hour, and certainly not without supervision or a chaperone of some kind, but there, in the corner, seated in a red armchair in front of a crackling fire, was Mae. Forgive me if I was no longer easily surprised.

I bid Phil a fond farewell, if only in my mind, and headed towards Mae, fully operating on the assumption that she would not only accept but appreciate my company. I would find out in short order if my perception was correct. Thankfully, on this night, it was.

"That was quite the little speech you gave the other day," she said as I shifted in my chair, seeking a comfortable spot. "I think your intentions are sincere, but I think you've got this all wrong. You're giving up your life, but you already know that," she said, sounding almost dejected.

"Wait, what? You heard that?" I asked with unfeigned surprise. "I know you understand some of this, Mae—I get that, I really do—but not all of it. I don't have a choice. I just don't."

"You *do* have a choice," snapped Mae, reaching the end of her tolerance with my stance on the matter. "But you're too stubborn and too concerned with doing the so-called right thing that you've become blind to the world in front of you. Alex, you know what, forget it. I'm done trying to convince you. From now on, do whatever you want. I won't be here much longer, and I can't bear to suffer through watching you piss your life away the same way I did, trying to connect with someone who is gone."

Mae's comments were cryptic, but I was drained of the energy necessary to really mix it up with her tonight, even though I should have.

The warmth of the fire complemented the lobby's decorations, the flames so mesmerizing that neither Mae nor I could take our eyes off them, even when we spoke to one another.

"Listen," she said like an exhausted boxer in the final round of a brutal bout, "you've made up your mind, and I won't try again to convince you otherwise. While we have time left together, let's have a little nip of the good stuff and enjoy some Christmas cheer."

With that, Mae pulled out a dull silver flask and, from God knows where, two glasses, filling them with the equivalent of about three fingers of golden goodness.

I was about to take a sip but quickly remembered the last time Mae had offered me something that looked like whisky.

"It's okay. Like I said, this is the good stuff."

Our glasses clinked, and we toasted to the future, whatever that might be.

"Mae, I've got to ask," I said with a sliver of concern and a heavy serving of apprehension. "When you say our time left together, what are you talking about? Is everything okay?"

"Oh, Jesus Christ, Sonny, you think and fret too much," she retorted. "If you get your way, and based on what you said to Autumn, you'll be a resident of the third floor in no time. You've seen how much we get to interact with the other floors in this place."

I wasn't convinced, but I also couldn't poke holes in that rebuttal.

"But if I may," she said. "I'll tell you one more story about John. It's not meant as an attempt to sway your position, per se, but it could, at the very least, open your eyes."

"Sure," I said. "If nothing else, I would love to hear more about the man who was willing to put up with you for a lifetime."

Mae smiled at my jest, perhaps more impressed that I had finally landed one than by the remark's actual quality. She withdrew a letter and, upon handing it to me, took me on a journey straight out of a history book.

CHAPTER 29

My Dearest Mae,

It is my sincerest hope this letter reaches you. I have just made it back to my barracks in the outskirts of the French city Caen. The British soldiers from the Second Army and the 3rd Infantry are doing all they can to keep the Germans at bay. I spent today waist-deep in a river, wading in thick reeds for over six hours. I fear my feet may never dry out. We were pinned in position by a German operation setting up on the north side of the river. It was not until darkness settled over the city that we were able to retreat to safety.

I fear, Mae, this war has changed me—that I am not the same man I was when I left. In fact, I know I am not that man. That boy. I have written to you faithfully my entire time overseas, and my love for you does not waver. But once more I fear that what I have seen, what I have done, has rendered me unsuitable for the love you have for me. When we are granted our short leaves, the men here take up with French women. I am ashamed to say I cannot blame them, for I too long for the tender touch only a woman can provide. I abstain, of course, for my heart only belongs to you. The men ridicule me for such devotion, and the women do their best to entice me. Neither particularly gets under my skin.

I do not know how much longer this war will be waged, and to be honest, I do not know how long I will make it in this conflict. I have had more close calls than I could ever describe but will spare you any details of the horrors and fears. Sleep is near impossible to come by, whether from the adrenaline of the battle or the air raids that seem to occur nightly. My mind is growing weary, but my commitment to our freedom remains. I will do anything to preserve it.

Mae, it is with sadness in my heart that I confess to you in this correspondence my desire for you to imagine a life without me. I do not wish to cause alarm with such a statement, for I do not intend on being laid to rest here in France or anywhere in Europe. But the boy you said goodbye to on that day in April is not the boy, the man, who will hopefully return home to you. I am battered. I am bruised. I am forever changed. I hope the man I am is worthy of your love, but as stated, I fear the demons I now carry with me will not be suitable to live in our home.

Morning will come soon, and having not heard more than the crickets, I hope to get some rest tonight. Your birthday is in a few days—this I have not forgotten. I will write you then: July 21, 1944.

With eternal love and fondness,

John D. Seasons

"That was the last letter he sent," said Mae, folding it on its original creases when I handed it back to her. It was dated July 21, 1944, the last day of the Battle for Caen. "John and his platoon, along with the allies he mentioned, captured the suburbs south of the river during Operation Atlantic. I read about the battle, found everything I could about it, but the reality of it was too much, knowing that John was killed in that battle. Not that it would have made a difference how he died. It was simply the fact that he did that caused me so much grief.

"You see, Alex, even as his time in the war went on, he knew things were changing, that *he* was changing. The person who was coming home—who, of course, never did—was not the same person I had fallen in love with. Through his letters, it became abundantly clear that the cheerful disposition and warm glow that had infused his character had been snuffed out by the traumas of war. I even wondered if the optimistic light that circulated in his eyes had been dimmed. I told myself it would never matter what nightmares came home with him, that I would always stay by his side and offer comfort. I told myself this lie to make myself feel better. I knew it wouldn't be that simple. I saw friends, neighbours, other women whose husbands did return, and with them came the war. Rarely was it ever a pretty sight. Who could blame them? The killing, the horror—it's not meant for us. John knew this, Alex. He knew it well, and though he told me, I was steadfast in my vow to stick with him."

Whether from the whisky—glasses had been refilled at this point—or the sheer rawness of the story, I could feel my lower extremities beginning to grow numb, and an understanding was slowly dawning on me: my vow to Autumn was the same as Mae's to John. It wasn't that it was without merit, but it was misguided. Just as Mae had held on to a version of her love she knew wouldn't come home, I too was holding on to a version of Autumn that no longer existed and would never be revived.

"Alex, I beg of you, do not make the same mistake I did." Mae's eyes, perhaps from the sting of the smoky flames in the fireplace, had a wetness to them that was as real and fresh as the story she had just recounted.

I struggled to comprehend the past few days, from my encounter with Autumn to the moment I now found myself in. A few days ago, I was so certain that my decision was sound, was right, was just. And now? Now I was questioning everything. What the hell was I doing? I was committing the rest of my life to a silent stranger. Autumn had barely even blinked at my presence when I spoke to her, let alone when I held her hands.

"Mae, what do I do?" I asked, totally sincere in my question and completely lost in my present. "I mean, what the hell do I do now? How do I live with myself knowing that Autumn is here because of me? I'm to, what, just abandon her? Again? I don't know if I can do that. What kind of a man would that make me?"

"An honest one. A human one. A man with the rest of his life in front of him."

The weight of such a simple response landed heavily, and there was nothing to do but stay quiet. Frank Sinatra had taken over the speakers, singing "Silent Night." As if by some twist of cruel and harmonious fate, the song famous for sparking the Christmas Truce in World War I was now the soundtrack to my own internal battle—and perhaps my truce with Mae.

Everything in the room had taken on a different aura. The Christmas tree, the wreaths with their bows, the empty boxes wrapped and scattered throughout the lobby as festive décor. It was all crystal clear one moment, a blur the next. I felt like I was having a stroke.

I hadn't noticed when it happened, but Mae had placed her hands on mine. Her hands were soft and cool despite our proximity to the fireplace, but they offered warmth and understanding.

"Alex, my dear boy, despite what you might think, I've grown quite fond of you, and I tell you these things because I know that life can be filled with nothing but loneliness and heartache, but it doesn't have to be. Chasing a ghost isn't impossible because we can't see it; it's impossible because they live where we cannot."

"I'm so sorry John never came home, that you never had your storybook life with him—or with anyone else, for that matter," I said, maintaining my composure. "I'm sorry you missed out. I don't want to miss out. My problem now, though, is that I'm not sure what I'm afraid to miss out on: the life I could have had or the life I could actually have. I know it should be an easy answer, but it's not. It's just not."

Mae was done trying to convince me; her austere look told me so. "I don't mind telling you at this point that you're being a complete idiot. You talk in circles, afraid to make a decision. You're afraid in general. But you know what? You have nothing to be scared of. John had something to be scared of; you do not."

"I thought you said you were done trying to convince me?" I shot back defensively. "You continuing to badger me about this is not fair."

The booze in our systems, especially mine, was tilting us towards combative, and escalation was teetering on a very unstable ledge.

"You're right. I am done. I'm very done," said Mae. "When you get to be my age, there's far less waiting for you. I've lived my life, or whatever you want to call my years on this planet, so it pisses me off to no extent that someone as young as you, with so much life ahead, is so content with just moping and pissing it away. We get one life. *One!* John barely got that, and that's what's not fair."

"Well, you know what, Mae? There's not much we can do about it, is there?" Mae seemed to know exactly how to get a rise out of me, even in seemingly tender moments. "John is gone, Autumn is gone, and here we are. I have a chance to spend time with someone

I love. You of all people should understand that. You're more of a hypocrite than a friend."

I'd crossed a line. I wasn't sure exactly when, but somewhere between hypocrite and friend I knew I had gone too far, and there was no putting that toothpaste back in the tube.

The solicitous portion of our conversation had long passed the threshold of being positive and productive. Sinatra finished crooning a few more carols as we sat, silently brooding in each other's presence. We both wanted to toss another verbal grenade at the other, hoping the shrapnel of our words would inflict persuasion to our viewpoint. Thankfully, for the sake of preventing another lifelong regret, neither of us pulled the pin.

"I haven't gotten your gift yet," I bawled without a prompt and completely oblivious to the raised volume of my voice. It was December 17, and shopping days were running out.

"Don't get me a thing," Mae said with contempt fueling her vocal cords. "It's bedtime, Sonny. Head on back to your room."

And just like that, Mae ended the night. She could have left, but her power play was to make me leave, sending me off like an impudent child. I did as I was told, except I didn't head back to my room; I headed to Fred's with the explicit purpose of asking him to help me get the hell away from here.

CHAPTER 30

"Listen, man, I've got to get out of here," was all I greeted Fred with when he opened his door. "I don't care where I go, but call me a cab or something."

"What the hell, Alex? Are you alright?" Fred opened the door fully and invited me into his room.

His suite was certainly homier than mine, but it was much smaller and didn't feature the same view I had. Turns out those who got stuck with Mae were pretty much bribed to stick around—why else would they stay?—because the woman was infuriating on the best of days. I was, of course, a little drunk at this point, and my review of Mae was nothing if not critical. It wasn't fair, but then again, what the hell was anymore?

"Look, can you just call me a cab?" I asked again, unsure about why I couldn't manage this simple task on my own. Perhaps it was proving a point—to whom, exactly, I have no idea—that I was grievously upset beyond the point of managing such a straightforward phone call without assistance. "I just need a night or two away."

"If you up and leave without a word, they may not let you come back, you know that, right?" he asked me. "I don't know what this is about, but you've been here a while now, a hell of a lot longer than anyone thought you'd stay, so there's a reason for that. Any observer can see that you and Mae are friends. And not just the transactional kind Mae uses to get what she needs."

Fred had no idea what we'd been through. I briefly thought about telling him, but before I could offer a response, he continued.

"But, if you don't think you can be talked out of it, or even want to be, I'll save my breath. As you can see, my shit is packed," he said, gesturing to the suitcases on the bed. "I'm out of here too, man, for good."

My head was spinning, and not solely due to the whisky, but it certainly played a large role. Fred's things were packed, and what was left in the room must have been the standard-issue Silver Springs décor.

"Wait, what?" I said dubiously. "You're out of here? To where?"

"Well, Alex, that's the thing; I have no idea. I came here without a plan, and I'm leaving here pretty much the same way. After Phil and Susanne made their announcement, it got me thinking, you know, that life has to be more than these walls, these people—that someone is out there for me to be as weird and crazy with as Susanne is with Phil. They're great, don't get me wrong, but I've been here as long as I have because I was afraid that if I backed out on the decision I made when I was eighteen, I'd be perceived as a coward of some kind. But by who? What the fuck do we know when we're eighteen anyway?"

"That's, uh, great, man," I said, steadying myself on the dresser and trying to ignore his comment about the kinds of decisions we make in our teenage years, knowing now that they're all basically ill-informed. "But where are you going to go? What are you going to do?"

"Don't know and don't know," he said. "Things worked out pretty well for me when I decided to come here, but times change, people change, *I've* changed. And with those changes comes the desire to do something different, to find a new path. And so here I am, charting that course."

Cartography analogies aside, Fred was unknowingly making a convincing argument to his audience of one. This was the same argument Mae had been trying to make, only I hadn't listened to her. I tried to compare both of their cases to see if they were, in fact, the same, but my blurred focus wouldn't let me drill down deep enough.

"So it's your lucky night; I'll save you cab fare. You can come with me and crash at the hotel. I got a last-minute reservation, which was pretty damn lucky, if you ask me, getting a room for a couple nights this close to Christmas."

"Let me grab my stuff," I said and headed towards my room. "Meet you out front in twenty."

Fred and I drove in the evening darkness to a Holiday Inn just over an hour down the highway. Somehow, he convinced me I was getting a good deal by having him chauffeur me in my own vehicle instead of us calling a cab.

The drive to the hotel was relatively quiet, mostly because I was trying to keep down the roiling bile that had floated to the top of my stomach, and was now threatening to project a violent and sour reminder of why you should never drink more than you can handle.

Snow started to fall as we pulled into the hotel parking lot, setting the scene for a snapshot of the season. Weary travellers were bustling in and out of the restaurant and bar attached to the hotel. Under nearly any other circumstance, grabbing a bite before checking in would have been a logical choice, but the pungent smell of grease from the pub fare being dished out turned my stomach.

Fred checked us in and we brought our bags to the room, which, thankfully, had a pair of double beds. I tossed my bag on the chair in the corner and kicked off my shoes, shooting them in opposite directions. I peeled off my jacket and dropped it on the floor with complete disregard for tidiness. I flopped on the bed and knocked off the extra blanket and pillows. Despite my unwillingness to hit the bar, Fred said he was going to find something to eat. I waved him off and felt my head compress deeper into the pillow.

I hadn't been asleep long, I don't think, before I heard a knock at the door. Waking from my boozy slumber, it took me a moment to figure out where I was, what was happening. But the repeated knocks on the door eventually got me out of bed, stumbling, to peek through the peephole.

I was shocked to see Autumn, chaperoned by the same orderly who was around the other day when I spoke to her. Without a moment's consideration of either my appearance or the state of the room, I opened the door with nervous excitement.

Autumn looked at me and smiled. "Are you going to invite me in?" she asked.

"Of course, come in, come in, please."

"Randy, thanks for the escort. I can take it from here, but feel free to wait outside if you'd like," she said to the orderly, who nodded in silent compliance.

Autumn wheeled herself in, looking around at the mess that constituted my corner of the room. Fred had not yet returned, but holy shit, would he ever be surprised to see that Autumn had also plotted an exit and followed us here.

"Looks like your room in high school," she joked. "I guess it's true that some things never change. This wouldn't have flown if we'd lived together, you know?"

"Uh, yeah, no, absolutely not." Words came out of my mouth, but they lacked coherent structure. I rubbed my eyes and blinked hard, trying to grasp and understand the moment.

"Alex, do you know why I'm here?" asked Autumn, her red hair falling perfectly on either side of her lightly freckled face.

"I, uh, no, but you are here." My linguistic abilities were not improving.

Of course, I should have asked her how she'd gotten here—outside of her escort, that is—how she was able to leave Silver Springs, how she knew I was leaving, and, more importantly, how she knew where to find me. However, none of this materialized in the form of words that exited my mouth.

"It's because of what you said to me the other morning. I heard every word. But I needed time to process everything. That's why I gave no acknowledgement to anything you were saying. You do understand, don't you?"

"Sure, I guess. Actually, no, not at all," I stammered. "But why? Why not at least acknowledge that you recognized me? That you knew me? Why not then or before? I've been at that place since September, and sure, there haven't been many opportunities to speak to you, but you must have seen me."

"I have seen you," she admitted. "But I'm at Silver Springs *because* of you." Despite knowing this, actually hearing it from her mouth was a blow beyond anything I could have anticipated. "I can't walk because of you. I'm sorry if that's too direct, but given my condition, when I choose to speak to someone now, I'm always very direct. Not speaking up before didn't turn out so well."

I realized I was still standing and slowly settled onto the corner of the bed. Autumn, with vibrant life in her eyes, was exquisite looking. Her beauty would never be lost on me, but this unexpected reunion, connecting with her again, had my heart racing and bolts of electricity shooting through my veins.

"Autumn, I am so sorry," I muttered. "I know it's my fault you're at Silver Springs like this," I said, pointing to her wheelchair. "I want to make it right, I truly do."

"I believe you," she said. "But don't you think it's just a little self-righteous to believe you can show up now and take care of me? What makes you think I need taking care of, I mean, outside of the obvious physical care I require? You've been around the place long enough to see how things are done, to know that we're all very well taken care of. My friends are here; they are my family. You saw what it was like for Phil and Susanne. What makes you think I'd want you here after all this time?"

I was stunned by this question; I had not once thought of viewing my actions through this lens. I had come here on the assumption that my arrival and daily presence would automatically be regarded as benevolent and received with gracious appreciation. Jesus, how fucking selfish, self-righteous, and self-absorbed was I?

"Autumn, I just figured that if I was here to take care of you now, I could make up for not showing up all those years ago. I could make things right, make sure you weren't alone."

"That's a sweet gesture, Alex. But again, you assume I need you now. I needed you *then*. You broke my heart. You shattered it, in fact. I never recovered from that abandonment. It led me down the dark path that put me in this chair. But you already know this. I know you've beat yourself up over it—as you should have. You failed to show up for me, for us. You fucked up." Autumn's bluntness was like a taser to the heart. Every point she made was incredibly valid, but the truth hurt. Immensely.

"But I fucked up too. I started drinking. And taking pills. I can't remember which ones, there were quite a few. I did a lot of irresponsible things to numb the pain. How stupid was I?" She laughed, thinking back to that previous time. "I mean, young love is meant to fall apart, right? It's one of those life lessons that hardens us for future heartbreak and softens us for future love. We were kids; we didn't know what the hell we were doing or what we even wanted out of life."

She was wrong. Yes, we'd been kids, and we hadn't known what life would hold, but I had known it was supposed to be us together, just as Mae had known this about John. I was just a little late to the party.

"Do you remember when we first met?" she asked.

Of course I did. How could I forget? It had been at a typical high-school party at Dillon Buchanan's house. His parents were always out of town, and he was quick to take advantage, supplying cheap beer for all and bedrooms for adventurous couples. I remember sitting on the stairs going down to the basement. There were only a few; the house was a sidesplit. I didn't know a lot of people there—it wasn't really my group of friends—but there were enough familiar faces and friendly acquaintances to make it worth my while. I had no idea that Autumn would be there, and prior to that night, it wouldn't have mattered one way or the other. At that point, she was just another person. I vaguely knew who she was but had yet to actually meet her. She ran with a different crowd at a different school.

I had seen her on the other side of the room, talking to her friends but glancing my way every now and then. I have no idea why I chose to sit on the stairs, but it had been my safe space before my life changed forever.

"I remember you coming up to me at one of Dillon's parties," I said to Autumn, who nodded in agreement. "You sat next to me and gave the simplest, sweetest introduction."

Sitting next to me all those years ago, she had sidled up close and said, "I'm Autumn, but you knew that, just like I know you're Alex. And tonight, we're supposed to finally meet." I remembered the way she had smiled at me for the first time. We'd talked on those stairs for the rest of the night, putting our budding love on display for all to see and not caring who did. We'd laughed. A lot. There'd been a comfort and ease with this stranger who was morphing into my soulmate.

"Do you remember what we talked about?" she asked me, leading me somewhere, but where, I wasn't yet sure.

"Actually, I remember talking about your ex-boyfriend at first."

Autumn laughed. "That's right, we did. What a great topic for our first conversation. But you kept it going anyway. Do you know why?"

I knew the answer. We'd talked about her ex because, as she'd told me later, she was giving me a list of things to never, ever do to her, without explicitly saying it. It wasn't a game so much as an obviously subtle way of saying don't break my heart. Needless to say, I didn't heed all the advice.

"Of course I know why. I kind of fumbled the instructions, though."

"We had some really great times together," she said. "I mean, we were everything to each other for a time."

"Yes, we were," I said, doing my best to keep the tear forming in my eye from completing its escape. "But we can have some of that again, or all of it. You don't have to stay at Silver Springs—or do you? I'm not exactly sure how the whole resident thing works there. It kind of seems like once you're there, you're there for life, but then again—"

"Alex, slow down. We can't have anything. It's all gone."

"No, it's not. We *can* have it again. I know we can. We're both here, and sure, things are different, but I came all this way. I need to—I have to make this right."

"There is nothing you can do, Alex," she said, moving closer to where I was now sitting—on the edge of the bed with my head in my hands. "We may both be at Silver Springs, but believe me, we're not in the same place, not even close."

My head was spinning, partly because I was actually talking to Autumn for the first time in what felt like a lifetime and partly due to the heady trip down memory lane we had been taking. I was surprised, if not a little offended, that my genuine attempt at restitution was being so actively spurned.

Autumn placed her hand on my knee, and it stimulated the same fire within as that first time she'd touched me at the party, when she had reached for my hand. My body lit up like fireworks, just as it had back then, unable to process the purity of her touch.

"Alex, it's okay." Autumn comforted me in a moment when I should have been comforting her. "Like I said, I'm okay at Silver Springs. I like it there. As you've seen, the natural surroundings are nothing short of amazing, the people are like family, and the staff love doing what they can for the residents, except maybe that Fred character who escaped in the middle of the night. It's nice you came, but we're not really a place for outsiders."

"I'll say. You don't have anyone come visit you. Hardly anybody there does," I said, somewhat indignantly, which was a very stupid thing to say given the reasoning behind Silver Springs's existence.

"I think it's time I go now," she said, moving away from me.

"No, wait, I'm sorry," I begged, not entirely sure what had triggered such an immediate response but knowing I wanted to put some glue on the floor to keep her from leaving.

Autumn reached the door, then turned back around and rose from her wheelchair.

"Alex, look at me. Really look at me."

I did. And I saw Autumn at fifteen—the young, beautiful girl I had fallen fervently in love with. She then transformed to the sad, distraught young adult that had been left standing with two keys in a one-bedroom apartment in Vancouver. From there, I saw the battered and bruised woman who had gone too far down the wrong road with the wrong partner. Her face was mottled with black and blue, her eyes puffy and lips split open. Her eyes had lost all the jubilant light I remembered them holding. Autumn as I knew her was gone.

I was failing to comprehend what I was seeing until Autumn returned to her present-day appearance—still beautiful but worse for wear.

"Alex, your monologue was heartfelt, but we'll never converse in real life like we are right now. You need to release your guilt. You're absolved. Accept that. I made terrible mistakes to cope with losing you. They weren't your fault. Sure, if we'd both made different choices, we'd be in a very different place right now, but we didn't, and we're not. I've never stopped loving you, Alex. I know you've never stopped loving me. But you have to leave Silver Springs. I'm not there anymore. You must know that, deep down. My life is over to a certain extent, but yours isn't. You can't stay here forfeiting your life, your future, for what we could have had. It's gone. Call Erica; go out with her again. And then again after that. She likes you. She looks at you the way I looked at you the first time we met. You're smarter now, Alex. Don't fuck this opportunity up too."

Autumn smiled at me and sat back down. I couldn't articulate a word or even a sound. I was frozen in place, ass firmly sewn to the burgundy-and-gold floral bedspread. I looked at her with sadness and relief, unsure which feeling exerted a greater pull. Part of me felt as though I needed her to set me free, because doing it on my own would weigh me down with a selfishness I couldn't move forward with.

"Autumn," I managed, swallowing the lump in my throat. "You're right. I've never stopped loving you. I still love you."

"I know you do, Alex. And I love you."

She blew me a kiss and dissolved, ensuring I slept fitfully the rest of the night. It would be two days later, December 21, that things would start to make sense.

CHAPTER 31

I woke up early the next morning, my mind racing like a greyhound chasing a rabbit. I was drenched in sweat, and a wave of misguided anxiety flooded my body from head to toe.

After several long, deep breaths to calm my mind and regain my centre, I hastily showered and got dressed, which curiously involved putting on the same clothes from the day before despite having a clean and complete outfit in the Adidas bag in the corner.

Waking up Fred was of no concern to me, so I wasn't timid about the sounds generated by my movements. I would have to wake him anyways to let him know I was abandoning him here, but that minor detail seemed trivial when you took into account the fact that he was on his way elsewhere with or without me.

"Fred, wake up man," I said as I shoved his sleeping shoulder side to side. "I gotta go. Thanks for everything. I mean it."

Fred grumbled something inaudible and rolled over. For good measure, I left him a note on the complimentary stationery on the desk. The note read, verbatim, what I had just said to him. I was sure he would know it meant more than the few words it actually was.

I fingered the elevator button, calling it to bring me down to the lobby. My forceful impatience was enough to break the button. Thankfully, the familiar ding chimed the elevator's arrival, and the doors opened before I could cause more damage or an outright malfunction.

Pressing the already-glowing button for the lobby, I was largely oblivious to the other passengers riding down with me. An older woman was clutching her purse as if I was a thief. A mother and son were holding hands, a white teddy bear protectively cradled in the child's other hand. He bopped along to whatever music was playing in the elevator as his mother stared straight ahead. She looked like she was on a mission—a look that would have been reflected back to her had she glanced my way.

My mother would have smacked me upside the head when the doors opened in the lobby and I took off towards the front entrance, failing to let women, children, and elders go ahead of me. Sorry, woman, child, elder. Sorry, Mom. This was one of those movie-scene moments where doing anything but exploding with frantic urgency to your final destination was too slow and unsatisfactory.

Snow had fallen throughout the night, blanketing all vehicles in the parking lot with at least thirty centimetres of powder; locating my car became an obstacle I had neither the time nor patience for. Thankfully, as with most modern-day vehicles, simply pressing the alarm button on my key fob was enough to reduce my search time to a mere fifteen seconds. I'm sure the sleeping patrons of the Holiday Inn and neighbouring Howard Johnson were less than thrilled by the incessant sound of a car horn blaring in the quiet winter morning.

I started the car, jacked the defroster and heat setting, and grabbed the snow brush from the trunk. After getting the top layer cleared off, I started furiously scraping the ice from the windshield and back window. I could have let the defroster do the job, and considering I wasn't wearing gloves, my hands would have thanked me. But did I mention that I was in the middle of a climatic movie scene? Wrecking my vehicle and dying en route because I was too rushed to properly clear my windows would really throw a wrench into things.

When the task of removing visibility hazards from the car was complete, I jumped in, cranked it into drive, and headed for the highway. My hands throbbed as they clutched the steering wheel, raw and red from the cold, white from the determination of my grip.

Thankfully, the plows had a head start on me, leaving the highways in relatively good shape considering the prior day's snowfall. Though I was cautious of the road conditions, I definitely drove a little faster than what was safely called for.

The drive disappeared in a flash. It felt like I went from the Holiday Inn to Silver Springs in the blink of an eye. Being in such a secluded part of the region and surrounded by old-growth nature, Silver Springs looked more like the set of a Hallmark Christmas movie than the health-care facility it really was.

I barely remembered to put the car in park and remove the keys from the ignition before dashing for the front doors. The snow in the open area between the parking lot and entrance was thick and deep. I was post-holing with every energetic step. I felt like Rocky Balboa training in the USSR in *Rocky IV*.

Flying through the automatic front doors, I was fortunate that I had enough sense to allow the sensors to register my presence, otherwise the staff would have been scraping me off the glass like a loveable klutz of a cartoon character.

Entering the lobby, I stopped dead in my tracks. Two things caused my impromptu immobility. The first was the stark realization that I had no idea what was fueling my current stampede. I'd had a dream that Autumn had absolved me of my sins, but I hadn't adequately addressed that information, let alone developed any type of plan for what to do with it. Maybe I should have read the script before the director called action.

The second thing that halted my momentum was Phil, or rather, the less portly, fresh-faced impostor posing as Phil at the front desk. I had never seen anyone else at that post in my entire time here; it was disorienting.

I composed myself, walked over to the desk, and eyed a young man whose nametag read Jeremy – Trainee.

"Hi Jeremy," I said, breathing heavier than I would have liked. "I'm Alex. I volunteer here. Let me ask you a quick question: where's Phil?"

"Hi Alex. Nice to meet you," he responded. "I'll need to see some type of Silver Springs identification before I can let you through." Phil had his hooks in this one already.

I rummaged through my bag and pulled out the lanyard with my ID card. As he studied it, I glanced around the lobby. Nothing looked different, but damn if it didn't feel different.

"So, Phil? Where is he?" I asked again.

Jeremy the trainee told me Phil was in Susanne's office—of course he was—and that he would be happy to call him should I wish to speak to him. Susanne had her hooks in him too; his robotic language had been memorized from one of her scripts. He was the perfect professional offspring of the soon-to-be newlyweds.

"Won't be necessary, but thanks," I said to Jeremy the trainee. I continued to eye him as I moved past him. His gaze, which was a little creepy, I have to admit, followed me until I was out of sight.

The same aggressive force that had pounded the Holiday Inn's elevator button was now being applied to Silver Springs's worn-out, illuminated up arrow. Things were moving in slow motion, and so my anticipation of the elevator's arrival was exacerbated by the strange *Groundhog Day* effect that seemed to be occurring.

The bell chimed and the door opened; the elevator here worked exactly like the one at the Holiday Inn, like every elevator everywhere, yet I was preoccupied with their nuances today.

Once inside, the door closed and—I didn't push a button. I didn't know where I was going. I didn't know what I was doing. Not wanting to be interrupted in the midst of this crisis of indecision, I hit the emergency stop button. I didn't know if this would work considering I hadn't selected a floor, which would have activated the elevator's ascent, but I pushed it nonetheless.

What was I doing? Was I here to apologize to Mae? Was I here to follow my planned path and stay with Autumn? Was I here to pack up and move on like dream Autumn had instructed?

It turns out the elevator wasn't shut down, and after a few minutes of inactivity that I used for contemplative solitude, the door opened and Phil pushed his way in.

"Hey Alex. Forget how to work an elevator? Here, let me show you. It's really easy. You just push the number four, and then it takes you up to your floor. Luckily for you, I'm headed there myself."

The night before, I had yearned for someone to make a decision for me, and now it had happened twice. First Autumn told me to fuck off from here—in a much sweeter fashion, mind you, but to fuck off nonetheless. And now Phil was telling me where to go: back to the fourth floor. My call was answered, yet I still felt unnerved about any decisions made one way or the other.

On the ride up, I thought about hitting the emergency stop button again. I needed time to think about my next steps before I so much as moved. The thought of crippling the elevator's functionality for even the briefest period of time while Phil was with me was reason enough to just let the machine do its thing.

The door opened to the fourth floor, and Phil stepped out. I stood cemented in place, paralyzed with fear, anxiety, uncertainty, you name it. I was at the crossroads of a major life decision, and I needed to finally talk about it. To really talk about it. To open up and be vulnerable and receptive to honest and firm suggestions. Mae had provided all of this to me in the past, but I hadn't listened. I'd heard her, but I hadn't listened. Now, more than ever, I realized that I needed to talk to Mae about this, that I needed to hear what she had to say. Because for the first time, I think what she had to say would actually sink in.

"You going to get off that thing or what?" asked Phil when he realized I wasn't in motion with him. "You might as well join me down at Mae's room. She probably would've wanted you to have some of the stuff in there."

"What?" I said. It was perhaps the most genuinely surprised question I had ever uttered. Phil's statement was so layered that there were catacombs under each word. He made the situation sound bad, but surely, he was just a poor communicator.

"She's gone, Alex. We're cleaning out her room."

CHAPTER 32

I followed Phil down the hallway that had become all too familiar. I knew where each loose spot of carpet was waiting to trip you up; where the paint colour subtly changed, the result of a time when the facility had been in such dire straits that entire hallways couldn't be repainted at once and someone had been left with the task of trying to match and blend previous colours; and where to nudge the wall to render a light sconce dark or spring it back to life.

Like a lost puppy, I continued to trail Phil. And truth be told, I felt like one. I needed Mae, and she was gone. What the hell did that mean, anyway?

Gone.

"Phil, what's going on?" I finally asked, with trepidation in my voice. "Where's Mae?"

"Like I said, she's gone, man," he replied dryly and without emotion, as if I had asked him what was on today's menu. "No warning either. Just like that, gone." He snapped his fingers to emphasize his point.

Had my mind not entered the state of shock my body would soon find itself in, I'm certain I would have punched Phil in the mouth. The insensitivity was beyond me. I was confused. I was furious. But most of all, I just wanted to see my friend. Before I could speak again, Susanne came up from behind me.

"Mr. Chambers, I am so sorry," she said, putting her hand on my shoulder. "I know you and Ms. Seasons were close. Unfortunately, despite our best efforts to keep her with us, this is not the first time something like this has occurred. We are trying to ascertain what happened so the others here can have some closure."

Susanne's tone was slightly better than Phil's, but I still wanted to scream at them: *What in the holy fuck is wrong with you?! Where is Mae? Can we cut the cryptic bullshit for a second and just tell me what the hell is going on?*

"Mr. Chambers, are you alright?" Susanne asked.

Instead of screaming out loud I had entered into a glazed-over, wide-awake comatose state.

"What? Yeah, I'm fine. No, wait, no, I'm not. What the hell is going on? Where is Mae? Why can't I get a straight answer?"

"Mr. Chambers, I understand your feelings, but these things do happen," comforted Susanne. "She is gone, and that is all we know right now. As soon as I know more, I will let you know. For now, the best thing would be to go to your room and get some rest; you look quite tired."

Oh, fuck you, Susanne.

"I'm not leaving here until I get some answers." I stood my ground, though it felt shaky and practically non-existent. "Where is she? Someone just tell me where she is."

I didn't want to ask the one question their ambiguous answers were suggesting I lead with. I wouldn't give them the satisfaction. Why I kept playing this me-versus-them game, I had no idea. My therapist would certainly be getting a call in the coming days.

"Mr. Chambers, please, we will let you know more information when we have it," said Susanne. "Right now, however, we simply do not have anything else we are permitted to share."

The rest of the day's numbing uneasiness could have been avoided by asking the question of whether Mae was dead or alive, but I never did. My day played out in solitary sadness, buried under the blankets of my bed in the Seasons room.

I had a repeating thought as I waited for the day to end, and it went like this: *Fuck this place. Autumn was right. I need to leave Silver Springs. Fuck this place. Autumn was right. I need to leave Silver Springs.* And so on.

Having skipped breakfast, lunch, and dinner the day before, I awoke from a thin, uneasy sleep with grumbles in my stomach more akin to a revving motorcycle engine than a simple case of hunger. I felt hungover even though I hadn't consumed an ounce of alcohol. As it turns out, a highly emotional day can have similar effects. At least with a booze-induced hangover, you might have a good story to go along with it.

I sat on the bed, staring at the carpet, thinking of the other night's dream, the one I so desperately wanted to talk to Mae about, the one with significance, both obvious and subtle, that I was ready to listen to. It had been one of those dreams that felt real until you were awake, and even then, you wondered if there were shreds of waking-life authenticity to it. Of course, seeing Autumn transform and progress from her teenage self to the Autumn of today had been enough to confirm it was nothing more than a subconscious vision, but everything before that had felt so damn real.

It left me wondering if Autumn had, in fact, heard what I said to her the other morning and if that dream had been some manifestation of the cosmos telling me as much. Whether or not her message had been distorted or clean, I would never know, but her advice was sound.

Despite my best intentions, I think I knew deep down that I didn't belong here for the long run, that perhaps my time really was up. I had just finished telling Autumn how I'd never leave, and here I was, ready to do just that. My guilt for what happened to her would never completely evaporate, but bearing it like Atlas holding the heavens was not doing anyone any good, nor was it a viable long-term plan.

Notwithstanding being by myself, I was growing increasingly agitated with, well, pretty much everything; my emotional hangover being most exasperating. I slogged to the bathroom for a shower, hoping a cleansing feeling would provide just that: cleansed feelings. It didn't.

Time was passing slowly. The last forty-eight hours played on a loop in my mind. I remembered the letter Mae showed me and the advice she had given. I'd say she was wise beyond her years, but she was wise *because* of her years. She had tried to pass her wisdom down to me as best she could, but like a stubborn child, I had dug my heels in and refused to listen, throwing a tantrum and pounding my fists and feet on the floor.

Reminiscing on my memories of Mae, I reflected on our time in Pineton and the diner, our dance in her room, and the many conversations we'd had in between about love, life, and what our futures might hold. And now, she was gone. I still didn't know where.

I sat to eat breakfast by myself. My usual dining companion, Fred, was also gone, making his way to whatever lay ahead in his life journey. I devoured as much food as an army—pancakes, cereal, a bagel, fruit, yogurt, juice, you name it—shovelling it down my gullet until a painful ache clenched my stomach and bowels.

It was this poor decision of overeating that resulted in me staying in the cafeteria long past everyone else leaving. No one was coming to kick me out or get me moving to my assignment of spending quality time with Mae. The minutes passed, and right on schedule, the occupants of the third floor emptied into the courtyard below.

The maintenance crew had been out while I was eating, clearing the paths and patio areas so that outdoor time could happen as usual. Despite the snow, it wasn't a particularly cold day, so taking advantage of the temperature and the sunshine this late in December was a given.

I watched as Randy escorted Autumn. I didn't know if that was his name, but that's what Autumn had called him in my dream; therefore, he would always be Randy to me, even if his real name was Tim or Jacob.

I pressed my forehead to the window, feeling its coolness and using it to soothe the feelings churning within. I watched Autumn now with less of a curiosity and more of a disorientation. The Autumn I knew, dream Autumn, had told me that it was time to leave, time to let go. The version below who sat in her wheelchair would never speak those words—or any others, for that matter. How could I possibly let the latter influence and drive my decisions? How had I not realized this sooner?

"Love will mess you up and make you do the craziest shit you've ever done in your life."

I didn't need to look to know who it was.

CHAPTER 33

As if my last forty-eight hours hadn't been surreal enough—with the last twenty-four being downright gloomy and intensely nerve-racking—I now sat staring at Mae as she settled into a chair opposite me. I wanted to hug her. I wanted to shout at her. Hell, I wanted to rough her up a little bit. Not in an abusive way, but more in that you-asshole-you-really-got-me kind of way.

For the time being, I did none of those things, which I guarantee was for the best.

"I'll be honest with you," began Mae, "I was going to give you the old French exit, and I almost did, but then yesterday morning, as I was waiting in the parking lot for Chandra of the Midnight Sun, I saw this idiot running from his car to the front doors in knee-deep snow. You were in such a blind, focused dash, you didn't even see me, and I admit, watching you flail and stumble your way in had me in stitches.

"In my defence, I didn't know if you were coming back," she continued. "Believe it or not, after we parted the other night, I went to find you, but Phil told me he saw you and Fred leave with bags. I figured if you guys had your bags, you would be long gone, never to be seen again. I decided to call up Chandra and have her come pick me up first thing in the morning. Had she understood my simple instructions and been on time, we would not be speaking right now."

"Well, in fairness, I didn't know if I was coming back anytime soon," I said, extending my olive branch by keeping my opinions about what I had just heard to myself. "It was on the spur of the moment, you know. But Mae, I left because, in that moment, I couldn't take you imposing your will on how I should live my life. I mean, if it wasn't for my decision to come here for Autumn, we would have never met." I let the words hang for dramatic effect and continued. I don't know if it worked, but I assumed it did. "And I'm glad we met, Mae. I really am. You've opened my eyes, broken me out of my shell, and brought me back to a reality I should have been living in all along but have been actively avoiding."

Mae just nodded as I spoke. I wasn't sure if this was in agreement to what I was saying or if it was more of an I told you so since she always believed that what she was doing was the right thing.

Either way, we weren't in the midst of a carryover argument, so I was taking that as a win and a sign to keep going.

"Don't get me wrong," I said, making sure she wasn't too embedded in her smugness, "I'm a little hurt you'd leave without saying goodbye. Yes, I technically did the same thing, but I was always going to come back sooner rather than later. But for you, I'm convinced that once *you* leave here, you're gone—that's the end of Mae Seasons as a guest of Silver Springs."

Mae nodded again, this time in sharp agreement—we were in fact on the same page. I looked out the window, down to Autumn, who hadn't been moved far from where she had originally been stationed.

"But hang on a second," I said, finally allowing the moment to catch up to me before asking the low-hanging-fruit question I should have started with. "Where did you go?"

"What do you mean, where did I go?" she asked, almost annoyed.

"Well, when I got back here yesterday morning, you were gone, and Susanne and Phil were getting ready to clear out your room, and you said yourself that you were outside waiting to get picked up. Obviously, you weren't back in your room this morning, and I doubt you hid out here all day and slept in the stairwell, so where the hell did you go with Chandra?"

"Turns out that Chandra couldn't get her act together and get her coked-up ass here the way I asked—something about her mongrel dog—so I called that off and shacked up with Francine instead. I shit you not, she's got a reclining chair that's better than any of the beds here," said Mae. "I won't say everything happens for a reason—I don't subscribe to that nonsense—but somewhere in the universe, someone requested that our story continue."

I pondered what Mae was saying, and though I had a list of follow-up questions rivalling an intrepid reporter, I didn't ask any of them. The last two days had been complicated enough up to this point, no need to continue the trend.

"So back to the situation at hand. You're still leaving?" I asked.

"Yes, Sonny, that hasn't changed since yesterday," said Mae. "But I'm glad I can say goodbye. And for what it's worth, I'm sorry for—you know."

Mae seemed genuine in acknowledging that leaving without saying goodbye would have been regrettable.

"Thanks, but as it turns out, you were right," I said, surprising her. "I'm not staying here either."

"Good, then you can drive."

Once in the car and on the road, I recounted to Mae the dream I'd had two nights prior. I told her about it in as much detail as I could remember. If anything was left out, it was unintentional, a reflection of a tired memory more than the withholding of details. Mae chuckled here and there, but in a sweet way, an aw-shucks kind of way. My story with Autumn had a really nice beginning, a storybook beginning. Our middle was more on the tragic side, and there would be no happy ending, at least not in a traditional sense.

Mae's directions were straightforward, but given where we were situated, it would have been tough to get lost on the way to the cemetery; the roads were mostly one way in, one way out this far north.

A happy sadness washed over me as we approached John's gravestone. Mae held on to my arm, stabilizing herself as we walked through the snow. I think part of it too was that we had reconnected, and this friendly touch was an unspoken way of saying we had finally buried the hatchet.

"I don't want to end up here," she said, looking at the plot beside John.

"Mae, I hate to be the one to tell you this, but we all end up here."

"Not dead, you imbecile," she said, smacking my arm but appreciating my humour, one of the few times she had in our time together. "I don't want to end up beside an empty headstone. Like I said, John's not here, just his name."

I believed her. Mae didn't want to end up next to no one, to nothing, even if, to my belief, once you're dead, you're quite finished with conscious thought. More than that, though, I think Mae wanted to be with John, or as close to him as she could get.

"Well, maybe in heaven you'll get your chance to be beside John again," I said. "That is, if Saint Peter lets you through those pearly gates. Your track record, and I'm only talking about the one I know of, does leave some room for penance."

"Oh, don't you worry about me, Sonny. I'm getting into heaven. And if old Saint Pete doesn't let me in on his own, I'll just kick him in the shins and run past while he hops around in agony." Of this, I had no doubt.

As we stood in front of John's gravestone, we reminisced about the past few months and the shenanigans that had taken place therein. The sun was trying to break through the grey clouds, but snow was just starting to fall in large, fluffy flakes.

A crowd was gathering by a gravesite about a hundred metres from where we stood, and I instinctively removed my toque out of respect to the departed stranger and his or her loved ones.

"We should head over there. That's Martin they're laying to rest."

Mae filled me in on who Martin was: a fellow patient at Silver Springs who used to be on the fourth floor but, as his condition deteriorated, was moved to the sixth floor where twenty-four-hour care was provided. Martin had been a friend to Mae, though I wondered exactly how that worked, as Mae was more of a taker in the give-and-take dynamic of her friendships.

I asked Mae how she knew it was Martin, and she told me she had heard about his passing a few days ago, that she knew he would be buried today. Her informative connections within Silver Springs were never in question; the woman knew everything that was going on. The second giveaway was the trio of white buses that were now rolling in, carrying Silver Springs staff and patients.

As we made our way to the plot where a casket sat, raised above the earth before its final descent, I realized that the group from Silver Springs was a fraternity, a sorority, a family coming together to say goodbye to one of their own. Many at Silver Springs could no longer comprehended some of the simple things, the common gestures and routines we take for granted—but this? This they understood implicitly. They had come today to pay tribute to someone as broken, unwanted, and perhaps unloved by the outside world as they were themselves. They never had visitors. No friends, no family kept in touch. They had each other. That was it. That was everything.

The reverend or priest—or whatever title had been given to the man with the white collar holding a big leather Bible—was motioning the crowd to draw in closer. He was soft-spoken, so this could have been careful avoidance of having to strain his vocals. Or it could have been a clever effort to try to keep everyone warm in the cold openness.

An enormous bouquet of white flowers lay atop the casket. They weren't red roses; therefore, I had no idea what type of flower they were. The casket looked large, but I knew nothing about casket sizes. Eventually, we were all within acceptable proximity for the white-collared man to start reading Psalm 23 from his King James Version of the Bible.

> *The Lord is my Shepherd; I shall not want.*
>
> *He maketh me to lie down in green pastures; He leadeth me beside the still waters.*
>
> *He restoreth my soul; He leadeth me in the paths of righteousness for His name's sake.*
>
> *Yea, though I walk through the valley of the shadow of death, I will fear no evil; for Thou art with me; Thy rod and Thy staff, they comfort me.*
>
> *Thou preparest a table before me in the presence of mine enemies; Thou anointest my head with oil; my cup runneth over.*
>
> *Surely goodness and mercy shall follow me all the days of my life, and I will dwell in the house of the Lord forever.*

I had no idea what any of it meant. I had been taken to church when I was young, but like most kids, I hated it. As an adult, I never went back. I had my reservations about religion, about the

Catholic Church—assuming this was a Catholic service, and I could not be certain it was. The words seemed fitting, though.

A few others made their way up to say some arbitrary funeral words. Nothing specific, just more scripture from the leather-bound book the minister or priest passed to those who spoke. I couldn't help but think about how much Mae would hate this when her time came. Not only would she not like the fuss, I don't recall her ever mentioning anything about religion or faith in general. Based on her basic viewpoints on life, I felt certain that organized religion would be in line to receive Mae's condemnation. It wasn't a morbid thought, Mae dying, but a realistic one. It's just what happens. Life eventually concludes.

The sun had finally broken through the light cloud cover and the snow ceased falling for the time being. I no longer noticed the cold or the melting flakes on the back of my neck sending small rivulets down my spine. I closed my eyes to bask in the sunshine now hitting me squarely.

When I opened my eyes again, Susanne was near the white-collared man, ready to speak. She was, as the textbook surely suggested, perfectly attired for the occasion. She wore all black, from boots to hat to gloves. Everything she wore was a step above what you would usually see her in. She cared. This much you could tell. And on a day like this, Susanne Rogers was going to look her best and honour her former Silver Springs resident as professionally and respectfully as she knew how. It made me rethink every negative thought and assumption I'd had about her.

"Staff, residents, friends, it is with sorrow we gather here today." Susanne took a moment to compose herself. "It is never easy to say goodbye to one of our own. We are a family at Silver Springs, and with family comes many things, loss included. But with family, most of all, comes love."

As Susanne wrapped up her speech, which was quite touching, and the service concluded, people milled about. I wasn't sure if this was common practice or just the nature of this particular goodbye to Martin. Regardless, Autumn was in attendance, and I made my way over to her. It was time for my last goodbye.

Randy, who turned out to be Terry, told me he'd give me an uninterrupted couple minutes once he learned who I was and Mae gave him her word that I was honourable.

"Autumn, hi," I said awkwardly, still half expecting her to return my greeting. "Listen, I know I said some things the other day, and I believed them wholeheartedly at the time. Part of me still does, actually. But the other night, you came to me in a dream. I know that sounds like the mystical stuff we would have once made fun of, but it felt so incredibly real. It was you, the real you, the you I remember. You told me, in a very nice way mind you, to fuck off. It was sweet, really.

"I will always carry you with me. What happened to you is my cross to bear until the day I die, but I can't stay here. I know this is a complete one-eighty from my recent declarations, but Mae was right, and you were right, at least the dream version of you. I feel selfish because I know you'll never have a second chance like I do, but I have to take it: I have to go. I will always love you, always. But part of that love means letting you be. I can't take care of you the way you need to be taken care of. I can't just watch you from afar, wishing for the feeling of days gone by, hoping that a time machine will let me go back to change my mistakes."

Terry had made his way back over, signalling my time was coming to a close. I held up my index finger to signal just one more minute, and he obliged.

"Autumn, I am so sorry for not showing up. I didn't show up for you, but if I stay here, I'm not showing up for me. I hope you understand."

I picked up her mitten-covered hands and kissed them gently. Terry started to move in, as if he were witnessing a grave offence, but Mae grabbed his arm and gave him a look that said, "let it go. It's fine." The look worked, and Terry stopped his advance.

I gently placed Autumn's hands back in her lap, and I'll be damned if I didn't see the corners of her mouth form the tiniest upward curvature.

"Mr. Chambers, what a pleasant surprise," interjected Susanne once I was standing upright again. "I thought you had left us, which would have been most unfortunate given that I have some good news for you—and for me. I am happy to say that you can refrain from asking me any longer about the third-floor position. It is now open again, and knowing your strong, to put it mildly, interest in it, I would like to offer that spot to you. I believe it will be a good fit, especially since Mae is leaving."

"Wait, you knew Mae was leaving?" I asked, shocked.

"Oh, yes, of course. There is a great deal of paperwork that must be completed when a resident chooses to leave Silver Springs. So what do you say about the position on the third floor? Can I pencil you in for tomorrow?"

I looked at Mae and then back to Susanne. Both looked like they knew what I would do, but only one of them was correct.

"Thanks, Susanne, but this will be my last day at Silver Springs too."

I hadn't heard Susanne speak a word out of turn since I'd been here, but I was certain she gave a perceptible, "Oh, for fuck's sake," upon hearing my answer.

CHAPTER 34

"Well, this is it," said Mae as we sat in the car after the funeral service. She said this with an ambiguous finality that left me with one of two roads to travel: ask her what she meant or just enjoy the moment and stay quiet, leaving the door open for her to elaborate if she so chose. But, as was often the case, Mae chose my path for me and directed me like I was her Uber driver, pointing us in the direction of The Oak Bean. A good choice, I thought, as it would be filled with the warmth of a fireplace and an assortment of beverage options to warm my insides.

It didn't take us long to get there, or at least it didn't feel like it took us long. The perception of time had been lost on me since I'd arrived at Silver Springs. Days seemed to blend into one another, especially since every day was pretty much the same, except for the ones that were absolutely not. If it hadn't been for the odd, rowdy weekend away or the lively holiday parties or the special celebrations, I'm pretty sure every day would have been identical.

We arrived at The Oak Bean and, before settling into a pair of oversized chairs, we argued about drink options and who would retrieve them once a decision was made. True to form, Mae's insistency to retain as much independence as possible won out.

"Well, Mae, what exactly is the next step?" I asked when she came back with our drinks. Mae set the mugs down on the small wooden table that separated us, her hands shaking as she carried the weight and warmth of them. To her credit, she didn't spill a drop.

"Senior's discount," she exclaimed as she motioned to the young man walking over with a plate of pastries. These weren't discussed during our original order, but when I saw the selection of goodies, I realized how hungry I was.

"Silent Night" filtered through the café. It wasn't Sinatra's version; it was some coffeehouse version, likely played by a teenager with an acoustic guitar and a haircut that didn't make sense to me, or so I assumed. Instantly, it reminded me of listening to the song with Mae at Silver Springs.

"Were you really not going to say goodbye, or at least try to say goodbye to me?" I asked again, not fully able to let it go. I could have left it alone, I suppose, but at that point, what the hell did I have to lose? I might as well get some closure while the possibility existed.

"Alex, you're right, I wasn't going to say goodbye. I could have told you it was my Irish goodbye, but like I said, I was making a French exit because that is more appropriate given where I'm headed. I took you to the cemetery today somewhat for Martin but mostly to tell John that I was coming to see him, to be with him, and to ask that he watch over me on my travels." As she said it, I realized it hadn't occurred to me why she had taken me there in the first place, and as bizarre a request as it had been at the time, I hadn't thought to ask.

"And besides, a hot number like me will have to be mindful of all the creeps out there. Having a former soldier as an angel on your side is pretty good protection."

Her joke landed softly, drawing a wry smile to my face. But it didn't make any sense to me. How could someone who had incessantly preached to me that what I was doing was a huge mistake now be going to do that very exact thing?

"I know what you're thinking," she said. "How could someone who preached to you about making a huge mistake go and do the exact same thing?"

"Sorceress," I muttered under my breath.

"I heard that," she scolded. "But I'll let it go. And in case you weren't aware, I am the elder of the two of us, though sometimes I'm not convinced of it. My days are numbered; yours aren't. I feel like a broken record repeating this to you, but I'm glad it finally stuck. Just in case you are wavering, I'll repeat it again: you have a lifetime ahead of you. I have, what, maybe a couple good years left before, if I'm lucky, I get hit by a bus after getting groceries? Lord help me if I stumble into some form of memory loss and start shitting myself. That's not how Mae Seasons is going out, no sir. It's my time to go be with John.

"Listening to you talk to Autumn the other day—which, yes, I know, I gave you the gears about already—actually struck a chord for me. John would have given anything to get back to me once upon a time. But he knew he had to prepare to let me go for me to move on with my life. Sound familiar to a particular dream you've had lately? He never came home, and I never moved on. I'm ready to move on, move on to where I need to be, where I'm supposed to be."

"So where exactly are you going then? And when are you going?" I asked her.

"I'm going to Caen," she said. "It's where John is buried. I've been doing some research, and I'm certain I have the information I need to find exactly where he was laid to rest or, at the very least, the most likely place he last stood on this earth. And I'm leaving tonight."

"Tonight," I repeated. It was as good a time as any, I supposed. I said it not as a question but a reaffirming statement to my subconscious, asking it to speedily come to grips with the fact that I would soon be losing my friend to her next great adventure.

"Benefit of modern travel, my boy," she said, pulling out a cell phone and showing me her e-ticket. "Couldn't get that done back in my day. Flying first class too. The rest of the peasants can whine about my privilege from coach. Do they still call it coach?"

"I have no idea, but probably not." I was sad at this news. Not because it was something of a surprise but because my friend was leaving—my unlikely, quirky, infuriating, fascinating friend. It was apparent enough for Mae to pick up on.

"Alex, I'm sorry." It was a rare Mae Seasons apology. "I've lived at Silver Springs for fourteen years, and believe it or not, I've loved every one of them. But I don't know if I ever enjoyed myself more than during these last few months with you. You've rekindled my belief in love, as injudicious as it can be, and you've given me a reason to finally do what I should have done fifty years ago. I could have moved to France and started over while still being close to John, found myself a nice, young French lover—you know how the French are in the romance department—and lived a pleasant life."

"Silent Night" had given way to "Jingle Bell Rock," which gave way to "Silver Bells," which gave way to some contemporary Christmas song that would never achieve the longevity of the classics.

By this point, Mae had finished her drink, her empty mug resting on the edge of the table, waiting for the same barista who had brought the pastries to come by and take it away.

A few minutes passed before either of us said anything. It wasn't an uncomfortable silence. It wasn't due to the fact that we didn't know how to speak to one another; it was because the inevitability of our conclusion was palpable. Getting up to make her exit, Mae broke the silence.

"Be good, Alex," she said.

I stood to help her with putting her coat on. I couldn't blame her for what she was doing; hell, I'd attempted to do the very same thing a few days ago.

"Goodbye, Sonny," she said, leaning in to kiss my cheek.

As she walked towards the door, the familiar light-blue LeSabre pulled up to the curb, Chandra of the Midnight Sun behind the wheel. How the hell did they time that?

When she got to the door, I realized this was it; this was how it ended. We weren't going to have a long, drawn-out, half-hour goodbye. Mae told me what she needed me to know, and I received it. What else was there?

"Hey, Mae," I called out. "I love you."

Mae stopped dead in her tracks.

"Everyone deserves to be loved," I said. "Moreover, they deserve to hear it. *You* deserve to hear it. I never knew John, obviously, but he was a lucky man. I hope you find love in Caen, whatever that looks like for you. Now, before you get all mushy on me, I'm only saying this because I don't want you to go even one more day without hearing someone say it to you."

The distance between us left room for uncertainty, but I was certain I saw a tear roll down Mae's cheek.

"Bloody hell," she mouthed, wiping away my confirmation. "Drink your coffee, and quit fucking around with that hot little number who is into you." Translation in Seasons: I love you too.

Mae walked out the door to the chorus of the bells above her and got into the LeSabre. I watched it drive away. Mae looked fixedly ahead and didn't wave. She didn't have to. We'd said our goodbye; why go through it again?

After the door chimed its signal of Mae's departure, it jingled again, announcing the arrival of The Oak Bean's next customer. As I drew my gaze to the door, I was surprised to see a snow-dusted Erica walking in, brushing fresh flakes off her hair and jacket.

I had just finished telling one woman that I loved her, and I could feel that I wasn't too far off from telling another one the exact same thing. But there was time to figure all that out. Life was ahead of me, not behind.

It was December 21, the first day of winter. It had taken me four months—well, sixteen years, actually—but I had finally said goodbye to Autumn.

The End

ABOUT THE AUTHOR

Marc MacDonald is an award-winning communications professional with a passion for storytelling. He has a background in journalism and minored in professional writing at Brock University. He has been recognized for his writing—appearing in print and online publications across Canada—by the Hermes Creative Awards and MarCom Awards. Outside of writing, Marc enjoys reading, coaching his kids, and being active outdoors with activities like camping and hiking. He lives in St. Catharines, Ontario, with his wife and two sons.

marcmacdonald.ca

@marcmacwrites